SILENT FOOTSTEPS

SILENT FOOTSTEPS

Jo Bannister

This first world edition published 2019
in Great Britain and the USA by
SEVERN HOUSE PUBLISHERS LTD of
Eardley House, 4 Uxbridge Street, London W8 7SY.
Trade paperback edition first published
in Great Britain and the USA 2019 by
SEVERN HOUSE PUBLISHERS LTD.

British Library Cataloguing in Publication Data
A CIP catalogue record for this title is available from the British Library.

ISBN-13: 978-0-7278-8864-8 (cased)
ISBN-13: 978-1-84751-984-9 (trade paper)
ISBN-13: 978-1-4483-0196-6 (e-book)

All Severn House titles are printed on acid-free paper.

Severn House Publishers support the Forest Stewardship Council™ [FSC™],
the leading international forest certification organisation.
All our titles that are printed on FSC certified paper carry the FSC logo.

Typeset by Palimpsest Book Production Ltd.,
Falkirk, Stirlingshire, Scotland.
Printed and bound in Great Britain by
TJ International, Padstow, Cornwall.

ONE

Benny Price finished his Christmas shopping, faced bloody death and met an Amazon warrior all on the same day. Since he worked in local government, this was possibly the most interesting day of his life.

It was also the day of the first significant snowfall. Apparently it was the wrong kind of snow, because the machine that should have removed it from the railway lines gave up in disgust somewhere between Birmingham and Norbold. So, in consequence, did the Norbold train.

Benny sighed, took his copy of *Birdwatching Magazine* out of his shopping bag and settled down to wait. He imagined that sooner or later the train operators would either dig out the track or provide buses to take their customers home, and in the meantime there was nothing to be gained by getting angry.

Some of his fellow travellers were equally philosophical, some were not. Behind him, the mother of two under-tens tried to engage them in a game of I-Spy. It might have been more successful if the watery sun hadn't set two hours earlier, limiting the view from the carriage windows to a pale, glowing panorama of snowy fields. When S and F had been used, the game ground to a halt much as the train had done.

Across the aisle, a young woman with fair hair and ear-muffs took a tablet out of her briefcase and keyed up some document Benny could see but – he was too polite to crane – not read. He got the impression that its contents displeased her. She pursed her lips and her fair brows drew together in a faint critical frown.

At the front of the carriage, two men in expensive coats traded anecdotes of Great Train Delays of Our Time in an increasingly competitive way. Taking seven hours to get from Coventry to Kidderminster beat five hours in the tunnel under Clover Hill, but was itself trumped by a derailment on the slow curve approaching Norbold. Apparently the driver had come in hot, jumped the tracks and attempted to enter the station sideways. The men in the expensive coats chuckled, and didn't understand why Benny – who remembered the incident, and remembered that eight people were injured, two of them seriously – was eyeing them with disapproval.

Behind Benny, someone was getting irritable. Voices were raised – at least, one voice was raised, and another was joining in, not with much enthusiasm but in a kind of placatory whine. 'Yeah, Trucker, it's a bummer. Don't see what we can do about it though, do you?'

'It's our mam's birthday,' snarled the first voice. 'You know how many of them she has every year? I promised I'd be there for tea. She's going to think I forgot. That really pisses me off. Like I'd forget our mam's birthday!'

'She'll know that, Trucker,' the second voice assured him. 'It'll be on the News.'

'Our mam's birthday?'

'The snow. It'll be all over the telly. She'll know the train's snowed in.'

'Snowed in!' snorted the voice called Trucker. 'That's what's wrong with this footling country. Two inches of footling snow, and the whole footling transport system grinds to a footling halt.' He did not say Footling.

Benny scowled into his magazine. He deplored bad language.

There was the sound of movement behind him, and someone pushed roughly past his shoulder, creasing his magazine. It was a large young man in dirty jeans and an anorak patched with gaffer tape, an incongruously seasonal bobble hat pulled low over his brow. 'Who's driving this footling thing anyway? I'm going to tell the footling cupcake what he can do with his footling train.' He did not say Cupcake.

There are times when a man has to do what a man has to do if he's going to respect the face he sees in his shaving mirror the next morning. Benny Price rolled up his battered *Birdwatching* and said firmly, 'Kindly moderate your language, young man. There are women and children in this carriage.'

For a spell that might have been only seconds but felt much longer, time stood still. Benny wondered if he hadn't been heard and was going to have to repeat himself. But it was more that Trucker – was that even a name? – didn't know how to respond to something he didn't believe he'd heard. People didn't speak to him like that. Fat middle-aged men reading magazines didn't even *think* about speaking to him like that. Not if they didn't want people in white coats retrieving their reading glasses with forceps.

Finally he managed, '*What* did you say?' in a kind of strangled shout.

Benny rose slowly to his feet. 'I believe you heard me the first time. If you want to complain to the train company, write them a letter. But the people in this carriage are not responsible for your frustration, so don't take it out on them.'

Trucker turned to his much smaller companion like a mastiff consulting with a terrier. 'He wants me to write them a letter,' he jeered. 'He wants me to write a footling letter to the cupcakes who run the footling train!'

A kind of recklessness overcame Benny Price. He travelled a lot by train. He'd been in this kind of situation before. He'd always done the sensible thing. Not got involved; not provoked someone who was clearly unpredictable; waited for the trouble-maker to become bored with him and go off to jeer at someone else instead. And all the way home he'd tormented himself with what he would have said if only he'd thought of it just a little bit quicker.

Today, he knew exactly what to say, and he was damned if he was going to go home without saying it. 'If you need help with some of the longer words,' he offered, 'I can lend you a dictionary.'

The large young man – and he was much larger than Benny; he might have been larger than Benny's coal-shed – leaned forward, enveloping him in a miasma of half-digested beer. Benny doubted if he was drunk, at least by his own standards, but he wasn't sober either. In a face approximately the same shape, texture and colour as a breeze block, the piggy eyes were hot with fury. Under one of them a small muscle was ticcing busily.

'Do you think I can't write a letter?' he hissed, offended and vicious. 'He thinks I can't write a letter, Rat. P'raps I'd better show him what I can write. Put your hand out, smart-arse, and I'll write my name on it real small and neat.' Steel winked in the carriage lights as a blade appeared like magic between his fingers.

Benny drew a deep breath and his chest swelled to meet the knife. A distant part of him thought: So this is how it ends . . . as foolish, as meaningless as this. Because he'd stood up to a thug on a train while everyone else pretended not to notice.

'Come on, lads,' said a clear voice behind Trucker's shoulder, 'it's Friday night and I'm supposed to be off duty. If I have to arrest you now, I'm still going to be filling in the paperwork come Monday.'

'And who the footling hell . . .?' demanded Trucker; and as he turned, Benny Price saw the girl with the fair hair, on her feet now, the tablet set aside and the ear-muffs round her neck.

She saw Trucker and Trucker saw her at the same moment. The young man gave a just audible groan, and the knife vanished as quickly as it had appeared. The girl – no, thought Benny, she was a woman, older than Trucker though younger than himself – let her face spread in a surprisingly amiable grin.

'Trucker! I should have known it was you. I haven't seen you for ages. Where've you been hiding?' And then, remembering: 'Oh – yes. When did you get out?'

'Three weeks ago,' mumbled the thug, like a schoolboy cornered by a cheery teacher.

'Then it's a bit soon to be trying to get back in again, isn't it?' She held out her hand, palm up. 'Knife, please.'

'Ain't got no knife,' muttered Trucker, shoving his fists deep into his pockets.

'And Admiral Nelson saw no ships,' retorted the young woman, leaving her hand where it was. 'Knife.'

'Aw, *miss* . . .!'

'How's this for a deal?' she proposed. 'I'll take the knife for safe-keeping, to give Winson Green a chance to paint your cell before you need it again. Ask me for it sometime when you're sober and you just might get it back. Then you and I can write a really rude letter to the train operators, listing all the places where railways manage to operate in real snow, not just a light dusting of Father Christmas's dandruff. And this gentleman here' – Benny Price, hanging on her every word

– 'can buy a round in his local and boast about the time he cheeked Trucker Watts and lived.'

All the tension had gone out of the situation. Stabbing anyone now would have seemed churlish, somehow, even to Trucker. He gave up the blade.

Unexpectedly the train started to move. They all staggered a little; then Trucker shouldered ostentatiously past Benny and went to find a seat where he didn't have to look at the woman who'd disarmed him. As he went, though, his companion hurrying in his wake, he growled over his shoulder, 'Happy Christmas, Miss Best.'

Benny Price drew a normal breath for the first time in a couple of minutes. When he felt his heartbeat beginning to slow he said, 'Is that your name? Miss Best?'

'Hm?' She'd been watching to see where Trucker went; but it seemed he'd had enough fun for one day. He made the men in the expensive coats shuffle up to make room for him.

Looking back at Benny she smiled. 'Yes. Constable Best, of Meadowvale Police Station in Norbold. Trucker and me are old . . . friends.' It wasn't entirely honest, but it was the best she could do.

'My name's Benny Price,' he said seriously, 'I'm with Norbold council works department. I hope you'll consider me a new friend. If you ever need a new wheelie-bin, or a bulk refuse collection, just say the word.'

She gave an appreciative chuckle. 'A girl can never have too many friends at the council works department, Mr Price.'

'Benny,' he insisted. 'Please.'

'Benny.'

TWO

'So how did the interview go?'

Hazel Best pursed her lips, considering. 'I'm not sure. Not great, I don't think. Nothing awful happened – I didn't wipe my nose on my sleeve, or yawn during one of Chief

Superintendent Forest's little homilies. They were polite to me and I was polite back. But there was no great warmth there. I think that, while no one was actually prepared to say it, they wanted me to go away with the understanding that they didn't see a future for me in CID.'

Gabriel Ash was brushing his dog. It was a nightly ritual, performed after his sons had gone to bed, which dog experts insisted reinforced the bond between pet and owner. Ash wasn't sure that the bond between him and Patience needed further reinforcement – he'd saved her from the council pound, she'd saved him from people trying to kill him – but she enjoyed their grooming sessions. And the boys' nanny appreciated his efforts to keep the short white hairs off their clothes, even though Ash suspected he was redistributing more than he was actually removing. When he'd finished, there always seemed to be more of them on his pullover than on the brush.

He cleaned the brush now and put it away before replying. 'You could be wrong about that.'

'I could,' Hazel agreed. 'I don't think I am. They kept harping on about different people having different strengths, and the importance of the right person in the right job. And the fact that Uniform is the foundation of all police work, that they couldn't afford to weaken the Uniformed Branch by transferring all their best officers to the specialities.'

She was right: it was hard to take much encouragement from that. Ash said, 'Would it bother you? Staying with Uniform?'

She had been asking herself that on the train home. 'Not as much now as it would have done a year ago. I always hoped to get into CID eventually. Now? I don't know. It's not like it looks on the telly. Anything resembling a major inquiry has such a big team running it, the contribution any individual can make is limited.' She grinned. 'Whereas, if you see a little old lady across the road and she makes it to the opposite kerb, you *know* you've achieved something worthwhile.'

This was disingenuous, and both of them knew it. She *was* disappointed. But it was not in Hazel Best's character to dwell on failure.

'I forgot to tell you,' she went on, putting aside the newspaper she'd been leafing through, 'I bumped into an old friend of yours on the train. Trucker Watts. You remember Trucker?'

Oh yes: Ash remembered Trucker. To the best of his knowledge, Trucker had only ever done one good thing, and that was to introduce Gabriel Ash to Hazel Best. Admittedly, he'd done it by beating the living daylights out him, leaving Constable Best to pick up the pieces; even so, Ash was not ungrateful. 'What's he doing these days?'

'Well, what he was doing this afternoon was working himself into a paddy because the train was delayed by the snow. Some bloke from the council told him to stop swearing, and Trucker pulled a knife.'

Ash regarded her levelly. 'And?'

'I asked him nicely and he handed it over.'

It terrified Ash, the risks she took. 'And if he hadn't?'

Hazel sighed. 'Gabriel, I'm a police officer. On duty or off, I can't pretend to be doing a crossword while Trucker Watts disembowels members of the public.'

'Maybe it's time,' Ash said carefully, 'you thought about being something else. Particularly if you're right, and Division intend to keep you out of CID. There are other things you could do with your life. Maybe this would be a good time to think about a change of career.'

She elevated one fair eyebrow at him. 'Another one?'

'Why not? You have transferable skills. What you learned as a teacher made you a good police officer; what you learned in the police will be of value whatever you decide to do next. These days, people don't have one career all their lives.' He gave a gentle, self-deprecating smile. 'Look at me.'

Hazel returned the smile with real affection; but being fond of him didn't keep her from teasing him sometimes. She thought it was good for him, stopped him taking himself too seriously. 'True,' she said. 'You were an insurance investigator, then you were a spy, now you run a second-hand bookshop. No one can accuse you of being stuck in a rut.'

Ash had put her right on this so many times he knew she was only saying it to annoy him. He still couldn't let it pass. 'I was a government security analyst. I was not a spy.'

'*I* could be a spy,' she suggested.

He believed – he hoped – she was still teasing him; but whether or not, he was knocking that one on the head. 'No, you couldn't.'

'Why not? You could get me an introduction . . .'

'You're far too honest to be any good at it,' said Ash. 'Spies have to be able to lie convincingly. You lie as convincingly as my eight-year-old when the biscuit barrel is empty and there are crumbs on his T-shirt.'

'I could come and work for you.'

'Say the word,' he said, and there was no mistaking the real warmth in his face and his voice.

'Oh Gabriel,' she chuckled. 'Rambles With Books barely makes enough for one person to live on, never mind two.'

'I have my pension . . .' It was an invalidity pension, because the post-traumatic stress disorder which ended his career was incurred in the course of it. Together with investments made in his high-earning years, he was financially secure – enough that his shop didn't actually have to make money. Some months, that was just as well.

'Now you sound like Methuselah!' Hazel headed for the kitchen to make coffee, wobbling on a pretend walking-stick. It was Ash's house they were in – the big stone house in Highfield Road which had been his mother's – but their friend-ship had been too strong for too long for her to stand on ceremony here. She helped herself freely to his coffee and biscuits – it wasn't always Guy who'd emptied the barrel – whether Ash was here or not. 'You're only fifteen years older than me.'

'Fourteen,' he murmured, barely audibly.

Through the open door, Hazel went on as if she hadn't heard him. 'Well, if I can't work for you, maybe I could work for Martha Harris.'

Ash suspected that Norbold's only private investigator had little more in the way of turn-over than he did. 'Do you see yourself as a private eye?'

Hazel reappeared with steaming mugs and rhubarb tart. 'In a sort of a way, I do. It would be a little bit like what you and I used to do.'

He heard the nostalgia in her voice and hastened to quash

it. 'What you and I used to do was find ourselves in the middle of a crisis and stumble around trying to find our way out. Martha, I imagine, spends a lot of time sitting in motel car parks, watching who goes in and out and whose lights come on. I don't think there's a lot of glamour involved.'

'Glamour I can do without,' said Hazel, 'if I have something interesting to sink my teeth into. Even if I stuck to my guns long enough to get into CID, I'm not sure I fancy working in a big squad of detectives. Even if what you're doing is interesting and important, just getting a tiny bit of it to do might be pretty boring.'

'Dave Gorman doesn't find it boring.'

'Dave Gorman's been lucky enough to find exactly his own level. As senior detective in a small station, he gets to deal with everything that comes his way, unless it's so far above his pay-grade that they send in Scotland Yard. There aren't many jobs like that. I could work my whole career and not find one.' She sniffed, discouraged.

'You enjoy what you're doing right now,' Ash reminded her. 'Seeing old ladies across busy roads, taking knives off thugs, and the rest.' The rest, in the case of Hazel Best, was invariably hands-on, often unexpected and always tackled with gusto. 'Maybe that's where your real talents lie. You could set your sights on Superintendent Maybourne's job.'

'Maybe,' said Hazel doubtfully. 'Unless . . .'

'Unless what?'

'Unless you can get me an introduction at MI5. I do quite fancy being a spy. I could work on the lying thing.'

Ash didn't think she was serious. But with Hazel, sometimes it was hard to be sure.

THREE

They were digging up the road outside Hazel's house. They'd been at it for a week now, and she was no clearer on why than when they'd started. Mrs Burden next door thought it was to do with the drains, while Mr Messenger on the other side thought it was for the phones. One of the men who arrived with a pickaxe each morning had heard a rumour that it might be for broadband, but it was hard to put much confidence in the opinion of a man with a pair of pretend reindeer antlers on his hard hat. All Hazel knew for sure was that she didn't like having to park her car round the corner, out of sight. It was a new car, and still shiny enough that she worried about things happening to it. She still tucked its wing mirrors in every time she left it.

By the time she got home, the workmen were long gone and there were flowers on her doorstep. She looked for a card, but there wasn't one.

Hazel lived across town from Highfield Road, in a small brick terraced house in Railway Street. It wasn't a smart address, but it was low-rent and she'd made it comfortable, and – after years in lodgings – she liked having her own front door.

Since, as with small brick terraced houses up and down the country, that front door opened directly onto the street, she'd found worse things on her step. Even so, the flowers puzzled her, until she remembered Benny Price from the train. He had been easily grateful enough to send her flowers. But why here, rather than Meadowvale Police Station where she worked? How did he even know where she lived?

Because he was employed by the council. The works department: he'd told her that. Perhaps he emptied her bins. She took the flowers inside and put them in water.

Then she sat in the little living room – which was smaller than Ash's kitchen; her kitchen was smaller than Ash's broom cupboard – and stared morosely at the empty grate. It was too late to light the fire. The house had rudimentary central heating so she wouldn't be cold, but a radiator isn't company in the same way as an open fire. These days Hazel lived alone; and while her lodger had brought more than his fair share of trouble, she missed him. She still believed that one day Saturday would knock at her door and ask for his old room back. It seemed less likely with every month that passed, but she kept the room free, and didn't use it to store her ironing board and out-of-season clothes, and an unexpected rap at the door still had the power to make her look up hopefully.

Tonight, though, she was not feeling optimistic. The tone of her interview over at Division had bothered her more than she had admitted, to Ash or even to herself. Criminal Investigation was something she had wanted, something she thought she'd be good at, and something she thought she'd earned. To be told in as many words that those who made the decisions didn't share her view felt like a slap in the face. Worse than that, it felt like a door closing.

When a door closes, you have various options. You can try to open it again. If it seems to be locked from the other side, you can shout for help. Or you can look for another way. Discouraged, feeling undervalued, Hazel stared into the empty grate and gave some serious thought to the possibility that her long-term future might not after all be with Norbold police.

She knew she had skills to offer. She was intelligent, diligent, considerate; she was fit, strong and prepared to get her hands dirty; she had advanced computer skills – she'd taught IT before joining the police – and she had both mental and physical courage. Oh yes: and she'd shown herself willing to kill if necessary. She didn't think she'd put that in her CV; probably better to leave it to the interview stage.

She could try another division. DI Norris, whose manor included Byrfield, where she grew up and where her father still lived, had expressed an interest in her. But would that too come to nothing if she tried to follow it up? The problem was, she'd drawn too much attention to herself. It hadn't been her fault, but time and again an unkind fate had put obstacles in her path that needed dealing with, and the dealing process had exposed her to both scrutiny and criticism. None of it was official. Officially, she'd done what any competent and dedicated police officer would have done in the same circumstances. Unofficially, though, she'd rattled cages. She'd made senior officers feel uneasy. This was not a good way to earn promotion.

Brooding on the past, worried about the future, she sat in front of the empty grate until the lateness of the hour, the weariness of the day and the lack of answers claimed her. She fell asleep on the sofa.

Hours later she woke to a body-cramping chill – even the rudimentary central heating had long since switched itself off – and the memory, already fading, of a sound at her window. She hauled herself off the sofa and pulled back the curtain, but the streetlight outside showed no activity, up Railway Street or down. It must have been a bird, confused by the reflections, bouncing off the glass. She staggered upstairs, threw off her clothes and fell into bed without ever completely opening her eyes.

Only in the last moments before sleep took her did it occur to Hazel to wonder how many birds fly at night.

In the morning there was a bottle of wine on her doorstep.

Having a secret admirer is one of those things which sounds more fun than it actually is. In fact, an admirer who won't declare himself is always an inconvenience and almost always an annoyance. An admirer worth having is one you can go places with, or not go places with, or listen to music or play Scrabble with. An admirer who doesn't make himself available for any of these functions is worse than useless: he's a source of stress.

To a police officer, a secret admirer is more of a problem than that. He, or she, can be a potential threat. Being compromised, or appearing to be compromised, is an ever-present concern, and one it's hard to guard against when you don't know where the danger is coming from.

Perhaps she was more than usually sensitive because the ripples caused by her past activities had just come back to swamp her boat. But Hazel thought it important enough to ask Superintendent Maybourne to record the fact that she had reported her unexpected gifts.

Grace Maybourne was a twenty-first century superintendent, a rather small woman in early middle-age with people-managing skills that more than made up for her inability to rugby-tackle beetle-browed criminals. She belonged to the first generation of women police officers who hadn't needed to match their male colleagues blow for blow, obscenity for obscenity, in order to progress their careers. She had brought different assets to the table. When the system finally, grudgingly, recognised the worth of those assets, a crack appeared in the glass ceiling that would make it easier for women of Hazel Best's generation to climb the promotion ladder.

Women of her generation but not Hazel herself, it seemed. She gave a sour sniff at the thought.

Maybourne heard her out politely. When Hazel had finished she just said, 'Flowers. And a bottle of wine.'

'The flowers on Friday night, the wine on Saturday morning.' It was now Monday morning.

'And nothing to say who they were from?'

Hazel shook her head. 'It had to be the guy on the train.'

The superintendent smiled. 'Well, it's not exactly bribery and corruption, is it? You were right to mention it, we'll log it in the Gifts & Gratuities Book, but I don't think you need let it concern you. If you happen to see Mr Price, thank him but say that enough is enough. Otherwise, I think you can safely forget about it.'

Hazel nodded. 'I just wanted to keep everything above board.'

Maybourne knew what she was saying. 'I take it your interview at Division didn't go entirely as you might have wished.'

'I think I can wave goodbye to CID,' Hazel said frankly.

'That's a pity. Not for me – CID's loss is my gain. But I know Detective Chief Inspector Gorman would like to have you, and I know it's what you were hoping for.'

Hazel shrugged. 'If wishes were horses . . .'

'Don't give up on the idea,' said Maybourne. 'Things change. Even at Division. If it's what you want, give the dust twelve months to settle then try again. If I get the chance to put in a good word, I will.'

Hazel knew she meant it. 'I appreciate that. Thank you.'

She had a school visit scheduled for the afternoon. It began, as they always did, with slightly overawed small people chanting, 'Good afternoon, Constable Best,' and nodding earnestly when she told them that the police were their friends and could be relied on to help in times of difficulty; and ended, as they so often did, with one of the older boys remembering something his dad had said and asking her outright.

'Is it true you shot your boss, miss?'

Hazel sighed. She'd been expecting it. Even so, she wouldn't have minded them disappointing her, just this once. 'No, Dwayne – it is Dwayne, isn't it?' It was. 'No, it isn't true. Somebody else shot my boss. I shot him.'

'Cor!'

After that the visit was only ever going to go south. They wanted to know if she had a gun on her today. The answer was no. They didn't altogether believe her. She tried to steer the discussion back to road safety and respecting other people's space, and who to tell if someone tried to bully you or do something else you didn't like, but it was like peppering an elephant's backside with a peashooter. They were oblivious. They only wanted to know who else she'd shot, and if she planned to do it again any time soon.

FOUR

She returned to Meadowvale at half-past three in desperate need of strong coffee and a doughnut.

But before she could do more than nibble at the jam leaking out of the side, Sergeant Murchison descended on the canteen, looking for bodies to throw into a developing situation in the Kingswood shopping centre on the edge of town. Hurrying out to the cars, Hazel asked what kind of a situation.

The sergeant didn't know, except that it appeared to be gang related. Half a dozen shopkeepers had phoned in, anxiously reporting that the mall was filling up with bellicose young men, half of them very hairy, the other half very bald. Even allowing for a certain amount of nervous exaggeration, there was clearly trouble brewing. Superintendent Maybourne wanted a big enough presence in the mall to stop it boiling over.

'It's not Hell's Bunnies, is it?' Hazel had rather a soft spot for the local biker gang.

Donald Murchison shook his head. 'They don't generally give us much aggro – they're just petrol-heads, they like looking tough but they're actually more interested in bikes than bovver. No, going off the descriptions it's going to be the Mill Street Maulers and the Canal Crew. They've never liked one another. Most of the time they have the sense to keep a demilitarised zone between them. I don't know why they'd suddenly start facing up to one another in broad daylight in a shopping centre.'

Hazel hadn't seen much gang-related activity in Norbold. 'Which are the hairy ones?'

'The Canal Crew,' said Murchison. He held the door of the people carrier for Hazel, squeezed in after her. 'They're easy enough to deal with. They're basically thieves: mobile phones, women's handbags, branded trainers – anything that's worth money and easily passed on. Casual violence rather than deliberate viciousness. That's more the Maulers' style.'

'They're the bald ones?' Now she thought about it, Hazel had seen them around. Not, as it were, on duty, crowding together for some purpose requiring big boot sizes and small IQs, just loitering in twos and threes on street corners and in tobacconists' doorways, glowering as she passed and flicking foul-mouthed epithets after her once she was safely out of earshot.

The sergeant nodded. 'They're modern skinheads. Anti-immigrant, anti-gay, anti-establishment – anti-us, of course; pro selling drugs and extorting money from people who're scared of them, which is most anyone with a modicum of sense.'

It was only a six-minute drive from Meadowvale, in the centre of Norbold, to the shopping centre on the ring road. But by the time they got there the car park was emptying fast. The sight of the Crew and the Maulers squaring up to one another was enough to persuade most people to finish their shopping later.

Meadowvale's finest piled out of the people carrier as soon as it came to a halt. But Sergeant Murchison blocked Hazel's exit for a moment. 'No heroics,' he rumbled in her ear. 'These are not nice people. It's no use appealing to their better nature – they don't have one.'

Hazel couldn't resist teasing him. 'You mean I should shoot first, ask questions afterwards?'

Sandy eyebrows lowered over his gaze. 'Given your track record, that would be pretty rash advice, wouldn't it? Just – stay close to me, stay alert, and don't turn your back on the beggars.' He did not, in fact, say Beggars.

The central concourse, with its bench seating for weary shoppers and its coin-in-the-slot carousel horses and fire engines for their toddlers, made an incongruous battlefield for some of Norbold's least desirable citizens. But a battle seemed to be in prospect, if not yet in progress. The ritual threats and gestures that accompanied most encounters of this kind were today conspicuous by their absence. Everyone present – fifty or more young men, aged from mid-teens to late twenties, and perhaps a dozen young women dressed to match – was there on business. The atmosphere was tense, hot with anger, primed for explosion if anyone was careless enough to strike a spark.

Murchison's first move was to create a physical barrier between the two sides. He led his thin blue line through the heart of the gathering, steering the odd errant Mauler or reckless Crewman back to his own side as he went. It wasn't a Riot Squad operation and they weren't in full riot gear, though they had all – Hazel included – pulled on stab vests as they left the vehicles. It was a calculated risk. If the situation deteriorated fast, they would rue the helmets, riot-sticks and tasers they had left behind.

But there were times when wading in like paramilitaries was enough to turn a bit of bad-tempered posturing into open warfare, and that was worth avoiding if it could be done with a clear conscience. Today, Murchison thought he could just about justify keeping things friendly.

So he led his colleagues down the fracture line between Crew and Maulers, firmly but patiently separating them; and Hazel, being Hazel, had a few words with those that she recognised, asking after mothers and girlfriends and, in the case of Jobber Bunting, his prize-winning ferrets.

Once the DMZ had been re-established, there was time to take stock. Murchison had a shrewd idea that if he could keep the rivals from physically reaching one another, sooner or later they'd get bored, and wonder if there was anything on the telly, and wander off. So it was that Hazel found herself in close proximity to someone she'd seen around Norbold on several occasions, most recently only a few days earlier on the train. The regrettable fact that the only name she knew him by was Rat didn't prevent her from greeting him cheerfully.

'Hello again! I didn't know you were a Mauler. Trucker's idea, was it? Is he here too?' She craned but failed to make out that substantial presence in the crush.

The Rat muttered something she didn't hear. She bent closer. 'Sorry?'

'I said, Trucker's the reason we're here.'

'OK,' Hazel said carefully. 'Did he want to see the Christmas decorations? Visit the Elves' Grotto down by the pound shop and have his photo taken with Santa?'

'They've done something to him.'

She frowned. 'Who have?'

'The Canal Crew. They've done something to him. We can't find him anywhere.'

The individual known as the Rat was so far from a reliable witness that he almost came out on the other side of disbelief. Hazel didn't think he was making this up. She sent a nudge up the line to attract Sergeant Murchison's attention. 'You're going to want to hear this.'

There had been a confrontation earlier in the day. Trucker had been spotted panhandling – well, demanding with menaces – outside an off-licence widely acknowledged as Canal Crew territory, and had been asked to leave. He'd sauntered away five minutes later with his pockets jangling, his unlicensed bounty supplemented by a Crewman's silver nose-ring, while its previous owner held a grubby handkerchief to his bloody face.

'And now he's disappeared. Vanished – gone.' There was no mistaking the genuine unhappiness in the Rat's tone. He may, Hazel reflected, have been the only person apart from

Trucker's mum to actually care about Trucker. 'They've done something to him, I know they have.'

'Have you asked them?'

'Like they'd admit it!' moaned the Rat. 'They have, though. We've looked everywhere. And he isn't answering his phone. Them bastards have done something to him.'

Donald Murchison frowned. 'So what are you all doing here? When you could be out looking for him?'

Another sotto voce mumble.

'Sorry?' said Hazel again.

'I *said*, we grabbed one of their scrubbers. Said we'd give her back when they let Trucker go.'

'Let me get this right,' rumbled Murchison, in a Scottish accent with girders in it. 'You've *kidnapped* a young woman associated with the Canal Crew, to hold as hostage until the Crew release Trucker Watts.'

The Rat nodded. He declined to meet either the sergeant's gaze or Hazel's; but then, he never met anyone's gaze, ever.

'And they've come here to get her back. All right, sunshine, where is she?'

The Rat wriggled. But he was never going to hold out against the moral authority of Meadowvale's station sergeant. He'd never held out against any form of intimidation in his life. 'She's in a van, round the back. Nobody's laid a finger on her, honest. We just want Trucker back.'

Murchison, with Hazel at his side, shouldered his way through the front ranks of the Canal Crew until he came to what looked like the combined chiefs of staff. 'I gather you people are missing a young lady.'

It took a moment for them to mentally translate. Hazel heard them whispering: 'Does 'e mean Fleabag?' 'I fink so. Yeah, 'e must.' 'Does 'e know where she is then?'

'We *do* know where she is,' confirmed the sergeant. 'I've sent someone to bring her here right now. So what have you done with Trucker Watts?'

One of the hairy young men appeared to be senior to the others. 'We 'aven't got 'im. We never 'ad 'im. We 'aven't seen 'im.'

There was something almost Shakespearean about it, Hazel

thought. But Sergeant Murchison was harder to impress. 'You saw him this morning, panhandling outside the off-licence in Arkwright Street.'

Yes, they admitted, they had. They'd seen him off – or, to be more accurate, they'd seen him leave. They hadn't seen him since.

'Is that the truth?'

'On my mother's grave.'

Murchison frowned. 'Your mother's still alive, Billy Barnes.'

'Yeah – but she's already bought a plot down the Municipal. Cost her an arm and a leg, it did.'

About then Constable Budgen returned with the Crew woman known as Fleabag. It was quickly established that she'd come to no harm, and since the Crew were content to take her and leave the mall, the sergeant took the executive decision that it was more important to defuse the situation than to charge someone with unlawful imprisonment, at least for now. The Crew drifted away. So, a few minutes later, did most of the Maulers.

Soon, there were only police officers, a few brave shoppers, and the Rat left in the mall. The Rat looked up at Sergeant Murchison. 'So who's going to find Trucker?' he demanded with a kind of nervous courage.

FIVE

T hey found Trucker the next morning.

Ironically enough, they would have found him earlier but for the face-off at the shopping centre. The rubbish skips lined up like so many landing-craft in a bay behind the mall were normally emptied in the afternoon. But though the area was closed to the public, the trouble inside meant that shoppers were flooding out of the nearby emergency exit. Calling the council for instructions, the drivers were told to leave Kingswood for now and go back first thing on Tuesday.

Trucker was behind the second skip they went to lift. It was

still dark, the work proceeding under a couple of strong lights
on the back wall of the mall that cast sharp-edged shadows;
and at first the council men thought it was just another bit of
rubbish that hadn't quite made it as far as the skip. They pursed
their lips disapprovingly, and pointed out to one another that
they would be within their rights to leave it there, lying on the
cracked tarmac. But Sid, who was the senior operative, finally
told Dale, who was the more junior, to sling it in anyway, in
the interests of doing a good job and because Christmas Box
season was fast approaching.

Dale went to do as he was bid. He had his thick gloves on,
so he wasn't too concerned what it was – if he could lift it,
it was going in the skip.

Sid heard the broken cry that was almost a wail and, glancing
in his wing-mirror, was puzzled to see his young colleague
stagger back and turn a white face his way, the mouth agape
with shock.

'Sid – Sid!' he heard. 'It's – it's . . . There's blood *everywhere*! I think he's dead.'

'BFT,' said the forensic medical examiner judiciously.
'Something heavy, but with a comparatively narrow profile. A
wheel-brace, a hammer – something like that.'

'One blow?' asked Detective Chief Inspector Gorman.
'Several?'

'More than one. What we scientific types would probably
describe as "lots".' The FME fancied himself as a bit of a
wag.

'Standing up? Lying down?'

'Both, I think. I'll be able to tell you more when I've had
him on the table, but this' – he pointed with his pen – 'looks
like the first blow, struck when he was vertical, and these
subsequent injuries were inflicted when he was horizontal, i.e.
on the ground.'

'A frenzied attack?'

'Yes,' agreed Dr Fitzgerald, 'and no. It takes a certain amount
of frenzy to go on attacking someone who's already unconscious at your feet. But the grouping is reasonably tight. He
didn't lose control.'

'He?'

Walter Fitzgerald gave him a knowing leer. He was a stout man in his early fifties who, as a bachelor, had never quite outgrown the mannerisms of a medical student. 'Balance of probabilities. How many woman do you know who use a wheel-brace as their weapon of choice?'

'Fair point,' acknowledged Gorman. 'Time of death?'

FMEs hate being asked for a time of death. 'When were the skips last emptied?'

'Late afternoon on Saturday.'

'Somewhere between late afternoon on Saturday and first thing this morning, then. Look' – he waved a hand at the depot, still dark beyond the reach of the floodlights – 'it's nearly Christmas. It's cold. Everything loses heat quickly in this weather. I might be able to do better after I've had a proper look, but you shouldn't count on it. Find someone who saw him alive: that's your best bet for working out when he died.'

Dave Gorman gave a sour sniff. He was a square, solid man of forty, and he'd been a detective for almost half his life. 'Right. That's what we criminal investigators call BBO.'

'BBO?' Though Fitzgerald knew it was a trap, he couldn't resist the bait.

'Blindingly bleeding obvious,' grunted Gorman, with a hint of satisfaction. 'Tell you what. You get him indoors and do your job, I'll get out and about and do mine.'

He was heading back to his car when Dr Fitzgerald called after him. 'Forgot to say. Congratulations on the promotion.'

DCI Gorman waved a hand without looking round. 'Yeah, yeah.' But it didn't take an expert to detect the note of complacency in his voice.

The same promotion, recent enough to be still shiny, made Hazel hesitate outside his door, knock and wait to be invited in. Over the last couple of years, circumstances had conspired to make them friends as well as colleagues, and away from Meadowvale that was how she still thought of him and hoped he thought of her. Here, though, he was a detective chief inspector, three whole ranks above her, and she didn't know quite how to address him now.

'Sergeant Murchison said you were looking for me – er – sir . . .'

'Close the door.'

In police circles, this is the invariable prelude to a bollocking. Hazel did as she was told and waited to learn what she'd done wrong this time.

'Don't you bloody *sir* me! I've *sirred* for England; when it comes to *sirring* I have no equals. I know *exactly* how much a *sir* is worth. So let's get this straight right now. Off-duty, and any time we're alone or with friends, I'm still Dave and you're Hazel. On-duty you can call me Chief. All right? *Sir* me again and I'll have you dressed as a panda teaching under-fives how to cross the road. Got it?'

It probably wasn't within his remit and both of them knew it; but it cleared the air and made Hazel grin. 'Got it.' She considered for a moment. 'That's why you wanted to see me?'

Gorman rolled his eyes. 'Of course it isn't. I wanted to ask you about this business with Trucker Watts on the train.'

'I did make a report,' she said virtuously.

'And I read it. I just wanted to hear it from the horse's mouth. So far, with the exception of the Rat and Trucker's mum, you're the last person I know who saw him alive.'

'As long as you're not thinking that makes me the first person to see him dead.' She cast her mind back and recounted the incident from start to finish, with all the detail she could remember. She didn't think there was anything there to explain what had followed.

Gorman regarded her soberly. 'You took his knife off him?'

'I asked for it. Nicely. He decided to be a model citizen and comply with the lawful request of a police officer.' She was still speaking lightly. Then something occurred to her and shock fell through her expression like a bucket of bricks. 'You don't think that's why he's dead? Because he wasn't able to defend himself? That he'd be alive today if I hadn't made him hand over his knife?'

Gorman shook his head. 'That was four days ago, plenty of time for someone like Trucker to tool up again. And in fact, he had a knife on him when he was found. I imagine he'd acquired it within fifteen minutes of leaving the train. Hell, he might have had it on him all along, as an insurance policy. It didn't save him. He was struck from behind. Even a skilful knife fighter, which Trucker Watts was not, would find it hard to fend off an attack from behind. The first blow put him on the floor. After that, he couldn't have defended himself with a bazooka.'

Hazel gave some thought to this, decided he was right. 'What was his name?'

The DCI frowned. 'You know who he was.'

'I know we all knew him as Trucker. But who names their baby Trucker? He must have had a proper first name.'

'Trevor,' said Gorman. 'His name was Trevor.'

'How's his mum holding up?'

Gorman's heavy eyebrows gave a kind of facial shrug. 'About how you'd expect. He wasn't Son of the Year even in Norbold, but then I don't suppose she won any prizes as a mother. She still shouldn't have lost him that way.'

'Would it be all right for me to drop in on her – see if she needs anything?'

'If you want to. She'll probably swear at you a lot. She swore at me a lot. Maybe it made her feel better.'

Hazel smiled. 'I've been sworn at before. I doubt she'll come up with anything too original.'

'Don't count on it,' muttered Gorman. 'I've been sworn at before, too. But some of what she called me I had to look up in a dictionary.'

Trucker's mother had had four husbands or none, depending on how strictly you define the word; and a child by each of them; and it told you everything you needed to know about her life that Trucker had been her favourite. Though she had never been to parenting classes, she'd heard it said that a mother shouldn't have a favourite child. But her eldest son was in prison for aggravated burglary, her eldest daughter was a career prostitute and her youngest daughter had changed her name and emigrated to Australia, so perhaps she had reason to consider Trucker her finest achievement.

And now he was dead.

She had been told hours before. She had already been to

the morgue at Norbold Royal Infirmary to make a formal identification of the body. Now she was sitting at her kitchen table with the only neighbour Gorman had been able to find who was willing to sit with her, working her way steadily, fiercely, through a bottle of gin. The neighbour wasn't sure she'd want to speak to Hazel, but Maggie Watts overruled her. 'Bring her in,' she called roughly through the kitchen door. 'Maybe she's got good news. Ha! That'll be the footling day.'

Hazel hadn't met the woman before, was surprised that she wasn't older. Then she thought: Of course she isn't older. Trucker was in his early twenties, his mother was probably no older when she had him. By most measures she was still a young woman, although there was a flinty hardness in her face and in her eyes that put years on her. Of course, she wasn't seeing Maggie Watts at her best.

'Well?' she demanded as Hazel stood in the kitchen door. '*Is* it good news? Do you know who did this?'

'No,' Hazel said quietly. There was nothing to be gained by prevaricating. 'But we will. We'll find out, and he'll pay for it.'

For some reason, Trucker's mother didn't react with the same bitterness as when DCI Gorman had told her the same thing six hours earlier. Perhaps it was the shock; perhaps it was the gin. 'Good,' she said savagely, pouring herself another.

Hazel took the chair the neighbour had vacated and seemed in no hurry to reclaim. 'Mrs Watts, can you shed any light on this at all? Do you know if' – she remembered just in time – 'Trevor was having trouble with anyone? If anyone had threatened him, or bad-mouthed him, or anything like that?'

'Threatened? No. People didn't go around threatening Trucker.' So even she had given up on his given name. 'Not more than once, anyway. Bad-mouthing? – yes.' She directed a secret smile into her glass. 'Nobody had a good word to say about him.' She might have been boasting about his skill on the pianoforte.

'Any names come to mind?'

Maggie Watts glanced up sideways at her. 'It was the Canal cupcakes.'

So this was where Trucker had acquired his vocabulary. 'Do you know that for a fact? Has someone told you that?'

The woman shrugged. 'Who else would it be? Maulers hate the Crew, the Crew hate the Maulers. It was only a matter of time before someone got his head beat in.'

'Are they violent?' asked Hazel. 'The Canal Crew? We have them down more as a nuisance – petty crime, loitering with intent, that kind of thing. They don't seem tough enough to start a war with the Maulers.'

'You're right there!' Then Mrs Watts thought about what she'd said. 'Yes, you are right – they're not. Bunch of petti-coats, really, with their long hair and those stupid hats they wear. You know – like bobble hats but without the bobbles, and flaps for their delicate little ears!'

Hazel hid a grin, not least because of all the crimes committed by the Canal Crew over the years, this was what Maggie Watts found objectionable. 'I think they're from Peru.'

Maggie shook her head. 'No – Norbold, born and raised. I've known some of them since they were tadpoles.'

Hazel decided against explaining. 'You can't think of anyone else who might have wanted to do this? Anyone Trucker was afraid of?'

Maggie Watts pivoted slowly on her bentwood chair until her eyes locked with Hazel's. 'My Trucker was never afraid of anybody in his life,' she pronounced emphatically. 'Except me. And once or twice . . .' She let the sentence die.

'Once or twice?' Hazel prompted her. 'Once or twice he let on that there was someone else he was . . . what, wary of? Who made him uneasy? That he wouldn't go out of his way to annoy – is that what you mean?'

'Pretty much, yes.' Mrs Watts returned to her gin.

'Who?' Hazel knew better than to expect a revelation. The best she was going to get was what a fish-wife thought her thug son might have been concerned about. It wasn't evidence as it was reckoned by the Crown Prosecution Service. But it might be a lead, and right now even a weak lead was better than no lead at all.

Trucker's mother did the secret smile into her glass again. 'You,' she drawled.

SIX

In the morning there were chocolates on her doorstep.

Hazel was woken by the sound of pneumatic drills. She hadn't set the alarm because she wasn't on duty until later. But the drills made it impossible to get back to sleep, so she splashed water in her face, splashed milk on cereal, dug out her running gear and decided to make the best of her rude awakening. She quite enjoyed running – just not quite enough to do it without some additional incentive.

Today the incentive was that she had four hours before she had to be at Meadowvale, which was too much to fritter away, so if she didn't run she'd have to do some housework. Hazel understood the necessity for housework without getting any pleasure from it. A brisk two miles round the park, up the tow-path and back via coffee at Rambles With Books was much more appealing.

The drills had opened a yawning expanse of roadway immediately in front of her door. Needing to pick a careful route past it, she looked down and saw the box, wrapped in brown paper. Even before she unfolded the wrapping, she knew what it was going to be.

There was no card.

A couple of the workmen were watching her covertly. They'd known the chocolates were there before she had. They assumed, as she did, that they were from an admirer, and for some reason that made them coy and shifty, watching her over their shoulders and from under their hard hats.

So they were surprised and puzzled when, instead of simpering girlishly, she looked up quickly, sharp-eyed, peering both ways up Railway Street with an almost pugnacious expression; as if someone had done something untoward.

When she realised they were staring at her, Hazel made herself smile. 'Did you see who left them?'

'Sorry, miss?'

This was disingenuous. They knew exactly what she was asking. Hazel tried again. 'The chocolates. Somebody must have left them early this morning. Did you see who it was?'

There was a chorus of mumbles and shaken heads before one of them found a voice. 'Sorry, miss. They were on your step when we got here. Er – you mean, there's more than one feller likely to leave chocolates on your doorstep?'

'I didn't know there was even one.' Her fair brows gathered suspiciously. 'I don't suppose it was one of you muffins?'

This caused considerable sly mirth and elbowing of ribs. 'Sorry, miss,' said the spokesman for the third time. 'Not on our wages. Them's pricey, them is.'

Hazel looked again, more closely. 'So they is . . . er, are. Well, I suppose it's nice to be appreciated.' But actually it didn't feel terribly nice at all. It felt as if she was being . . . tailed. Watched. Stalked. She put the box on the hall table and closed the door. 'Tell you what. If you see someone hanging around, could you try to get a photo for me? Or anyway a description? Then I'll know who to thank.'

'Certainly, Miss Best. We'll keep our eyes skinned.'

The voice was familiar, and peering through the little knot of workmen she spotted a face that was also familiar. Now perhaps the chocolates made sense. 'Hello, Mr Price. So this is what you do when you're not standing up for civilised behaviour on trains.'

'Benny, please.' He nodded and indicated the excavation. 'A hole has opened up in Railway Street – council employees are looking into it.'

Hazel smiled dutifully. It might not have been the joke of the year, but the council works department probably wasn't very fertile ground for comedy. The man deserved marks for trying. 'Can I have a word?' She beckoned him aside, out of earshot of his colleagues.

He went with her obediently, eager to oblige. 'Something I can do for you?'

'Actually, yes. The flowers were a nice idea. The wine was pushing it, and the chocolates are definitely a bridge too far. I was just doing my job, and you thanked me at the time. I can't accept presents, however kindly meant.'

Benny was looking at her in a kind of puzzled embarrassment. 'Miss Best, I didn't leave you any flowers. Or wine. And like the lads said, the chocolates were there before we arrived.'

It was Hazel's turn to be embarrassed. 'I'm sorry. I just assumed . . . And then when I saw you here this morning . . .'

'I should have thought of flowers,' said Benny Price regretfully. 'I'm sorry I didn't.'

Hazel shook her head. 'No, I'm sorry – forget I mentioned it. Please?'

He smiled. He had rather a nice, kindly smile. 'Consider it forgotten. Was that everything?'

'Yes,' she said. Then: 'Actually, no.' He was a funny, slightly pompous man with the heart of a lion and a nice smile, and he deserved not to hear about Trucker Watts over a burger in the council canteen. 'I don't want this coming as too much of a shock. But you remember the young man on the train? The one with the knife?'

'Of course.'

Hazel recognised it was a stupid question. Benny Price was unlikely ever to forget him. 'His name was Trucker Watts. And he was found dead yesterday morning, behind the skips at the Kingswood shopping centre.'

There was no earthly reason for Benny Price to regret the passing of Trucker Watts. But it's human nature to reel when confronted with the eternal truth that all of us are going to die sometime and some of us are going to die quite soon. His mouth opened in a shocked O; then he closed it and looked for something appropriate to say. Finally he managed, 'He must have drawn that knife on someone who had a bigger one.'

'Someone who had a wheel-brace, actually. And he didn't get the chance to draw his knife. He was attacked from behind.'

Benny shook his head regretfully. 'I suppose, the kind of circles these people move in . . .'

Which was exactly what she would have expected a middle-ranking council employee with a steady job and a monthly salary and a pleasant house containing a wife and two-point-four children and a cocker spaniel to say. That too was human nature. Acts of sudden savagery had to be the fault, at least in part, of the victim. The terrifying alternative was to believe that anyone could be overtaken by them at any time. That Benny Price, or Mrs Price, or the little Prices, could have been found dead behind the skips at the mall.

'I didn't want you seeing his picture in the *Norbold News* tomorrow, without any warning.'

'No. Thank you.' He seemed touched that she would consider his feelings like that. 'Well, whatever next? Have you any idea who was responsible?'

Hazel shook her head. 'It's not really my department. CID may have a lead by now – I wouldn't necessarily hear. Trucker's gang thought it was a rival gang, but braining Trucker seems a bit out of their league.'

Benny walked her past the roadworks to the end of the street. 'Anyway, we'll keep an eye out for your secret admirer.'

'Thanks, Benny.' She went into her warm-up jog and quickly left him behind, standing on the corner of Railway Street, watching until she disappeared from sight.

'Well, if it wasn't Benny, who could it have been?' asked Hazel.

Ash was ringing up a sale. A young man with a silver bar through his nose had surprised him by choosing a volume of Elizabethan love poems. He tried not to be judgemental – some of the books he sold he wouldn't have chosen to read, but in principle he was in favour of anyone reading anything. Still, he found himself making certain assumptions, and it was good to be reminded that they weren't always right.

He returned to the kitchen where Hazel had poured out the coffee. 'Will you join us?' he asked, proffering a mug; but the young man with the nose bar had already left, clutching his volume of Tudor sonnets to his breast.

Hazel was still waiting for an answer, but of course Ash had no idea. 'Someone else you've done something nice for in the last few days?' he hazarded.

She couldn't think of anyone. Not because she had done nothing nice, but because she had done nothing nicer than usual. Being nice to people was part of her job description, even if it was a part some of her colleagues had never got round to reading, but think as she might she could come up with nothing likely to be marked by more than a grateful smile.

'Then could it be . . .?' Ash hesitated, frowning.

'What?'

'A bit of reverse psychology? Someone you've annoyed, or harassed, or put to some trouble. Someone who'd really like to set his dog on you, but knows that would get him into trouble. But little anonymous gifts might come to feel threatening if you didn't know who was sending them and you didn't know why. Do you think?'

Hazel was staring at him in astonishment and something like delight. 'I *love* the way your mind works! It makes mine seem so *normal.*'

References to his mental processes that would once have been wounding, even from a close friend and however carefully phrased, no longer troubled Ash. He knew she meant it as a compliment; and even if she hadn't, he had enough stability in his life now to look back on that phase of his life with some equanimity. 'Well? Have you been annoying anyone?'

'More than usual, you mean? I don't think so. Division are probably still pissed off at me, but I can't see the deputy chief constable creeping round after midnight to scare me into submission with a box of chocolates.' She favoured him with a sweet smile. 'Which leaves you.'

He hadn't seen that coming. 'Me?'

'Am I wrong?' Though she was smiling still, there was a note of challenge in her voice. 'Don't I annoy you? Don't you secretly wish I'd grow up and stop playing at cops and robbers? Either become a sensible high-achieving career woman like Superintendent Maybourne, or else settle down with a sensible high-achieving career man and have a litter of kids and worry about things like vacuum filters and cosmetic dentistry and getting an appointment with the manicurist. Be honest, Gabriel – don't you?'

Ash regarded her through the steam off the coffee mugs. Then he put his own down carefully on the counter, and took Hazel's from her and put it there too. Then he put his long arms all the way around her and hugged her tight against his chest. Speaking into her hair he said, 'I have never, ever wanted you to be any different to how you are.'

She didn't know what to do with the chocolates. She didn't think there was anything wrong with them, but not knowing what baggage they brought spoilt them for her. If she was going to consume that many self-indulgent calories, she wanted to enjoy them. She thought she might hand them in as Lost Property, in which case she confidently expected to see them making the rounds of Meadowvale Police Station by the end of the week.

Then she had a better idea.

On her way to work she stopped at the garage for petrol. Returning to her car, still enjoying the satisfaction of trading up from the battered old blue hatchback to this sleek and snorty hot hatch in glorious glinting sapphire, she spotted a familiar figure slinking out of the adjacent off-licence, the cheapest six-pack in town under his skinny arm.

If even Trucker Watts had a proper name, it was certain that the Rat had one too. If she checked back in the Incident Book she was sure she could find it. But his nickname suited him so well, describing both his physical appearance and the shape of the space he filled in the world, that she'd never been tempted to.

Except that sensible high-achieving police officers could hardly call out, 'Oi – Rat!' in a public place in the middle of the day. So she had to trot after him and tap him on the shoulder, and give him her most reassuring smile because no one had ever run after him in order to do something nice before.

'I'm sorry,' she said, 'I don't know your name.'

When the Rat realised she wasn't going to hit him, or arrest him, and wasn't even making fun of him, he replied with a shy little smile of his own. ''S Neville,' he confided.

Oh dear Lord, she thought – keeping the thought out of her face – some poor woman had held this little pink, or possibly slightly anaemic, baby, and beamed at it in pride, and named it Neville. Whatever would she think to learn what it was universally known as now?

'I'm Hazel,' she said aloud. 'You probably knew that. I'll tell you what it is, Neville. Have you seen Trucker's mum today? I keep wondering how she's holding up.'

The young man – and that's all he was: he wouldn't have been as old as her, though she'd always thought he was older – hefted the cider. 'I'm on my way round there now. We'll keep an eye on her, miss, don't you worry. Trucker was one of us. We'll keep an eye on his mum.'

And Hazel knew they would. There wasn't a lot to be said for the Mill Street Maulers, but there was this: they looked after their own. She reached into the car. 'Will you give her these? Someone gave them to me, but I don't eat chocolate.' God will forgive me, she thought parenthetically. 'Tell her I'm thinking of her, and if there's anything I can do to help, she must let me know.'

'I'll tell her, miss. But she won't. If she needs anything, she'll come to us.'

Hazel smiled again. 'I'm sure she will, Neville.'

They had already parted, Hazel opening the door of her shiny new car and the Rat heading for Mill Street with his commission, when she saw him hesitate, and half-turn back towards her, as if there was something he wanted to say and he wasn't sure if he should.

'Was there something else, Neville?'

He still wasn't sure. The conflict was etched in his pale, narrow face. But her gesture had taken him by surprise, and he was feeling the unusual urge to reciprocate in some way. It was a now-or-never moment – if she hadn't seen him pause, it would have been never – but she had, and it was now.

Speaking mostly to the cider and chocolates held in front of him, he said, 'You were asking if Trucker had any enemies.'

When he didn't go on, Hazel said, 'And everyone told me, Of course he had.'

The Rat gave a proud grin. 'Yeah – that was our Trucker.'

'Neville – was there someone in particular? Someone he was at loggerheads with? Maybe you've no reason to suspect him of hurting Trucker, but still, his name came to mind?'

'Yeah,' murmured the Rat. 'That's about it. I've no reason to suspect anybody, but . . .'

'But?'

'But if you've nothing better to do, you might see if Leo Harte was in town at the weekend.'

That was it: that was all she was getting, and from the way the Rat hurried away, head down and not looking back, she was lucky to have got that much.

SEVEN

'**W**ho's Leo Harte?' Dave Gorman looked up from the sports pages of last week's *Norbold News*. It's something to do with testosterone, apparently, this urge to read newspapers backwards. 'Why do you ask?'

'I heard the name today and didn't recognise it.' Without waiting for an invitation, Hazel pulled out a chair and joined the DCI in the corner of the police canteen. It was the middle of her shift, the end of his – he was eating here to avoid having to cook when he got home. He'd thought he'd be able to read the sports reports in peace while he ate.

'In connection with the death of Trucker Watts,' she added, expressionless.

That got his attention. He folded the paper at the rugby results and put it aside. 'Who were you talking to, and what did they say?'

'Trucker's friend Neville, otherwise known as the Rat. And all he said was, did we know if Leo Harte was in town around the time Trucker died.'

Gorman regarded her speculatively. He'd known Hazel Best for a while now, and knew it was reckless in the extreme to let her get her teeth into anything resembling a mystery. On the other hand, people told her things that they wouldn't tell him. Because she was a woman, perhaps; because she was friendly and approachable; because she made people feel that their concerns were important enough for her to devote time to, and if he was honest – and Gorman tried to be honest, with himself most of all – he knew that wasn't his strong suit. He cared about solving crimes. He tended to forget that, before a crime was his puzzle, it was someone else's disaster.

'The Rat thinks Leo Harte brained Trucker with a wheel-brace?'

'You think he's a non-starter? Why?'

Gorman pulled a face as he drank his coffee. The coffee available in the Meadowvale canteen had only one thing to recommend it: it wasn't made by the coffee machine on the landing outside the CID offices upstairs. 'Because Leo Harte isn't a criminal.'

He said it so deliberately, so positively, he almost certainly didn't mean it. 'You know that, do you?'

'Oh yes,' said Gorman firmly. 'It's been proved in court on a number of occasions. Lots of people who wouldn't dream of lying, like solicitors and accountants and a man who founded a church in Paraguay, have staked their reputations on it. Leo Harte is a law-abiding businessman. He has interests in property development, shipping and motor racing. There is no time left in his busy schedule for illicit gambling and the bulk distribution of mind-altering substances.'

'I see,' said Hazel slowly. 'So it wouldn't come as *that* much of a surprise if he and Trucker knew one another.'

'Actually, it would. Leo Harte might employ someone like Trucker – lots of people like Trucker – but I doubt he'd know them if they met in the Royal Enclosure at Ascot.' The thought of Trucker Watts in such surroundings made both of them pause for a moment. 'It's like . . . like me and ACC-Crime. We might work for the same organisation. We might be working towards the same goal. But he's at one end of the scale, and I'm rather closer to the other. In the normal way of things, my face wouldn't look even vaguely familiar to him.'

That wasn't strictly true. It might have been true once but it wasn't any more. It would be a long time before the Assistant Chief Constable (Crime) managed to forget DCI Gorman's face.

Hazel grinned. 'So why haven't I heard about Leo Harte before?'

'Because he's not local. He has offices in Birmingham, and he lives somewhere in the Cotswolds, I think.'

'So how come the Rat *has* heard of him?'

'That,' said Gorman, 'is a really good question. I'll make sure it's one of the very first ones I ask him.'

Hazel hesitated diplomatically.

'What?'

'Yes,' she said slowly, 'you could interview him. Do you think he'll talk to you?'

Gorman scowled. 'I suppose you're going to tell me he's more likely to talk to you.'

'He's already made the decision to talk to me. He didn't have to say anything at all. He certainly didn't have to implicate a man with the means and the motive to string him up by his ears and use him as a piñata. He wanted us to know about Harte. But if he'd wanted *you* to know about him, Chief, he'd have found a way to talk to you instead of waiting until he saw me. Maybe he finds me less intimidating. I don't know. But if we want to find out what he knows about Trucker's dealings with Leo Harte, I think he's more likely to open up to me, over a bag of chips on a bench on the tow-path, than if you put him in Interview Room One with the video running.'

Dave Gorman had no illusions about his qualities as a detective. He wasn't a brilliant investigator, leap-frogging ahead of his colleagues by peerless skill and intuition. What he had achieved, he'd achieved by hard work, long hours, and trying to do a good job even when the rewards for doing a mediocre job would have been higher. So if his pride took a dent from recognising that on this occasion a PC might get further with an informant than Meadowvale's DCI, it was only the latest of many and he could live with it. 'Do you want me to square it with Maybourne?'

'You probably should. She already thinks I'm trying to join CID through squatters' rights.'

Above the broken nose that is obligatory in rugby players, his eyes were unexpectedly kind. 'I'm sorry your interview didn't go better.'

She shrugged. 'Maybe they're right. Maybe I'm not cut out to be a detective.' But it cost her blood to say it.

*   *   *

Hazel didn't know where the Rat lived. But if he used the offie beside the garage, it was only a matter of time before he showed up there again. She left her phone-number with the cashier and asked for a buzz next time he came in, and the call came only a couple of hours later.

She was on her way home, already in civvies, which was fortunate because – whatever it was he wanted her to know – no one in the Rat's position could be seen talking to a uniformed police officer.

By the time she reached the off-licence he'd paid for his drink and left. She turned the way he'd turned last time they parted, and a minute's slow driving brought him into sight. Even from behind, there was no mistaking that crouched, anxious gait, as if he couldn't decide which was most important: not being noticed, or getting off the street before anyone who had noticed him did something about it.

She thought about calling his name, but that would leave him open to ridicule as well as the casual abuse he was accustomed to. So she parked her car and followed on foot, fifty metres behind, until he turned under a narrow arch between two brick terraces in Crimea Street, and put his shopping down on a doorstep while he fumbled for his key.

Hazel was quietly impressed that the Rat owned anything worth locking up.

She came up quietly behind him as he opened the door. 'We need to talk, Neville. Can I come in? Or shall we go and get a burger somewhere? My treat.'

He hadn't realised he was being followed, started so violently she swore his feet left the ground. Then he shot an urgent glance past her and back to the street. 'Come inside. But stay away from the window.'

Hazel hurried past him, staring. 'Someone's trying to shoot you?'

The Rat gaped at her. ''Course not. The bailiffs are after Auntie's telly again.'

'This is her house?'

'I rent a room.' The Rat added virtuously, 'I pay her for it.'

And what he got for his money was the front living room turned into a bedsit, with use of the kitchen behind and the bathroom that had started life as an outhouse in the back yard. It wasn't gracious living, but it was a roof over his head and there were the ashes of a fire in the grate, and it represented as much comfort and stability as anyone in the Rat's position could probably hope for.

There were thick net curtains, none too clean, at the window. Before he turned the light on, the Rat pulled a second set of heavier drapes across. Unless someone was paying close attention, from outside it would not have been obvious that the room was occupied. 'Is your aunt at home?' asked Hazel.

The Rat shook his head. 'She's at work.'

'What does she do?'

'She cleans offices. What is it you want, miss? I can't tell you anything.'

'You've already told me something I didn't know,' Hazel pointed out. 'That Trucker had dealings with Leo Harte.'

The Rat was regretting that already. 'I don't know nothing,' he responded automatically. 'Whether he did or not.'

'Neville,' Hazel said patiently, 'Leo Harte is a wealthy entrepreneur working from a posh office in Birmingham. I didn't know that until what you said made me ask around. I don't want to be rude, but the only way you'd have heard his name is if Trucker mentioned it. And the only way *he'd* have heard the name is if Leo Harte had a job for him to do. Was that it? Was Trucker working for Harte? Or had he *been* working for him, only it ended badly?'

'I don't know,' insisted the Rat. 'Trucker never said nothing to me.'

'He must have done. Why else would you even have thought Harte might know something about his death?'

'Because I want to get my head beaten in with a wheel-brace too?' muttered the Rat.

'Has he threatened you?' asked Hazel. 'If he has, the safest thing you can do is tell me what it's all about. That way there's no point him coming back and threatening you again.'

'Leo Harte don't even know I exist,' said the Rat with conviction, 'and that's how I want to keep it. All right?'

'All right. Well, there's no one here but us chickens. Tell me what it is you want me to know, and I'll go away and

never tell anyone I heard it from you.' Which was, she realised
in retrospect, a little more than she could honestly promise.
But then, the Rat would make such a terrible witness in court
that he was probably more valuable as an anonymous source
anyway.

'Oh *miss*!' He squirmed in an agony of indecision.

'Come on, Neville, spit it out. Trucker was your mate. A
fellow-Mauler. If you even *think* you know something about
who killed him or why, you owe it to him to get him some
justice.'

That seemed to chime with him; he gave a troubled nod.
But then he seemed to change the subject entirely. 'I know
where Leo Harte gets his hair cut. That swanky place in Fleet
Lane, with leather chairs and windows you can't see through.'

Hazel felt her mental wheels spinning. 'Lassiters? Well,
that's . . . interesting. Did Trucker tell you?'

The Rat nodded again.

'How did Trucker know?'

'He seen him in there. He talked to him.'

'Did he?' Hazel was trying to imagine the circumstances
in which Trucker Watts had been allowed over the threshold
of Lassiters. Had he helped old Gordon Lassiter bury a body?
'What did they talk about?'

'Mohawks,' the Rat answered immediately.

The wheels were hardly gripping at all now, and the cliff
edge was coming closer. 'The Indians?'

The Rat smiled, a transient sweetness that momentarily
transformed his pinched, sharp-nosed face. 'The *hairstyle*,
miss. You know, like a Mohican – shaved at the sides, standy-
up in the middle?'

'Leo Harte was getting his hair shaved at the sides so it
would stand up in the middle?'

'Don't be silly, miss! He's too old for a Mohawk – got to
be forty-five if he's a day.'

'So it was Trucker who wanted the Mohawk?' This was
even more problematical: for as long as Hazel had known him,
Trucker Watts had no visible hair at all.

The Rat sighed patiently. 'Neither of them wanted a Mohawk,
miss. They were just talking. Passing the time of day.'

She paused to consider for a moment. But no, absolutely nothing was becoming any clearer. 'Did Leo Harte ask Trucker to meet him there?' That would at least explain him being allowed inside.

'It was more, Trucker saw his chance and grabbed it. This flash car was parked in Fleet Lane, and Trucker recognised it as Leo Harte's. He said he'd been waiting his chance to ask Mr Harte for a job, and he'd never get a better one than this.' He looked down, embarrassed. 'He made me wait outside. But he told me all about it afterwards.'

Hazel tried to picture the scene. 'So Trucker asked to speak to Leo Harte while he was getting his hair cut. They talked about hairstyles. And then Trucker said he'd like to work for Harte. What did Harte say?'

The Rat was still studying the pattern of his well-worn carpet. 'Somefink about hell freezing over.'

It was all Hazel could manage not to laugh out loud. Trucker had seen his chance and taken it, and been rebuffed. As the dogs in the street had known he would be. Men who travelled from Birmingham to Norbold in flash cars in order to get their hair cut at Lassiters did not employ the likes of Trucker Watts, on a whim or probably at all.

'Was Trucker disappointed?'

'A bit. But then he brightened up. He said, now they'd broken the ice he could talk to Mr Harte again, and next time he'd be ready with some sure-fire arguments.'

'And did he?' asked Hazel. 'Approach Leo Harte again?'

'He was going to,' said the Rat. 'A few days later. We were going to the footie together – local derby, Norbold v. Allstars, Saturday last. But then he said he wasn't coming, that Mr Harte was going to be in Coventry for some trade do and he was going to have a go at cornering him as he came out.'

'Any more luck that time?'

'I don't know, miss,' the Rat said mournfully. 'I never seen him again. By Monday we realised he was missing, and the next day he turned up behind the skips at Kingswood.'

Which could mean anything or nothing. People like Leo Harte didn't have to murder people like Trucker Watts in order to stop them being a nuisance – they just sent a bit of muscle round to warn them off. Of course, if Trucker hadn't wanted to listen, and the muscle got carried away . . .

'OK, Neville,' said Hazel. 'We'll try to find out what happened. I'll let you know if we find anything.' Just before she left she asked with a smile, 'By the way, who won the match?'

The Rat beamed. 'The Maulers, of course – by two broken jaws and a smashed knee-cap in extra time.'

EIGHT

'What do you think?' said Hazel. 'Anything in it?' She'd been waiting outside Dave Gorman's office when he arrived first thing the next morning. He still hadn't got a new sign made for his door. Someone had inked in a letter 'C' between the 'D' and the 'I' with felt-tip pen.

Gorman shrugged. 'Could be. If Trucker wouldn't take no for an answer, one of Harte's minders might have got carried away. On the other hand . . .' And there he stopped. He regarded her levelly. 'You want to be a detective? You tell me why the picture doesn't quite fit the frame.'

Momentarily nonplussed, Hazel gathered her thoughts and rose to the challenge. 'Because he ended up dead. A dead body was always going to be investigated, and someone like Leo Harte wouldn't want investigating.'

'He also wouldn't want pestering by someone like Trucker every time he needed a haircut.'

'And he could certainly have sent one of his minders to explain that to Trucker. But Leo Harte wouldn't employ amateur muscle: that's *why* he'd no use for Trucker. Whoever he sent would know not to get *that* carried away.'

'There's always the chance that the first blow kills,' Gorman reminded her. 'Even in a friendly knock-about, sometimes one blow is all it takes.'

'If Trucker had been hit in the face, that would have been

a possibility. But he wasn't. He was hit from behind, with something hard and heavy, and then again while he was on the ground. Whoever did that wasn't passing on a friendly warning. At the very least, he meant to cause serious injury. He waited until Trucker was looking the other way because that was the easiest and safest way to get it done.'

Gorman nodded his approval. 'He wasn't passing on a message, he was taking Trucker out of the picture. It was over-kill – in every sense – from the point of view of Leo Harte.'

Hazel was disappointed. 'So it was nothing more than coincidence that Trucker was on his way to see Harte the last time he was seen alive?'

'I don't know. But it doesn't feel right. If Trucker had got his teeth knocked in or his fingers broken, maybe. But he was beaten to death. That's not how you warn someone off. And if Harte had wanted him dead, he'd have gone to more trouble to stop him being found.'

Hazel could see he was probably right. 'You'll interview Harte anyway?'

'I can't not. Even if Trucker never got to Coventry, we know he talked to Harte in the week before his death. I'll ask Harte what they talked about, try to get some idea of how bothered he was by Trucker's attentions.'

'Can I come?' asked Hazel hopefully.

Gorman scowled at her. 'What do you think?'

'I think I'm going to end up as the oldest uniformed constable in Britain,' said Hazel glumly. 'Giving advice on responsible use of a Zimmer frame to other octogenarians.'

She got home at a quarter to nine. Mrs Burden next door was watching out for her. 'I took a parcel in for you, dear.'

Tired as she was, Hazel was immediately alert. 'Who left it? Can you describe him?'

Mrs Burden was clearly surprised, but she did her best. 'Average height, dark hair, maybe about thirty?'

That rang no bells. 'Did you see what he was driving?' Of course, he'd probably had to park round the corner in Alfred Street, the same way she had.

'The post van, dear, same as always,' said Mrs Burden.

Hazel felt both foolish and relieved. 'Sorry. I thought you meant . . . Sorry.' She took the brown paper parcel, studied the label, learned nothing except that it had been posted in Norbold. 'Thanks, Mrs B.'

She took it inside, left it on the kitchen table while she put the kettle on. Then she opened it. But carefully: being delivered by the postman didn't mean it hadn't come from the same place as the flowers, the wine and the chocolates.

At first she thought it was a book. But there was nothing printed on the leather-cloth binding, and when she opened it she saw why. It wasn't a book, it was a photograph album.

'Who the hell buys albums these days? When every photo you ever took can be sitting on a memory stick ready to plug in to your laptop at a moment's notice?'

'Well – actually, I do,' said Gabriel Ash. 'It's different. I have pictures on my computer as well. But actual physical photographs in an album are more, well, permanent. You can leaf through them. You can show them to people. I started a new one when the boys came home. It's nearly full already.'

'A new one?' Hazel tilted her head on one side like a curious bird. 'You mean, you had one before that?'

Immediately Ash's eyes dropped. 'Mm.' He topped up their mugs in what looked suspiciously like displacement activity.

A slow smile spread across Hazel's face. 'Can I see it?'

He shuffled uncomfortably inside his clothes. 'There's nothing special in there. Just . . . family snaps, you know . . .?'

She did know. At least, she was pretty sure she did. 'They're pictures of Patience, aren't they?'

He didn't deny it, but nor did he meet her gaze. He knew she was laughing at him. 'Another biscuit?'

They were sitting at the long table in Rambles With Books. Five days a week Ash walked his sons to school, then he and Patience continued into town to open the bookshop. On Saturday mornings they came via the park. The shop was officially open from nine-thirty, although it was rare to see customers before ten. Of course, it was comparatively rare to see customers.

Hazel had been waiting for him when he arrived, the brown

paper parcel, roughly wrapped again, in her hand. He'd asked if she'd had breakfast, or possibly supper since she was on nights, and she'd said that she had, but Ash didn't entirely believe her. He thought she drank too much coffee and didn't eat enough proper meals.

He may have been right, because she was going through his custard creams as if the government was about to ban them. 'Gabriel,' she said through a mouthful of crumbs, 'there's nothing wrong with taking photos of your dog. Everyone does it.'

'Do they?' He'd never had a dog before so he didn't know.

'Of course they do. They're a big part of your family. Until the boys came home, Patience *was* your family.'

Under the table, the slim white lurcher heard her name and pressed up against Hazel's knees. They weren't close in the way that Patience and Ash were close, or even Hazel and Ash, but a dog always knows where its next biscuit is coming from.

Ash steered the conversation back to safer ground. He nodded at the album. 'Are there any pictures in it?'

Hazel shook her head. The first thing she'd done on receiving it was leaf through the plastic sleeves. 'Not one.'

'Yet,' said Ash.

Hazel didn't follow. Perhaps she didn't want to. 'What do you mean?'

He didn't mean to alarm her. On the other hand, if she really hadn't seen where this was going, Ash didn't want it to come as a complete shock. 'If someone who wants to remain anonymous has sent you an empty photo album, it's because he's going to send you some photographs to put in it.'

Hazel frowned. 'Photographs of what?'

Ash gave an apologetic shrug. 'If I had to guess, I'd say photographs of you.'

For half a minute her expression vacillated between disbelief and indignation. She looked at Ash as if she thought he might be making it up. Anger drew her fair brows into a deep V; a rebounding wave of surprise smoothed them out again. Finally her features settled into a kind of pained incredulity. 'Nobody has taken any photos of me!'

'Maybe they haven't, yet. Or maybe they've just been careful about how and when they took them. With a telephoto lens, he could have been so far away you wouldn't have known he was there.'

'Him?'

Another shrug. 'It's probably a safe assumption. It's mostly men who stalk women. The flowers, the wine and the chocolates make it almost certain.'

'And now he's going to send me photos of myself? *Why?*'

'Mostly, to show that he can. That he can watch you, and you don't see him. That he can get close to you, and you can't stop him.'

'But why would he want to?'

'Stalking usually starts off as a kind of shy admiration. Someone admires someone else but daren't make an approach for fear of being rebuffed. At first, proximity is reward enough. He gets his satisfaction from getting close to his subject without her knowledge. From watching her, observing her everyday activities. As time passes, though, just watching isn't enough. He wants to be part of her life, exercise an element of control. Look at what I can make you do. I can make you sniff flowers, drink wine, eat chocolate. I can make you look twice at everyone you know, wondering which of them is me.

'After a while, though, even that isn't enough,' continued Ash. 'The stalker starts to feel slighted. *Why* haven't you guessed it's me? Do you think so little of me? Do you think I'm not capable of this, either the strength of feeling behind it or the clever things I'm doing? That's when resentment starts to build, and the nature of the stalking changes from inappropriately expressed regard to intimidation. That's when it starts to get dangerous.'

None of this was exactly news to Hazel. Her Police Studies course had covered the psychology of stalking somewhere between domestic violence and drive-by shootings. But then it was an academic subject, something to be remembered and remarked on and recalled if ever someone came into the police station and asked for help. This was different. This was personal, and a scruple of Hazel's back-brain was embarrassed at *how* different that made it. 'Dangerous? You really think I should take this seriously, then?'

Ash nodded sombrely. 'I do. I think you need to tell Superintendent Maybourne that it's still going on and it's escalating. I think you need to take care of your personal security.'

'I'm not going to strap on a six-gun, or hang out my washing in a stab vest!'

She was making a joke of it, but Ash knew her well enough to see that, whatever his intentions, he'd succeeded in alarming her. Perhaps it was as well. Checking her car before she got in it and avoiding unlit areas late at night would do her no harm even if there was no strict need for it. Dismissing a committed stalker as someone with a teenage crush could get her hurt.

'You could move up to Highfield Road for a few days.'

Once, he could have made that offer to everyone he knew without running short of space. Now the big stone house was full to the brim with what seemed much more than just two young boys. Of course, there was also their live-in nanny; and Ash needed a study to conduct the business of the household and his shop; and the dusty echoes and pervasive sadness that had occupied the house when first Hazel knew it were long gone. Even so, she knew he was entirely serious about his offer – that he'd sleep on the kitchen sofa, using Patience as a pillow, if there was no other way to put her up – and she appreciated it even though she had no intention of accepting.

'I'm not being driven out of my home by some sad individual who doesn't know how to conduct normal relationships,' she said quietly. 'I will be careful, Gabriel, and I will tell Superintendent Maybourne, and I'll take the appropriate measures the moment I figure out who's behind this. But I'm not going to change how I live, or how I work. I'm not going to start jumping at shadows, and looking under my bed last thing at night. I'm not going to let him make me feel like a victim. If he doesn't get the response he's looking for, hopefully he'll get bored and find something better to do with his time. And if not . . .'

'If not?'

'I hope he's a decent photographer. I've been promising my dad I'd get some new pictures taken.'

When she'd gone, Ash was arranging a fresh display of

books on the long table when he became aware of the steady golden gaze of his dog. Her eyes were the same colour as the speckles in her coat: caramel shading to toffee. He kept working. But after a moment, without looking round, he said, 'Apparently it's perfectly normal to take photographs of your dog. No one will take it as a sign that I'm losing my marbles again.'

Patience said nothing.

Ash went on reflectively, 'I must take some more pictures of the boys. It would look less odd if I didn't have three of you for every one I have of them.'

Still Patience said nothing.

'What I should do,' said Ash, 'is book a studio session with a professional photographer. Children grow up so fast. Happy snaps are fine, but in years to come I'd like to have a really good photograph of the three of us.'

The four of us, said Patience reproachfully.

NINE

Superintendent Maybourne said nothing while Hazel recounted the latest development.

Hazel had rather dreaded this second interview, was afraid that updating her boss so soon might seem neurotic. Someone was leaving nice things on her doorstep. It was not unknown for police officers to find bullets, bombs, even body-parts on their doorsteps – and she was worried about after-dinner mints? But it felt oppressive. It felt like an opening salvo from someone who had much bigger guns hidden below the skyline.

Somewhat to her surprise, Maybourne took the delivery of the photo album at least as seriously as Ash had. She too seemed to feel that the tacit promise of ongoing surveillance was a significant escalation in the stalker's campaign. And they were now using the term *stalker*. These were not random acts of kindness: they were evidence of someone covertly watching her, and intending to go on watching her, whether she liked it or not.

'And you've still no idea who it could be?'

Hazel shrugged helplessly. 'I can't imagine. There's no one in my private life and no one in my professional life who seems to fit the bill even remotely. No new boyfriends, or old ones come to that. No one I've helped who might have mistaken professional assistance for personal kindness. No one, so far as I'm aware, that I've annoyed, who might think haunting me with unexplained gifts was a sneaky way of getting his own back.'

'We annoy people all the time,' Maybourne reminded her. 'We aren't doing our job if we don't.'

Hazel thought some more, but the result was the same. 'There was Trucker Watts, but I don't think flowers were his style even when he was alive.'

'Sometimes,' said the superintendent slowly, 'these things are closer to home than we want to believe. Hazel, don't misunderstand me when I say you have some interesting associates.'

For a second, when Hazel realised what she was saying, her jaw dropped. Then she shook her head decisively. 'No.'

'I know you think of Gabriel Ash as a good friend,' Maybourne persisted. 'Has it occurred to you that maybe he's thinking of you as something rather more?'

'No,' Hazel said again. 'For so many reasons. He's married – and though his wife treated him abominably, he's still in love with her. I know our friendship puzzles people, but that is all it is. We're not romantically involved. We're not going to *be* romantically involved. It's not what I want, and it's not what Gabriel wants.'

'I don't need to remind you that Mr Ash has a history of mental illness. He may not be entirely sure *what* he wants. Or, if he is sure, how to go about getting it.'

But there was not a shadow of a doubt in Hazel's mind. 'I'm sorry, ma'am, but you're wrong. Gabriel would never do anything to frighten me. It's not in his make-up. And he can't lie to me – I know him too well. We've talked about this. I'd know if he knew anything more than he was admitting to.'

Maybourne appeared to accept that, at least for the moment. 'Then there's that homeless youth who used to live with you. Could he be behind it?'

It's always interesting to see ourselves as others see us, and rarely an unmitigated delight. Hazel got a sudden insight into how her life appeared to people on its periphery. It wasn't normal, there was a pervasive hint of questionable judgement, and it explained some of the wariness with which colleagues treated her. She took a deep breath and swallowed the sharp retort that was forming.

'You never really got to know Saturday, did you, ma'am? He left Norbold soon after you came here. It's a pity: I think you'd have liked him. You'd certainly have been surprised by him. I know I was. He was living proof that anyone can make a future for themselves if they try hard enough.'

'That's why you took him in?'

'I took him as a lodger,' said Hazel, with a not-too-subtle shift of emphasis, 'because he needed somewhere to live, and Gabriel and I owed him a favour. He was sixteen years old, and life had shafted him again and again, and still he was willing to risk what little he had to do the right thing. He deserved a chance. He never made me regret being the one to give it to him.'

'And yet he left.'

Hazel swallowed. She knew Maybourne was aware of the circumstances. 'He left because I got him hurt. Because a man I had a relationship with raped him.'

'Yes, I remember,' said the Superintendent quietly. 'It was me who sent you to meet that man. You're not the only one to harbour feelings of guilt about what happened. But being an innocent victim then doesn't mean the boy can't be a suspect now. He could be looking for some kind of payback.'

'No.' There was nothing Hazel could add to explain why she was so sure. But she was.

'Then you've no idea who could be doing this?'

'Ma'am, I haven't. I'd tell you if I had. I'd tell you even if I thought I was wrong. I've asked the guys digging up the road outside my house to keep an eye open. They say they haven't seen anyone yet, but they might. Apart from that, I can't think what else to do.'

'We could get the computer geek to rig up a camera.' He had a name: it was Melvin Green. But everyone, even the superintendent, called him the computer geek.

'It's worth a try. Though the stalker may have thought of that too. That might be why he sent his last delivery by post.'

Superintendent Maybourne took her point. 'Well, let's do it anyway. Have a word with the geek, tell him what you want. And watch your personal security on the way to and from work, too, Hazel. Perhaps we should keep you off the streets for now. There's always plenty of paperwork waiting to be done.' She paused for a moment, a tiny frown clouding her brow. 'Anyway, it isn't paperwork these days, it's computer work, and IT is your thing, isn't it?'

'Yes,' agreed Hazel reluctantly. 'But I don't want this man stopping me from doing my job, or telling me which bits I can do and which I can't. Besides, so far his focus has been on my home. I've no reason to think he's been following me around town. I don't think staying off the streets would make any difference, except that it would look as if he was getting to me.'

'Isn't he?' asked Maybourne. 'Getting to you?'

'Yes, he is rather. But I don't want him knowing that, and I'd rather my colleagues didn't either.'

'You could always go away for a couple of weeks. A bit of winter sun. Or go down to Cambridgeshire and visit your father.'

'Same problem – it would look as if I was running away. What I'd like to do, what I think would be best, is exactly what I always do, on duty and off – but keep watching, and wait for him to make a mistake. He will, sooner or later. Then we'll know who he is and what to do about it.'

The superintendent nodded slowly. 'We can do that, for now. But Hazel, you know as well as I do that stalkers don't always settle for making their victims uncomfortable. We used to feel that it was a fairly benign form of harassment, that those who stalked and those who attacked were two different sorts of people. We know now that isn't the case. Many stalkers will go on to attack if they aren't stopped. Many attackers begin by stalking.'

'Which makes it all the more important that we find him and stop him,' Hazel said firmly. 'Going off on holiday, or staying out of sight, will do nothing but spin this out. He'll start again when things return to normal. We'll just have wasted time we could have been using.'

In fact, Superintendent Maybourne agreed with her. 'All right. Just . . . don't be brave about this. If anything or anyone is making you uncomfortable, get out of that situation and let me know. If you start suspecting someone, even if you have no evidence, tell me. I want to get this sorted out as much as you do.'

Hazel risked a wry grin. 'Well – nearly as much.'

In spite of which, when she thought of something that might help, and it was within her superintendent's gift and wouldn't even cost anything, she didn't go back and ask to be kept on nights for a while longer. Working nights meant that when she was sleeping alone in the house there were other people about in the street, and that when the town was dark and quiet enough for mischief she was awake and capable of dealing with it. If it had occurred to her while she was still in Maybourne's office, she would have suggested it. But it only occurred later, and it seemed such a trivial thing that she didn't like to go back and ask. Two days later her night-shifts came to an end.

Among the other investments in his portfolio, Leo Harte owned a golf course. He was not himself a keen golfer, but given a nice day it was a good place to entertain clients. He had given them a meal in the restaurant and then, as the cold grey morning gave way to a crisp bright winter's afternoon, he steered them out onto the greens and, still talking business, made sure they outplayed him by just enough to be feeling generous.

Glancing back from the twelfth tee towards the clubhouse, he saw his social secretary heading purposefully towards him. John Carson was not a man to interrupt a business meeting on a whim, so Harte knew something either awkward or urgent had come up. He turned to his guests with a smile. 'I'm sorry, gentlemen, but I think I'm needed back at the clubhouse for a moment. I'll be right back. But do play on – I think we can all agree, I was always going to come last!' With that he walked to meet Carson.

'Sorry, boss. But there's a copper in the office asking for you. If I hadn't come for you, he would've, and I didn't think you'd want that.'

Carson was not most people's idea of a social secretary. He was pushing fifty now, with a broad, scarred face, and under his dark suit he appeared to have been constructed out of boulders. He was, and everyone who knew him knew he was, Leo Harte's principal minder. But giving him the job description of social secretary achieved two things. It amused Leo Harte, and it made it easier to claim him as legitimate expenditure on his tax return.

'You were right,' Harte confirmed briefly. 'Who is he, what does he want?'

Carson shrugged. 'Detective Chief Inspector Gorman, from Norbold CID. Wouldn't say what he wanted.'

That seemed to surprise Leo Harte. 'Norbold? Apart from getting my hair cut, I've never done anything in Norbold. Nothing the police could possibly know about; in fact, nothing they couldn't.'

They walked together back to the clubhouse. 'Do you want me to take an urgent call for you after five minutes?' asked Carson.

Harte considered. 'No, I don't think so. I'd like to know why he's here.'

The visitors had been shown into the club secretary's office. Harte nodded to the secretary as he arrived, an amiable but definite dismissal. 'I'm Leo Harte. I understand you were asking for me.'

'Detective Chief Inspector Gorman.' Gorman stumbled fractionally over his new title. 'And this is Detective Sergeant Presley.'

'What can I do for you?'

Dave Gorman looked at Leo Harte, and Harte looked at Gorman.

What Gorman saw was a man a few years older than himself, clean-shaven, tall and slender without being disagreeably skinny; even if he had been, the beautiful cut of his clothes would have disguised the fact. His hair was fox-red with traces of grey at the temples. He had widely-spaced eyes of an almost turquoise blue, netted by laughter-lines, which offended Gorman even more than the man's conspicuous wealth. From what he knew of Leo Harte, he had no business laughing that much.

What Harte saw was a man of slightly more than average height and considerably more than average bulk, with a square face overshadowed by heavy brows and rather less forehead than the higher primates usually exhibit. A casual glance, at least from someone in Leo Harte's line of business, might have dismissed him as a plod, except for two things. One was that plods don't get made up to detective chief inspector, even in Norbold where there wasn't a lot of competition. And the other was the unmistakable glint of intelligence in his gaze. Leo Harte had dealt with many policemen in the course of his career. He'd developed an instinct for when he could afford to have fun with them and when he needed to take them seriously. Improbably enough, he was wary of DCI Gorman.

'I understand you were in Norbold ten days ago. At Lassiters, in Fleet Lane.'

'That's right,' said Harte. He added, somewhat unnecessarily, 'Getting my hair cut.'

'There aren't any barbers in Birmingham?'

Harte smiled. 'Of course there are barbers in Birmingham. I'm sure many of them are very good. But a man's barber is like the cordwainer who makes his shoes: when he finds one he likes, he sticks with him. I like Mr Lassiter. I would continue to visit Mr Lassiter if he moved his premises even further into the sticks.'

Gorman became aware that Harte was looking at his shoes. Gorman had never bought handmade shoes. He'd never wanted to, even with his recent salary enhancement. But somehow the fact that Leo Harte knew that was a real irritation to him.

'Who did you speak to while you were there?'

'Gordon Lassiter, of course,' said Harte. So far, he seemed not to mind being questioned. 'Mr Lassiter's assistant Harry. And I believe' – he turned to his social secretary for confirmation – 'that

Mr Carson here and I exchanged a few words, on the weather and the consequent state of the roads.'

'No one else?'

'I don't think so.' He paused until he saw that Gorman, believing he'd finished, was about to jog his memory, then he added: 'No, wait, there was. A rather uncouth young man. He said he was looking for work. I think he was just looking for hand-outs.'

'Which did you give him?'

Harte smiled again, broadly. 'Neither. I asked Mr Lassiter to show him to the door, and Mr Carson to ensure that he found it.'

'And then?'

'And then nothing. Mr Lassiter finished cutting my hair, and Mr Carson drove me home.'

'Mr Carson didn't – for instance – follow the young man outside with a wheel-brace?'

Leo Harte's turquoise eyes widened with well-feigned surprise. 'He had a flat tyre? He didn't mention it.'

British policemen have a reputation for being stolid, and this is why: sometimes it's the only alternative to slapping someone, which is frowned on. Dave Gorman said woodenly, 'So you had no further dealings with him.'

'None.'

'You didn't see him again last Saturday, in Coventry?'

'I was certainly in Coventry on Saturday,' said Harte. 'I was speaking at a property seminar. I'd be surprised to learn that particular young man was in the audience. But perhaps he was hiding his light under a bushel. Perhaps he was a major international developer, travelling incognito. If so, it was a really good disguise.'

Gorman hung onto his patience. 'So you wouldn't know who beat his head in and left him behind the skips at the Kingswood shopping centre?'

'Someone attacked him?' Harte's tone of shocked regret was too perfect to be sincere. 'Is he all right?'

'No, Mr Harte, he's not. He's dead. And the last person we know he talked to reckoned he was on his way to Coventry to see you again.'

Leo Harte seemed to have lost the inclination to joke about it. 'I can't imagine why. There was nothing more for us to talk about. I had no intention of employing him.'

'Maybe he thought he could change your mind.'

Harte shrugged. 'Hope springs eternal, I suppose. Perhaps he did try to see me again. But he didn't succeed. He wouldn't have been allowed through the front door of the conference centre. But by all means speak to the door staff. Maybe they'll remember him.'

'I'll do that,' growled Gorman. 'And I'll ask them what time you left, as well.'

'Actually, I didn't leave until Monday morning. It was a weekend seminar. When was the young man killed?'

Gorman didn't answer that, but he might as well have done. 'So you were still at the conference centre on Sunday night?' Harte nodded. 'What about Mr Carson?'

'Right there with me. I'd be lost without my social secretary.'

'Can anybody confirm that?'

'Lots of people, Detective Chief Inspector. I suggest you start with the events manager at the conference centre, and work your way down to the lad who parked the cars.'

Short of compering the Policeman's Ball, Leo Harte and his minder could hardly have had a better alibi. Though he would indeed check it, Gorman knew it would check out. A manufactured alibi would have been a handful of people Harte knew well enough to have some power over, not a random cross-section of the business community.

'That's probably all we need for now, then,' said Gorman, heading for the door. 'Don't bother to see us out.'

'If there's anything else I can help you with, do let me know,' said Leo Harte politely.

TEN

Sergeant Murchison, who organised the rotas, tried to ensure that officers switching between night- and day-shifts got forty-eight hours off duty to adjust their body clocks. Finishing at 8 a.m. on Saturday, Hazel had until 8 a.m. on Monday as down-time. Her first priority was to get some sleep. But it was best to start conforming to the norms of diurnal existence as soon as possible, so she set her alarm to wake her for a late lunch and then looked for something meaningful to do with the afternoon.

Before doing anything, though, she checked her doorstep. Nothing. She cast a shame-faced little grin in the direction of the road crew, who grinned back. They were always cheerful on Saturdays: they got paid extra.

'Nobody's been to your door since you came in this morning,' said Benny Price. 'Even the postman gave you a miss today.'

She'd already looked on the mat in the hall so she knew that. 'Thanks, Benny.' She looked past him to where the hole in the road appeared to be acquiring a life of its own. Every time she looked it was longer, wider, deeper and contained more workmen. 'Er – any idea when you're going to get finished?'

Price gave a rueful shrug. 'How long is a piece of string? These things take as long as they take. The lads are doing their best – they'll get out of your way as soon as they can.'

Hazel caught a rebellious mutter from the depths of the hole. 'We'd get done a damn sight quicker if that daft bugger would stop watching us and go count the ducks on the park pond instead.'

She wasn't sure if Price had heard or not; but perhaps he recognised the note of criticism, because he said jovially, 'Now then, lads, Miss Best's entitled to ask. That's her doorstep you're excavating underneath.'

Hazel smiled at him, and smiled at the workmen, and left them to it, walking round the corner to her car.

So what, she found herself wondering, was the hold-up? She'd got the album two days ago. Had her stalker photographed nothing worth putting in it yet? Quite possibly. She'd had a particularly uninteresting few days, from her own point of view as well as any observer's. She had done nothing photogenic during her shifts, which had in any event all taken place during hours of darkness, and most of her time between shifts she'd spent in bed. She'd stuck her head in at Rambles With Books a couple of times; she'd done her grocery shopping; she'd been to the laundrette in Crimea Street because her own washing machine was on the blink. Cecil Beaton would have struggled to capture an image worth preserving out of that lot.

So what was he waiting for? Could she draw him out by staging a scene he couldn't resist? Like what? Was she really going to have to ride a horse naked through the streets of Norbold? She might have been tempted, except that the stalker wouldn't have been the only one taking photographs. One of the mental welfare gurus from Division would certainly have been there too.

With nothing better to do, and hours to fill before she should sleep again, she thought she'd have coffee with Ash then take Patience to the park. Conscious that she was inclined to finish the biscuits he provided for his customers, she stopped at the first corner shop she came to and stocked up.

Maggie Watts came out of the shop behind her, carrier bags heavy in both hands. 'Can I give you a lift home, Mrs Watts?' The last time this woman had done a big shop, perhaps Trucker had carried it home for her. Although, knowing Trucker, perhaps he hadn't.

It took Maggie Watts a moment to recognise her, but less than that to accept her offer. 'You can that, dear.' Hazel opened the boot and Maggie deposited her bags with an audible sigh of relief. 'Oh. It's Constable . . . Sorry, I can't remember your name.'

Hazel reminded her with a friendly smile. 'So how are you managing, Mrs Watts? There's a lot to do when someone dies, I know. Are you getting the help you need?'

Maggie shrugged. 'Trucker hadn't that many affairs to put in order. He hadn't a lot of property to be divvied up. I sent most of his gear round to the Maulers, to let them share it out as they thought best. I don't think the Inheritance Tax will be much of a burden.'

Hazel gave her a quick sideways glance. This was an uneducated woman, in many ways an ignorant woman; what she wasn't was a stupid woman. 'I'm sure you've been thinking about what happened to Trucker—'

'Like I'd be thinking about anything else!'

'Of course not. I just wondered if you'd thought of anything else that could help us find who killed him. Even a vague suspicion would be worth investigating.'

'If I'd even a vague suspicion,' said Maggie Watts, 'I'd be doing something about it myself. I haven't.'

'Did Trucker ever mention a man called Leo Harte?'

'Leo Harte from Brum?' She barked a humourless laugh. 'Who told you about him?'

'I don't know,' lied Hazel. 'The name just came up. Did Trucker know him, then?'

Maggie shook her head. 'Leo Harte's big league, Trucker was little league. He dreamed of working for Leo Harte. He talked about it like other people's kids talk about going to university and getting head-hunted by a bank. But it was never going to happen. He hadn't the class. And that's me saying it. There were things about Trucker that only a mother could love.'

Hazel stopped the car in Mill Street and helped Mrs Watts gather her shopping. 'Do let me know if there's anything I can do. A message left at Meadowvale will always find me. If you need help with the funeral, or anything . . .?'

'I don't know when I'm getting him back yet.' Maggie sniffed. 'But thanks anyway.'

Hazel watched her go inside, then got back in her car.

She was about to drive off when someone tapped on her window. Two men were standing on the pavement, a tall thin one and a short thick one. The thin one leaned down to her window and said, 'This must be yours. It fell out when you opened your boot.'

It was a stiff brown envelope. Hazel took it from him, but there was no name on the front. She started to say, 'I don't think it's mine.' But before the words were even out, she knew that it was, and also what it must contain. 'Ah . . . yes. Thank you.'

The tall man nodded and smiled, and Hazel drove away.

The stiff brown envelope lay on the long table between them. There was no one else in the shop.

Ash said carefully, 'You shouldn't have brought it here. You should have taken it straight to Dave Gorman.'

'Why?' asked Hazel. 'Do you think it might be a bomb?'

He flicked her a worried smile. 'Of course it isn't a bomb. We both know what it is.'

'A photograph. Of me.'

'And evidence of a crime.'

She thought about that. 'Put your gloves on before you open it.'

Ash's deep-set eyes flared briefly wide. 'Me? Why do I get to open it?'

'So I won't have to.'

'Dave . . .'

Hazel didn't let him finish. 'Gabriel, I *know* I should have taken this to Meadowvale. If it *had* been a bomb, or a bullet, or a threat, or someone's ear, I would have done. But we know it's none of those things. It's a photograph of me. If it's a photograph of me in the shower, I don't want to be the second to know after Dave Gorman.'

That worried Ash even more. 'You think this man's been in your house?'

'I've no reason to think that. If he has, the camera didn't catch him and he left no trace. But I don't want to run the risk. I want to know what it's a photograph of before I start showing it round.'

Ash's brows drew together in a pensive frown. 'You don't want Dave seeing a photograph of you in the shower, but you don't mind me seeing it?'

Hazel breathed heavily at him. 'You may be a bit of a muppet sometimes, Gabriel, but you are always a gentleman.

If this photograph shows something I wouldn't wish people to see, *you will not see it.*'

Her trust in him warmed his heart. 'Well, if you're sure . . .'

It was mid-winter: his outdoor gloves were too heavy for delicate work. He fetched the washing-up gloves from the bookshop kitchen, and a fruit knife.

It's amazing the things a man can learn as an insurance investigator and security analyst. Gabriel Ash had learned how to open an envelope while causing the minimum of disturbance to any fingerprint or DNA evidence it might carry. He began in one bottom corner, opening a small aperture, then worked along the bottom. At that point it was possible, without disturbing the flap where some trace evidence might linger, to make the envelope gape wide and to see the photograph inside.

'You're not in the shower,' said Ash. He sounded relieved. 'You have all your clothes on. In fact, no,' he added, peering closer, 'you haven't. Isn't that my sweater?'

Hazel looked too. 'You never wear it,' she said defensively; which was of course another way of saying Yes. 'It's pink.'

'It's claret,' he said with dignity. 'No, don't take it out – take it to Dave so he can run it by Forensics.'

Hazel nodded. But she hesitated. 'I'm trying to figure out where it was taken.'

'When did you last wear my claret sweater?' asked Ash pointedly.

'I wear it quite a lot,' Hazel confessed. 'You left it at my house a couple of months ago. I never got round to returning it.'

'Well, the photo was taken in daylight, so you weren't on your way to or from work. So it must have been one of your days off. But you couldn't have been far from home or you'd have needed more than just a sweater at this time of year.' He squinted obliquely at the photograph. 'The background's out of focus, but isn't that the corner of a shop window? There seems to be some kind of a display . . .'

The same thought occurred to both of them. They trooped silently outside. Ash looked at his own window from a few metres away, then said sheepishly, 'I thought it looked familiar.'

'Stand by the door. A bit further to your left. Yes, there.'

Hazel was moving backwards across the pavement, stopping just before she went off the kerb. 'He was right here. In full view of anyone who was passing. Someone must have seen him.'

'Lots of people probably saw him. The question is, did anyone notice him? And without knowing when the photo was taken, there's no point either looking for CCTV footage or questioning passers-by. You're in here three or four times every week, and you've had the sweater for two months. It's too big a haystack to start combing for needles.'

They went back inside. Ash studied the envelope some more. 'It hasn't been through the post. How did it get in your car?'

'Maybe it didn't. The man said it fell out of my boot, but maybe he was mistaken.'

'Or maybe he was lying. Maybe it was never in your car. Maybe that was your stalker. Had you ever seen him before?'

She'd hardly looked at him long enough to know. 'I don't think so. Besides, if he'd wanted me to have it, he'd have been waiting a long time outside Maggie Watts's house! Much easier, and much safer, to stick it in the post.'

That was unarguable. 'Your car was locked?'

'I think so.'

'You only think so?'

'I couldn't stake my life on it! I hit the button on the fob when I leave it, I hit it again when I come back. I expect it to lock and unlock the car. But I don't check that it's worked. It's just possible that I thought I'd locked it when I hadn't.'

'Or maybe he wedged it somewhere. Under the rear windscreen wiper, or behind the bumper. Maybe it really did fall down when you opened the boot.'

There was no way, now, that they were going to know.

'All right,' said Hazel. 'I'll run this over to Dave, tell him what little we've figured out. Maybe Forensics will come up with something more positive.'

ELEVEN

'Nice sweater,' said DCI Gorman absently.

He'd pushed aside the file he was studying when Hazel brought in her envelope. Noting with approval the way it had been opened, he armed himself with gloves, tweezers and evidence bags before taking the photograph out. Now it lay on the desk in front of him while Hazel looked over his shoulder.

'You don't often wear pink.'

'It's not pink, it's claret. And most of the time you see me I'm wearing navy-blue with a stupid little bowler hat.'

'Fair point.' He looked at the back of the photograph. 'It's a DIY job rather than commercial stock. Good DIY, but DIY. No point asking round town if anyone printed it for him.'

'The joys of the digital revolution,' sighed Hazel.

'So when were you in the bookshop in your claret sweater?'

She shrugged an apology. 'Once or twice a week for the last couple of months? Gabriel and I tried to narrow it down, but we couldn't. Neither of us could remember what I was wearing when.'

'You haven't got a coat on.'

'I can usually park at the door. So I leave my coat in the car.'

'And you don't remember anyone pointing a camera at you?'

'It probably wasn't a camera. It was probably a phone. He probably looked as if he was making a call, not taking a picture.'

Gorman looked more closely at the image. He couldn't tell, but Forensics might be able to. 'Well, I think you can say you've got yourself a fully paid-up stalker. The question now is whether he means you any harm.'

'Nothing he's done so far suggests that he does,' Hazel ventured.

'No. That, unfortunately, is no guarantee of his future intentions. Have you given any more thought to that holiday?' He didn't wait for her to reply: her expression was answer enough. 'No, I suppose not.' He considered for a moment. 'I probably shouldn't be the one to suggest this, but is your firearms certification up to date? You could ask to draw a personal protection weapon.'

Hazel looked at him as if he was mad. 'I'm not taking a gun home so I can feel safe in my own house! Not because someone's left me chocolates and photographed me in a public place in broad daylight!'

'Fair enough,' agreed Gorman reluctantly. 'I just . . . I don't have a good feeling about this, Hazel. If he is an admirer, he's not content to admire from afar. I'm worried he'll get bored with leaving you presents and try to get up close and personal.'

'In which case I'll find out who I'm dealing with and know what to do about it. I don't think we should over-react, Dave. Yes, it's a bit unpleasant and I'm feeling a bit twitchy about it, but in terms of what he's actually done, it's very small beer. It's probably some pimply teenager suffering his first hormone rush. Either he'll get himself a real girlfriend and lose interest in me, or he'll pluck up the courage to ask for a date. In which case I'll give him an ear-wigging and send him home to his parents, with the suggestion that they confiscate his camera-phone for a while.'

'OK. Just . . . be careful.'

She smiled. 'I'm always careful, Dave.'

'That must be why you never get into any kind of trouble,' growled Gorman.

He reached for an evidence bag to slide the brown envelope inside. As he did so, his cuff caught the edge of the file he'd been reading when she arrived, tipping it over the edge of his desk and spilling its contents on the floor.

Hazel bent to gather them up. As she handed them back, though, she froze.

'What?' asked Gorman, trying to see what she was looking at.

'This man. Who is he?' Her voice held an odd edginess.

'Leo Harte. The Birmingham operator Trucker Watts was trying to get in with before he died.' He frowned. 'Why?'

'Because that's the man who handed me that envelope.'

*   *   *

'What possible business could someone like Leo Harte have with Maggie Watts?' Ash had his worried face on again.

'What possible business could he have with me?' countered Hazel. 'And if he *was* looking for me – and I can't imagine why he would be – why would he look in Mill Street? At Meadowvale, yes; at my house, possibly. But nothing more than random chance took me to Mill Street. I didn't know I was going there, so how could he?'

Ash had no answer for that.

'He *might* have had business with Maggie,' said Hazel slowly, 'if he was lying to Dave Gorman about his meetings with Trucker. If more passed between them than just an approach and a rebuff.'

'You mean, if Trucker's approach worked and he was already on Harte's pay-roll?' Ash thought about it. 'In that case, something he was doing for Harte might be what got him killed.'

This time the coffee pot they were sharing was at Highfield Road. Ash had already put his sons to bed, and with very little encouragement would have tucked Hazel up under a quilt on the sofa. The latest development, concerning as it was, was still only just enough to stop her nodding off: she was struggling to stay awake long enough to sleep until morning and rise with her body clock reset.

'Maybe he was killed by someone Harte had him put the frighteners on.' Hazel had a certain fondness for pulp fiction.

'Well, maybe,' said Ash diplomatically. 'Although if Leo Harte wanted to put the frighteners on someone' – he pronounced the phrase carefully, as if he'd never heard it before – 'why would he send Trucker rather than the highly professional muscle we know he employs?'

'John Carson,' nodded Hazel. 'Maybe it was a test for Trucker, to see if he could do the job as well as he said he could.'

Ash was unconvinced. 'An entrance exam? But Harte wouldn't send an untried wannabe up against someone dangerous. He wouldn't mind Trucker coming away with a cauliflower ear, but he wouldn't want the inconvenience of him turning up dead. If he had issues with anyone that violent, he would send Carson.'

'Probably. Then why would Leo Harte visit Maggie Watts?'

'Two possible reasons,' mused Ash. 'Trucker had something which Harte wanted. Or he felt guilty about how Trucker died and wanted to do right by his mother.'

Hazel gave a hoot of mirth that turned into a yawn. 'This is still Leo Harte we're talking about, is it? Leo Harte who organises illegal gambling and sends John Carson to collect his debts. Leo Harte who ships goods all over the world, with who-knows-what hidden inside them. I'm not sure guilty is in his emotional lexicon.'

Put that way, it didn't seem too likely.

Another possibility occurred to her. 'You don't think he'd hurt Maggie, do you?'

'Conceivably. If Trucker had taken something of his and he wanted it back, and now he couldn't ask Trucker himself where it was? – yes, I imagine he might. But would he go in person, in broad daylight, and be seen near her house? – no. Not to hurt her, and not to threaten her. For either of those purposes he'd send John Carson, and he'd send him after dark.'

'What's left? He wanted to express his condolences?' One canted eyebrow said how likely Hazel thought that was.

'What did Dave say?'

'Dave thought I should go away on holiday.'

'*I* think you should go away on holiday.'

'Why? Because I bumped into someone on the street who might, but equally well might not, know something about Trucker Watts's murder? Even if he does, why would that make Leo Harte a danger to me?'

'Perhaps it doesn't,' conceded Ash. 'But Leo Harte isn't the only one you need to worry about. There's also the man who's been leaving you presents and taking your photograph.'

Weariness was now overtaking Hazel like a flood tide. She hauled herself to her feet, groped her way into her coat and headed for the door, her car and home. 'Tomorrow,' she promised. 'I'll worry about that tomorrow. Tomorrow is another day.'

And, being Sunday, it brought no post. But Monday morning did. It brought another stiffened brown envelope, which Hazel

opened when she got home from work. This time the photograph showed her parking her smart new car round the corner,
which was still as close as she could drive to her front door;
and this time she knew when it was taken. Workdays she'd
been leaving home and getting back in darkness. The photograph was taken in daylight. And she'd worn that coat as
recently as yesterday.

Yesterday. She could cast her mind back to pretty well the
exact moment that picture must have been taken. Even knowing
that someone had been watching her, had been taking photographs of her, she couldn't remember seeing anyone in Alfred
Street. 'Oh, you're good,' she murmured. 'And you're not just
a pimply teenager with a crush, are you? Have you done this
before? This, or something like it? Or are you just putting a
lot of thought into making it work?'

TWELVE

T uesday, Hazel wasn't due at work until after lunch.
She didn't set the alarm. She thought she'd sleep until
ten o'clock in the morning and wake like a giant
refreshed.

In that she was wrong. Perhaps she was more concerned
than she'd let either of them think, DCI Gorman or Gabriel
Ash. Worry will murder sleep more effectively than anything
except pain. In the darkness and the silence – Railway Street
did not on the whole keep party hours – she lay cocooned in
her winter-weight bedding, comfortable enough, waiting for
sleep to return. Growing irritable when it did not.

It was all so *stupid*. None of it made any sense. Not the
death of Trucker Watts; not the involvement of Leo Harte; not
the advent-calendar visits of her secret admirer. They made
no sense considered as separate episodes, and even less as
parts of a greater whole. And her friends wanted her to feel
threatened by this nonsense? She was damned if she would.
No one had any reason to harm her. The only one who might

conceivably have borne her some ill will was Trucker, and he was no threat to anyone now.

She turned on her side, drawing the quilt up under her ear; sleep remained elusive. She couldn't think why. She'd been tired enough when she fell into bed, and morning was still hours away. She found herself listening, although there was no sound from the street to disturb her rest. Even Mrs Burden's Alec, who had a habit of singing Gilbert & Sullivan on his way home from the pub, liked to be tucked up with his cocoa before midnight. Perhaps there was a stray dog raiding bins just on the edge of hearing. Perhaps there was a fox. They were getting bolder, becoming more urbanised, all the time. Perhaps . . .

That wasn't a dog, it wasn't a fox, and it wasn't a sentimental Glaswegian claiming to be three little maids in an improbably high falsetto. And it wasn't as far away as the street. There was someone in the house.

Hazel's first instinct, the one that came from that primitive part of the brain shaped in a time when human beings were not top of the food chain, was to freeze. Her muscles cramped up so rigid that she had to fight them as if there was another person holding her down. But if someone had broken in here intending her harm, she had to move. She had to not be where he expected to find her. She had to be ready to fight back.

Then, when she'd battled through the fear paralysis to regain command of her own body, her second instinct was to turn on the light, and that was wrong too. Right now, in all her hand she held only two good cards. She was awake when the intruder expected her to be asleep; and she was familiar with her surroundings in a way that he was not. Together, they gave her an edge that would disappear if she turned on the bedside light. Tonight, darkness was her friend.

When she'd lived in student lodgings, she'd kept a cricket bat to deal with unwelcome night-time incursions. That bat had become evidence in a criminal case, and though the case had long ago been resolved, she didn't think it had ever been returned to her. She tried to think what else she could use to defend herself. She didn't play golf, and both brass candlesticks and marble statuary were rather Victorian for her taste.

But she had what no Victorian damsel defending her honour could resort to: she had a mobile phone.

There was no lock on her bedroom door. Her heart thumping in her throat, conscious that he might already be upstairs, that as she emerged onto the landing she could find herself gripped by unseen hands, she had to force herself to open the door anyway and seek a refuge that was more defensible. Silent on unshod, chilly feet, she crossed the landing to the bathroom – no hands reached for her, as far as she could tell – and with infinite care shut and locked the door behind her. With the phone to her face and a towel to muffle the sound, she called not 999 but the number of the front desk at Meadowvale, which she thought would get help to her quicker.

Wayne Budgen picked it up. 'This is Meadowvale Police Station, Constable Bud—'

'Wayne,' she whispered urgently. 'It's Hazel. I need the area car. Someone's broken into my house.'

'Hello?' he said. 'Is there someone there?'

'Wayne!' she hissed again, her voice quivering with fear and impatience and adrenalin. 'It's Hazel! Hazel Best. There's someone in my house. I can't speak up, I don't want him to hear me.'

'Hazel?' Then the penny dropped. 'Hazel! You've got an intruder? Are you somewhere safe?'

'I've locked myself in the bathroom.'

'Good. Stay on the line. The area car will be with you in three minutes.' There was a pause in which she could hear him talking to the patrol car. Then he was back on the line. 'Is he downstairs or upstairs?'

'Still downstairs, I think,' she whispered. 'I haven't heard the stairs creak.'

'Is there anything you can wedge behind the door?'

It was a small house with a tiny bathroom: all the furniture there was room for was a towel-rail and a linen-basket. 'Only me.'

'No – stay away from the door. Is he armed?'

'I've no idea. I haven't seen him. I just heard someone downstairs. What time is it, anyway?'

'Twenty past three. Listen, Hazel – get in the bath.'

She wasn't expecting that. 'What?'

'I know those houses. My aunt used to live in Railway Street. Have you still got the old cast-iron bath? Because if he's armed, and he starts shooting, the door won't stop bullets but that bath will.'

She hesitated no longer. She threw everything off the towel-rail in first – cast-iron is a cold prospect in winter, which is why so many old baths have been replaced by warmer but less bullet-proof materials – then eased herself over the edge, trying not to rattle the toiletries on the rim. Then she waited.

If he was just trying to freak her out, he might place his latest present on the kitchen table and leave whatever way he'd got in. (How had he got in? She knew she'd locked both front and back doors, left no downstairs windows ajar, and didn't have a cellar.) It was already a big step up from leaving chocolates on her doorstep, a photograph on her car. But if she heard footsteps on the stairs, his purpose here was more sinister still.

If he'd been watching the house, he knew which room she slept in. That was the first place he would go. He wouldn't turn the light on, so it might take him a minute to realise she was no longer in bed. (If she'd thought quicker and panicked slower, she might have done the old thing with the pillows under the quilt: let him drool over that for a while, or shoot it, or jump its bones – whatever he'd come here for. But she hadn't.)

He might try the other bedroom, the one that had been Saturday's, next. But probably he would realise that, aware of his presence, she'd headed for the one room in everyone's house that has a working lock. She'd know he'd found her when the doorknob turned.

What would he do when the door didn't open? If he'd any sense he would run, try to get away from the house before help arrived – because he would know by then that it must be on its way. The house phone was in the hall downstairs, but everyone sleeps with their mobile beside the bed, don't they? (Except Gabriel Ash, she thought parenthetically, who left his on the hall table with his car keys whenever he came in.) So the sound of the doorknob – she wouldn't see it move in the dark, but in the small-hours silence she should hear it – should be followed in quick succession by the sound of someone running back downstairs, no longer trying not to be heard, anxious only to be away from this house before the police arrived.

And if he didn't run? Well, that was bad news of a whole new order. That meant that what he had come here to do mattered more to him than getting away with it. The bathroom door, with or without the linen-basket behind it, wouldn't stand up to a determined assault.

Three minutes, Wayne had said. Surely at least one of them had passed already?

In her ear he said, 'Are you all right, Hazel? They're on their way. They're passing the park already. Another minute and you'll hear them. So will he.'

And if he wasn't prepared to run, would the sound of the siren drive him to an act of desperation? Would he attack the bathroom door with a hatchet? Would he start shooting through it? Hazel flattened herself against the bottom of the bath, cold along her breast and belly despite the towels, keeping her head below the level of the rim. She could still catch a ricochet. And if he'd come armed with both a hatchet *and* a gun . . .

Surely that must be another half-minute gone?

The creak of old timbers, that she heard so often she never normally heard at all. 'He's on the stairs,' she whispered into the phone. 'Oh Jesus, Wayne . . .'

She heard her bedroom door open. Seconds dragged past. She heard Saturday's bedroom door open. Then she heard the sound, part creak, part rattle, of a hand on the bathroom doorknob.

In the tucked-up silence of the long winter night, undisturbed even by Alec Burden being the very model of a modern major general, the sound of a police siren carried half a mile through the sleeping town. Deep in her cast-iron bunker, Hazel heard it and her heart rallied. Outside the bathroom door the intruder heard it too. There was an intake of breath, a muffled curse, and then heavy-booted feet heading down the stairs much less carefully, much more noisily, than they had come up.

The area car would come to the front door – the back gardens in Railway Street were little more than yards giving access to a ginnel – so, whatever way he'd got into the house, he had to leave by the back door if he didn't want to run straight into the arms of two large policemen. Suddenly Hazel wasn't prepared to let him get away scot-free. With the promise of support already within earshot, the fear that had been clutching her innards in a cold hand turned in a heartbeat to hot anger, and she rose from the depths of the bath like Venus rising from the sea-shell, only crosser and wearing pyjamas.

She vaulted over the bath rim, threw open the door, flicked on the landing light as she flew past and took the stairs two at a time, saved from disaster only by her familiarity with their treads and the fact that she was now too furious to be afraid. She wanted to see his face before he got clean away. She wanted to know who was persecuting her.

If she'd caught up with him, she might well have tried to arrest him, though she knew that would be deemed reckless by DCI Gorman and insane by Gabriel Ash. In the event, however, she never got that close. She saw a thick-set body in a thigh-length khaki parka, fur round the raised hood, standing at the back door as he fumbled the latch. Then the door flew open and he leapt the two steps, crossed the yard in three paces, wrenched open the back gate and was gone.

THIRTEEN

'I made a complete cock-up of it!' declared Hazel bitterly. 'I behaved like an amateur. Worse: like a girly amateur!'

It was now mid-morning. She'd been thoroughly debriefed by DCI Gorman and Superintendent Maybourne, and the adrenalin rush that had left her shrill and shaking for the first hour had long since receded. Now she was able to review the night's events with a cold and critical eye, and she wasn't pleased by what she saw.

Ash had taken one look at her when she arrived at the bookshop, drawn the blind and taken her back to Highfield

Road, where he was now plying her with hot chocolate for the shock.

They had the big stone house to themselves. The boys were at school and their nanny was shopping in town. Hazel sat down beside Patience on the kitchen sofa while Ash heated the milk. Over his shoulder he said, 'Is that what Dave said?'

'It's what he must have thought.'

'What did he *say*?'

She vented a weary sigh. 'He said I'd done the right thing by locking myself in the bathroom and calling for help.'

'What did Superintendent Maybourne say?'

'Pretty much the same thing. But Gabriel, he was there – right there, within a few feet of me. If I hadn't panicked, if I'd thrown open the door while he was trying the knob, I could have seen who it was. I could have put an end to this.'

'He could have killed you,' Ash said.

'He hasn't been sending me presents because he wants me dead!'

'He started off by sending you presents. You don't know what he wants now. Only that he thought it was worth risking being caught, and all that would follow from that. You cannot afford to underestimate what this man is capable of.'

Hazel knew he was right. It didn't make her feel any better about cowering in a bath while an intruder prowled her house.

'Do you know how he got in?' asked Ash.

Hazel nodded. 'He used a glass cutter to make a hole in the pane in the back door. Then he reached through and turned the key.'

'Which was in the lock.'

'Which was in the lock,' she agreed. 'All right, this time it was a bad idea. If there'd been a fire, it would have seemed like a good idea.'

'I suppose fingerprints are out of the question?'

She nodded glumly. 'Gloves.'

'And nothing on the camera?'

'Only Railway Street with nobody in sight. We put the camera at the front – that's where he was leaving his little presents.'

'You can't cover every possibility,' said Ash. 'But you saw him as he left.'

'I saw his back. I can give a fair description of his parka, that's about all.'

'Tall man? Short?'

Hazel shrugged. 'Somewhere in between. Maybe on the solid side. Or that might just have been the parka.'

'He never looked round?'

'Not while I was there. And the hood covered his head – I don't even know if he was bald or bearded.'

'Did you see any kind of a weapon?'

'I hardly saw anything at all,' she repeated. 'I can't say he *wasn't* armed.'

For a moment neither of them said anything more. They sipped the chocolate, explored the contents of the biscuit tin.

Ash broke the silence. 'You know you can't go back there?'

'Of course I can,' said Hazel, surprised. 'The glazier replaced the panel in the door.'

'For God's sake,' exploded Ash, 'I'm not worried about the draught! I'm worried that next time he does it, you won't hear him. You cannot sleep in that house again until he's been found and dealt with.'

'And how long's that likely to take?' demanded Hazel. 'Weeks? Months? I'm not sleeping on your sofa for the fore-seeable future.'

'You can have my room,' he offered in a low voice.

His diffidence still had the power to charm her. She touched the back of his hand with her fingers. 'Thank you. But no. I told you before, I'm not running scared from this man.'

'Weren't you scared?'

She was about to lie, thought better of it. 'Of course I was. There's no need for everyone to know, though, is there?'

'You should be scared. A week ago you had a secret admirer: last night you were threatened by an intruder in your house. That's too big a progression in too short a time. What's he going to do next? He's not going to be content with leaving small tokens of appreciation on your doorstep any more.'

Much as she wanted to dismiss his concerns, Hazel knew he was right. Whoever was doing this had crossed a Rubicon when he broke into her house and padded round looking for her. The arrival of the area car might have scared him off, but it wouldn't keep him away. Something was drawing him to her, something that perhaps he understood no better than she did but which he could not resist. He would be back. Or he would find her somewhere else.

'What do you think I should do?'

Ash dared to hope that she would listen to reason. 'I think you should get out of Norbold for a while. Go and visit your dad. The investigation will go on just as well without you. When Dave Gorman makes an arrest, you can come back and see if it all makes sense when you know who's been doing it.'

At least she was considering it. 'What if he follows me? It wouldn't be that difficult for him to find out I have only one close relative, and where he lives. I don't want to take my trouble to his door.'

Fred Best was an old soldier: Ash thought he was probably still capable of dealing with most forms of trouble. But he understood her reluctance. 'What about Pete Byrfield, then? He wouldn't have to give up his bed for you. And you'd be close enough to see your dad without being under his roof.'

The idea had a certain appeal. Hazel had grown up on the country estate where her father was handyman to Peregrine, 28th Earl Byrfield, widely known as Pete. She'd ridden his sisters' out-grown ponies and he'd pulled her pigtails. Meeting again as adults, he'd been rather surprised that (a) Hazel Best the grubby tomboy had turned into a notably good-looking young woman, and that (b) the old easy friendship had survived a decade apart.

'I suppose I could ask him,' she said slowly.

'Hazel,' said Ash sternly, 'you solved a mystery that was tearing his family apart. You really think he's going to begrudge you B&B for a couple of weeks?'

'All right,' she decided. 'I'll ask him.'

Ash drove her to Cambridgeshire. There were three good reasons for Hazel to leave her car in Norbold, although Ash thought she was only aware of two of them. If the stalker saw her car in its usual place, he might venture to approach the house again, and although Meadowvale couldn't spare the manpower for a 24/7 surveillance, frequent drive-bys in unmarked cars might spot him. As well as that, she didn't want her car to be seen anywhere near her father's house – if the stalker realised she was missing, he might think it worth the three-hour drive to check if she was visiting her father.

The third reason, the one Ash hadn't mentioned to Hazel, was that if she didn't have her own transport at Byrfield, she couldn't get bored after three days in the country, wonder how the investigation was progressing and nip home to check.

'What did Pete say when you called him?' asked Ash as he drove.

'He seemed pleased, and a little concerned, and said we were going to have a cracking good time.'

Ash liked the 28th earl. Not because he was a snob but because Byrfield wasn't either. They both recognised that the only difference between the earl's domain and the farms of his neighbours was a hamper full of ceremonial robes mouldering gently in the attic, and that a rowdy bullock was unlikely to be impressed by ermine and strawberry leaves. Pete Byrfield was a farmer: not just in name, in welly boots as well.

'That was nice of him. He must have been missing you.'

'Well, maybe,' murmured Hazel. 'Mainly, I think he was happy his mother's spending Christmas in London.'

'And you're going to spend it with your father and the Byrfields.' There were three of them, or four if you counted David Sperrin, who was the 27th earl's by-blow. It was a tribute to the family how well they all got on, mostly by being very pragmatic and slightly eccentric and not giving a toss what anyone else thought. If it was true that the dowager countess had proved less generous than her children, it was also the case that she never showed much generosity to anyone so David didn't feel it as a particular burden. Also, his own mother didn't like him much either.

'I don't know about that,' Hazel retorted sharply. 'It's three weeks to Christmas – surely this will be sorted out before then?'

Ash shrugged. 'It'll take as long as it takes. Enjoy the break. If you're still there, I'll bring the boys down for a visit on Boxing Day.'

'Yes, do – that would be nice.' Hazel was watching the winter landscape pour steadily past the car window and thinking: Don't count on it.

Pete Byrfield met them at the front door of his ancestral home, but they didn't go in that way. He led them round the side to the kitchen door. He'd been TB-testing cattle, and several of them had left their mark on him.

'I'm glad you're here,' he called from the scullery, where he was stripping off boots and overalls to reveal a cleaner – rather than a clean – layer of sweater and cords underneath. 'I've been worried. Are you all right? What the hell's going on?'

He sounded so troubled that Hazel attempted to make light of it. But Byrfield wasn't fooled. The plain facts were unavoidable. Someone had broken into her house, at night, while she was alone and asleep. And it wasn't a random burglary attempt: it was personal.

'Thank God you're safe. And I'm glad you thought to come here. You're always welcome at Byrfield – I don't need to say that, do I? We'll look after you, I promise.'

He was a tall, narrow man in his mid-thirties, with fair hair already thinning and rather more teeth and less chin than might have been considered ideal. But for the fact that an earlier Byrfield distinguished himself at the battle of Bosworth in 1485, he might have been a middle-ranking academic at a red-brick university.

He turned to Ash. 'Are you staying tonight, Gabriel?'

Ash shook his head. 'I'd better get back. I've left my nanny trying to outfit one archangel and one shepherd from the contents of the dressing-up box plus some of my mother's old curtains, and the nativity play's on Friday.'

They waved him off from the top of the steps. 'I've booked dinner in Burford,' said Pete. 'We're picking your dad up on the way past.'

FOURTEEN

I t was true about the nativity play, and nanny Frankie Kelly was glad of her employer's help. In fact both costumes were comparatively simple – brocade and a bit of tinsel for the archangel, a dressing-gown and a tea-towel headdress for the shepherd – but the two boys kept being distracted by treasures they'd unearthed in the attic. At one point it appeared that their father's namesake was going to announce the birth of the Christ-child while wearing roller-skates, and the second shepherd would insist on the protection of a motorcycle helmet in case the star fell on his head.

But being true didn't make it the only reason Ash had wanted to get back to Norbold. After the boys were finally in bed and asleep, and Frankie had retired to her room to listen to a concert on the radio, Ash filled a flask with coffee and looked out a spare quilt against the cold. He knew Dave Gorman would be as good as his word and organise drive-bys as often as he could, but Ash could do what the police could not. He knew where Hazel kept her spare key: behind a loose brick in the shed behind her house which had once been the privy. He could let himself in, and sit in the dark all night in the hope that her stalker would return.

He left a note for Frankie on the kitchen table. With luck he wouldn't be missed, but he didn't want anyone worrying if he was.

Patience was sitting expectantly on the doormat as he went to leave. I'm coming too, she said.

Ash shook his head. 'Not this time. Stay here. You don't want to get cold.'

The lurcher pointed her long nose at the bundle under his arm. That's a pretty big quilt you're carrying.

'It's going to be a long night. And probably a fruitless one.'

Dogs can sleep anywhere.

'But if something does happen, it could get violent.'

Exactly, said Patience. And you'll need someone to watch your back. Preferably someone with teeth.

There was a limit to how long he could argue with his dog without being overheard. It wasn't as if they had the house to themselves any more. 'Oh, all right then. But you'll regret it before the night's out. Do you want to bring Spiky Ball?'

Ash carrying bedding and refreshments, Patience carrying her only treasure, they slipped out of the house and headed for Railway Street.

Hazel remembered Christmases at Byrfield. Nearly twenty years ago, when she was a child and the head of the family was the 27th earl, a bluff cheery man upholstered in tweed, the old house had twinkled its way through the darkest part of the year: candles in every window, the tree in the great hall weighed down with baubles and fairy-lights.

There was always a party for the children of Burford village on the Saturday before Christmas, and presents wrapped in glittering foil tied up with tinsel under the tree. Hazel remembered waiting with baited breath, the tension mounting, until jovial Henry Byrfield – wearing a Santa suit over his own wellington boots, still damp from the courtyard tap – read her name off one of the gift-tags and, shy but thrilled, she stepped forward to collect her parcel. Pete's mother thought the little boys should bow and the little girls curtsy, but Hazel's father, who worked on the estate, said she just had to take it without snatching and say, 'Thank you, my lord.'

Usually it was a colouring book and some pencils, a board game or a toy; but one year it was a pony-sized head-collar which delighted and puzzled her in equal measures. Then Pete's older sister had sidled up beside her and said she was getting a sixteen-hand hunter for Christmas and her outgrown pony needed someone to ride him in case he felt jealous. That was the best Christmas ever.

This year's tree – the best and biggest on the Byrfield estate – was already in place, rising through two storeys of the house with the grand staircase looping round it. Although they habitually used the kitchen door, after Ash had left Pete Byrfield brought Hazel back in again through the main entrance so she could see it at its best. 'I thought we might decorate it after dinner. It's a good tree, don't you think?'

'It's a fine tree,' she agreed warmly, and he shrugged his narrow shoulders happily. 'When did you cut it?'

'A couple of days ago. From that stand over by the lake. Your dad helped me set it up.'

They were alone in the hall. Hazel turned to face him. 'Pete, I haven't thanked you properly for taking me in.'

Byrfield's smile transformed his thin, rather aesthetic face. He didn't look like a farmer. He looked like an Eng. Lit. graduate who'd written his thesis on the romantic poets. 'What are friends for?'

'I don't think they're for holding your hand when you've had a sudden attack of the vapours,' said Hazel, embarrassed.

'I do,' said Byrfield stoutly. 'I think that's pretty much exactly what they're for.' And he reached out and folded hers in his long, slender, surprisingly strong fingers – a gesture that might have been more poetical if he hadn't been forking silage in to his suckler herd, so that his hands were greeny-brown and smelled like vinegar. 'Assuming that I accept your premise, which I don't, I think the whole point of friends is that they take your side regardless of the merits of your case. That they tell you you're right even when they know you're wrong. That they cover your back, even if they've nothing to cover it with except their own.'

Hazel appreciated that more than she could put into words. She squeezed his hand instead.

'Besides which,' added Byrfield, 'the last time we had this conversation it was me having the attack of the vapours. I don't remember you calling for a taxi.'

'That was different,' murmured Hazel.

'It *was* different. You were helping this family out of a hole of our own digging. Whereas you've been threatened in your own home by some kind of a weirdo, and until he's rounded up it would be the height of foolishness to keep sleeping where you know he can find you.' He even talked like an Eng. Lit. graduate. It would have been pretentious if it hadn't been entirely unconscious, the product of a sad sojourn in one of the cheaper public schools.

'I have to go back sometime.'

'If you go back before he's caught, I'm coming with you. To stand guard with my trusty twelve-bore while you catch up on your beauty sleep.'

Hazel grinned. 'Who's going to feed the bullocks?'

'My mother,' said Byrfield firmly, and both of them laughed. The dowager countess didn't do livestock. She didn't do people any more than was strictly necessary.

'Seriously . . .' began Hazel.

But Byrfield would brook no argument. 'It's three weeks to Christmas. At least stay until then. If only to see me in a cotton-wool beard and my dad's old red dressing-gown, doling out iTunes to the village children.'

'ITunes?'

'Colouring books don't cut it with modern kids,' he said ruefully.

It was tempting. In fact, it was too tempting to resist. 'Christmas then,' she said. 'But I'm going home on Boxing Day.'

'We'll talk about that on Boxing Day,' murmured Pete Byrfield.

Ash was right about one thing: it felt a long night. Because he wanted to mimic the normal pattern of life in the little house, he sat downstairs until about eleven, then he put the upstairs lights on for another forty minutes, and after that he turned everything off and sat in the dark, bundled up in his quilt, feeling the house go cold around him. Patience dug herself under a fold of the quilt, her slim form warm against his thigh, and went to sleep, snoring softly. Every couple of hours, by the minimal light of a pen-torch, he poured himself a cup of coffee; the coffee was colder each time, as was he; and when he started to hear sounds of activity in the street outside, a little before seven o'clock, he accepted that nothing was going to happen now and got up to go home for a hot shower and a cooked breakfast. Both knees folded under him and he had to grab the back of the sofa to keep from falling.

You're getting old, remarked Patience.

'Yes? Well, you're getting old seven times faster.'

He excused himself, apologetically, from taking the boys to school. Frankie Kelly took over without a word; and when she got back, Ash still hadn't left to open the bookshop. In fact, after his hot breakfast and his blessedly hot coffee, he'd sat down on the kitchen sofa to tie his shoelaces and promptly fallen asleep.

Frankie made no attempt to wake him. But after a minute he became aware of her scrutiny and opened his eyes.

'I found your note,' she said, expressionless.

'I didn't want you to worry.'

'I didn't say I didn't worry. But I gather nothing much happened?'

'Nothing at all happened,' admitted Ash.

'Will you go back tonight?'

Stifling a yawn, Ash nodded.

Nothing happened the next night either.

On Thursday morning, they'd been at Rambles With Books for forty minutes when Ash noticed Patience getting restless. 'Do you want to go out?'

Sequestered in the corner with the Brontës, Miss Hornblower – who was one of his regulars – found it amusing how Mr Ash talked to his dog as if she understood every word he said; as if any day now she was going to answer back.

No, said Patience; but she didn't sound very sure.

'Then what do you want?'

She looked up at him with mournful, toffee-coloured eyes. I left Spiky Ball at Hazel's house.

Gabriel Ash had never had a dog before. He didn't know you were supposed to give them toys and play with them. He fed her, and took her for walks, and brushed her fine white coat, but there was not at that time much room in his heart for play and it never occurred to him to buy her a ball. When the boys came home, that changed. They'd never had a dog before either, and they made up for lost time by haunting the local pet shop, showering her with balls and chews and a raincoat for wet weather and the car restraint that she so disliked wearing.

Of all these presents, Spiky Ball was the stand-out success. He was fluorescent pink, squidgy, easy to grasp, easy to keep clean, and he floated if dropped in the park pond. (He was also, from their earliest acquaintance, male – it made no sense, but Patience referred to him as 'he' and Ash found himself doing so as well.) The lurcher rarely went anywhere without him now.

Ash was going to make her wait until he closed the shop at six o'clock. He didn't shut at lunchtime: it was often the busiest hour of his day. And he knew Patience would be true to her name, and not make a fuss, and accept that it was her own fault. He also knew that she would be unhappy until she and Spiky Ball were reunited.

He sighed. 'I'll shut up shop for ten minutes when we've no customers.'

Patience beamed at him. So did Miss Hornblower, if for slightly different reasons.

It was, he freely confessed, no way to run a business – to lock out potential customers in the middle of the morning because your dog was missing her favourite toy. But you can do things as the proprietor of a second-hand bookshop you couldn't possibly do if you sold groceries or shoes. A certain degree of eccentricity seemed to be tolerated, even expected of him. It was an expectation Ash never had any difficulties in meeting.

The workmen were still excavating their hole. At least, the hole was still there – the workmen were having a brew-up in their shelter halfway up the street. Ash sidled past the warning tape and went to open Hazel's door with the spare key that he'd never put back behind its brick.

The door wasn't locked. It swung open under his hand.

It was only four hours since he left here, and he knew he'd locked up then. Had Hazel returned without telling him? Well, she might not have told him if she intended to return, guessing he'd try to talk her out of it; but she wouldn't have left the door unlocked. Not right now. Someone else had been here.

And was perhaps here still.

Feeling his pulse climb, Ash really wished he'd brought Patience with him. She didn't look much like a guard dog, but she was fast and she was smart and there were a lot of teeth packed into that slim muzzle. He'd left her at the shop so anyone seeking admittance would see her through the window and know he'd be back in a matter of minutes. Right now, that felt like a really bad decision.

He had three options: to leave quietly, to call the police, or to search the house. But he'd spent two long, uncomfortable nights waiting for this opportunity – he wasn't going to throw it away now. He could certainly call the police – but he was going to look pretty silly if there was no one here, no evidence that anyone had been here, and the likeliest explanation of the unlocked door was that he himself had omitted to lock it.

Which left searching the house. Ash was not deeply concerned for his own safety. Men who stalk women are usually much less inclined to tackle other men, and Gabriel Ash was a big man, both tall – when he remembered not to stoop – and reasonably substantial now he was eating properly. He wasn't a natural street-fighter, but if fate had presented him with an opportunity to stop whoever had been harassing his friend, he would risk a bloody nose to take it.

Railway Street was a late-Victorian terrace, built to accommodate the workers who fed the industrial revolution in towns like Norbold. A hundred and forty years ago the houses were aspirational for a class of people who were mostly born in slums. They were still remarkably sound, cheap to run and convenient to the town centre; but they were small. The fact that families had raised vast quantities of children in them didn't alter the fact that, by modern standards, they were small dwellings with two bedrooms and a tiny bathroom upstairs, a living room and a kitchen downstairs, a front door that opened onto the street and a back door that opened onto a small enclosed yard. Today when they came up for sale they were advertised as starter homes. When Hazel had had a lodger, she'd had to keep the vacuum cleaner under her bed – there had been nowhere else to store it.

Today, the bijou nature of the residence was a bonus. There was almost nowhere an interloper could hide. Ash could check each room just by putting his head round the door, and if the intruder was upstairs he was already trapped – there was no question of him pushing past Ash to make his escape.

The door to the living room was on his right. It was the biggest room in the house, but there was still only room for a couple of two-seater sofas, a gate-legged table and two bentwood chairs, and a small sideboard with the television on it. Seeing no one, Ash moved quietly down the hall to the kitchen at the back. No one there either.

So if he was still here, he was upstairs. Just in time, Ash remembered how the stairs creaked: he kept his feet close to the edges, shifting his weight carefully. His ascent wasn't silent, but it was quiet enough that someone with his mind on other matters wouldn't notice.

The main bedroom was at the front of the house, the smaller bedroom and the bathroom at the back. Ash expected that Hazel's room would be the focus of any intruder's interest: he paused just long enough outside the door to fill his lungs and steel his nerves, then pushed it open and stepped inside.

He didn't know what he was likely to find. Some kind of pervert by definition – normal men don't draw satisfaction from haunting young women. But what form that perversion might take, he had little idea. He tried to be ready for anything, from a two-metre paratrooper in full camouflage gear to a rampant transvestite posing in front of the mirror in Hazel's best party frock.

Still what he found managed to surprise him. He was so geared up for the confrontation that finding no one to confront left him momentarily nonplussed.

And because of that he spent too long staring round the empty room. It took a sound behind him to remind him that there were still two rooms he hadn't checked and he was no longer between them and the stairs.

Even as he moved towards it, he didn't know what the sound was that he'd heard. Then he did. It was the sound of bedsprings sagging under someone's weight. He was in the back bedroom. And now he couldn't get out without Ash seeing him.

It was a very small room. When the door was open, the headboard and the top third of the bed were behind it. What Ash saw when he pushed the door open was a pair of jeans, a pair of socks, and on the floor by the foot of the bed a pair of trainers that might have attracted admiring glances in London but were hardly up to a Midlands winter.

To see the rest of the man, he had to close the door. So he did.

Indignation almost overtook the burgeoning anger in his breast. The creep had not only broken into Hazel's house, had not only made himself at home in the guest room, but had had the unmitigated gall to fall asleep! Torn between allowing him to wake and find himself cornered, or ripping him from sleep by one hand fisted in his shirt front, Ash stood over him for a moment, literally shaking with fury, studying him, wondering if he'd seen him before.

He'd fallen asleep with his back to the door, so it was hard to get a proper look at his face. But the whole lazy, languid disposition of his body said he was a younger man than Ash had been expecting. In spite of which he was obviously in funds. It wasn't just the trainers: the leather coat he'd thrown over himself in lieu of a quilt had clearly been expensive, and the heavy chain of the identity bracelet about his bony wrist was clearly gold. Only the tangle of straw-coloured hair spoiled the picture. This was someone who could afford a decent haircut if he wanted one, so it had to be that looking like a small haystack after a high wind was a fashion statement.

With the drowsy sigh of someone who had got far too comfortable for the situation he was in, still sleeping the young man rolled onto his right side, the bed-springs groaning again, and Ash saw his face for the first time. And realised that he had indeed seen him before.

An unconscious awareness of when we're being watched is a part of the self-preservation instinct that goes back to a time when human beings were popular items on other creatures' menus. These days it's what makes us peer across a crowded room for the individual who's staring at us, or look round on a bus because someone we know is sitting further back. Now that same sixth sense that warns us when we're under scrutiny warned the slumbering youth that he was no longer alone. Ash saw his peaceful expression begin to break down as the world started to intrude into his sleep, and he climbed back towards consciousness with a visible effort. Finally his eyes flickered open.

'Oh – hi, Gabriel,' he yawned. 'Have you seen Hazel?'

For most of the last ten minutes Gabriel Ash had been prepared to do violence to whoever it was had been stalking his friend, and he wasn't ready to forgo the option yet. The tremor was still in his hands, and in his voice.

'Saturday,' he said tersely. 'What the hell are you doing here?'

FIFTEEN

'I live here,' said Saul Desmond, universally known as Saturday. 'Remember?'

'I remember,' Ash said tersely, 'that you buggered off to London, without a word of explanation, without so much as a postcard to say you were OK, leaving Hazel distraught with grief and guilt.'

'I never blamed Hazel for what happened.' Saturday's voice was low.

'Well, you could have stuck around long enough to convince her,' snarled Ash, entirely unappeased. 'You broke her in half, running off like that.'

'It wasn't the easiest time in my life, either,' retorted the young man rebelliously. 'You know that. Why are you angry with me?'

'Because that was more than a year ago, and this is the first either of us has heard from you since! We thought you were dead. No,' Ash corrected that, '*I* thought you were dead. Hazel always thought you'd come back. For months she kept your bed made up, changing the sheets although no one had slept on them. She kept this house on because she believed you'd show up one day needing your old room. Why didn't you *call*? Or text, or e-mail, or write? *Anything*, just to let her know you were alive and' – he paused in his tirade to look Saturday up and down – 'well.'

'I should have,' admitted the youth. 'At first, I couldn't face doing because it was all too raw. And later, I couldn't face doing because I should have done it sooner. I'm sorry, Gabriel. I'm sorry if I hurt her. I didn't think . . . I didn't expect . . . it would matter to her that much.'

'Of course it mattered to her!' shouted Ash. 'It mattered to both of us. *You* matter to us. *Anything* could have happened to you. You could have been dead in a ditch somewhere, for all we knew. And now' – his anger revived like a stoked fire – 'you turn up out of nowhere, without a word of warning, just roll up here and let yourself in and go to sleep as if this was still your bed!'

Saturday looked around him, trying to see what harm he'd done. 'I was tired after the drive. I left London at seven this morning. So I fell asleep: so shoot me.'

'Don't tempt me!' yelled Ash. Then, scowling: 'Drive?'

Saturday had never been easily chastened. At that he looked positively chipper. 'Yeah. I got a new car.'

'You can drive now?'

'Of course I can drive. I'm eighteen, you know?'

'And you can *afford* a car?' The last time they met, Saturday had been stacking shelves in an all-night service station. The first time they met he was living on the streets.

'I got me a proper grown-up job. I've got my own flat and everything.'

The echo of his earlier remark came back to Ash. 'You drove up this morning? So you haven't been in Norbold this last week? You didn't leave flowers and wine on the doorstep? You didn't let yourself in a couple of nights ago?'

The teenager's face, a fraction broader than Ash remembered it, was a picture of confusion. 'I told you: I got here about an hour ago. I still had my key, so I thought I'd wait for Hazel inside. Do you reckon she'll be long?'

Ash considered. 'Actually, yes. I took her down to stay with the Byrfields for a while. Things have been going on here that she needed to get away from. I have to get back to the shop now – I left Patience holding the fort – but we need to talk.'

'What shop?'

Almost more than anything else, that brought home to Ash

how long Saturday had been gone. 'I opened a second-hand bookshop. I'm never going to get rich, but it's good. Give me a lift down, and I'll bring you up to speed on what's been happening.'

Saturday locked the front door, and Ash made sure he'd done it right. In his mind, Saturday was still an irresponsible adolescent, not to be trusted with anything important. They walked round the corner into Alfred Street, where Saturday stunned Ash to his boot-soles by nonchalantly opening neither the maroon hatchback nor the grey van parked there, but the sunshine yellow sports car.

Like most sports cars, it was designed for people like Saturday, not for people like Ash. Which is odd, because most people who can afford sports cars are more like Ash than they are like Saturday. But Ash finally folded his long legs into the well and shrugged his broad shoulders together enough to get the door shut. 'This proper grown-up job you got,' he ventured.

'Cyber security,' Saturday said complacently. 'They pay me silly money to hack into corporate systems and figure out where the weaknesses are. Which is a riot, because if they weren't paying me silly money to do it, I'd probably still be doing it and they'd be trying to put me in gaol.'

He started the car. The throaty rumble made curtains twitch all the way up the street. But instead of driving off, he twisted in the close confines of his seat so that he could see his passenger's face. 'Just one thing, Gabriel. In all the circumstances, that was a bit tactless.'

'What was?'

'Accusing me of buggering off.'

Ash looked at him in sudden horror, the enormity of the gaffe making his jaw drop. He was still trying to stammer out some kind of apology when Saturday grinned, an impish grin as sunny as his car; and the griefs and recriminations of the missing year turned to pixie-dust and blew away.

DCI Gorman was in his office – paperwork, he'd discovered, mounted in direct proportion to rank – when DS Presley stuck his head round the door. 'We've got another one.'

Gorman considered. This could mean almost anything:

another visit from the IPCC, another strongly worded letter from a local solicitor, or Ralph Percival making off with another unsecured bicycle. 'No, I'm going to need more of a clue,' he decided.

'BFT,' said Presley.

Like a Labrador at the sound of a gun, Gorman was immediately alert. 'Who? Where? Another Mauler?'

Presley consulted his notebook. 'Who: Gillian Mitchell, aged forty-three, of 81 Park Crescent, Norbold. Where: at her home, sometime last night. And definitely not another Mauler. She was a journalist.'

That too could mean almost anything, from international correspondent to writing up the racing pigeon results for the *Norbold News*. 'Do we know her?' asked Gorman.

'Not really. She's always lived in Norbold but she's a freelancer, working mostly for the London press. One of the neighbours called it in. He noticed that she hadn't opened the curtains by mid-morning. He couldn't get a response to either a knock or a phone-call, so he used his key – they kept one for each other – to check that she was all right. And found that she wasn't.'

'What happened?' Gorman was already shutting his computer and reaching for his coat.

'Somebody beat her head in, quite possibly with the same wheel-brace he used on Trucker Watts,' said Tom Presley.

Which was so odd that Gorman had the forensic medical examiner confirm it. Journalists *do* get murdered occasionally, but not usually by the same people who murder criminal fringe wannabes like Trucker Watts.

But Dr Fitzgerald had already noted the similarities: lesions of the same dimensions, delivered in a similar manner, ending in an almost right-angled indentation into the skull that suggested a fashioned tool rather than, for instance, a length of wood or metal piping.

Gorman viewed the body before they bagged it, but experience told him he'd see nothing that Fitzgerald wouldn't have noted and be able to expand on in his report. All he saw was a middle-aged woman in a dressing-gown, face-down on her sitting-room floor, the blood pooled under her head already dark and congealed. One slipper had come off when she fell.

'So she knew her attacker,' said Presley slowly, 'but they probably weren't intimately involved.'

That was an unusually discreet way of putting it, at least for Presley. 'And you know this how?' asked Gorman.

'Because she was wearing her dressing-gown. If he'd been a stranger, she wouldn't have let him in after she'd gone to bed. But if they were an item, she probably wouldn't have bothered with the dressing-gown – we'd have found her in just her pyjamas.'

It was good thinking, except for one thing. 'It's the middle of winter. Once the central heating's gone off, the house will go cold pretty quickly. Check what time the heating goes off – an hour later than that, she'd need a dressing-gown if she was only nipping to the bathroom.'

Presley grunted a fractional disappointment. 'So it could have been someone she was shacked up with.'

'Right now it could have been anyone. Mind the picture.'

Presley looked around him. There were pictures on every wall: mostly prints, some watercolours. 'Which one?'

'The one on the floor. The one you're about to put your foot through.'

It was a small watercolour in a black frame, reared up beside the fireplace. It might have been a crowd scene; it might have been a woman's hat. Presley tried looking at it sideways. 'Is that what they call Impressionism?'

'Either that, or somebody's pet monkey got at their paints.'

The truth was, they were two single men with more interest in sports than art, not qualified to comment on a creative woman's taste.

'OK,' said Gorman, moving on, 'let's talk to the neighbours, see what they can tell us. Oh, and bag that.' There was a laptop on the coffee table. 'If this isn't random, if it's something to do with her work, maybe the reason's in there.'

Careful in his plastic gloves, Presley went to pick it up. It fell apart in his hands. He raised shocked eyes to his chief, who nodded glumly.

'Let's say, the reason *was* in there.'

But what Gorman and Presley knew, and many people don't, was that data is not necessary destroyed by trashing the equipment containing it. They bagged all the pieces as gently as they could, and hoped that the skill of their IT experts would prove greater than the fury of the man with the wheel-brace.

Colonel Aykhurst had spent the fourteen years of his retirement being considered a nosy neighbour. This was unfair, since most of Park Crescent had benefited from his observational skills at one time or another. When there was a spate of break-ins, Colonel Aykhurst it was who knew everyone's routine and was able to alert the police to the unauthorised activity in time to catch the culprits. When Mrs Delaware's Lhasa Apso gave birth to a litter of curiously marked puppies, Colonel Aykhurst it was who had noticed the clandestine visits of Mr Wilson's Jack Russell terrier to her garden nine weeks earlier.

And today it was Colonel Aykhurst again who wondered why Miss Mitchell still hadn't drawn her curtains by eleven o'clock in the morning, and – not out of nosiness but out of concern – took steps to find out.

As a serving soldier, he had seen action in Bosnia, Northern Ireland and the Gulf. He was no stranger to the mayhem one individual can wreak on the body of another. But seeing it in Bosnia – even in Northern Ireland – was one thing, and seeing it in Park Crescent, in the house next to his, when the body in question belonged to a woman he had known for seven years, was something else again. He was still clearly shaken when the detectives arrived to speak to him.

He might have been shaken, he might have been growing old, but he knew what the policemen needed to learn and he went straight there. 'I did not see anyone approach or leave Miss Mitchell's house. But last night I heard voices raised in what might have been an argument, and a noise that I took to be a slammed door.'

Presley was scribbling fast to catch up. Gorman said, 'What sort of time would this have been?'

'Approximately twenty past ten,' said Colonel Aykhurst. 'I was watching the television news. They'd finished with the important items but hadn't yet gone to the weather.'

'You heard this argument above the sound of your TV?'

'Yes, sir. They were not shouting – I could not hear what they were arguing about – but the tone of disputation was unmistakable. They were in the sitting room, on this side of the house. The curtains were imperfectly drawn and I could see the light through the gap.'

'Was Miss Mitchell one of the parties arguing?'

'I could not vouch for that, although it seems likely. I believe I heard one female voice and one male voice.'

'How long were they arguing for?' asked Gorman.

'They were arguing loudly enough to attract my attention for just a minute or two. They may have been arguing more quietly for some time before, of course.'

'And then someone slammed a door. But you didn't see anyone leave.'

'No, sir. And I did look. I went to my window, which' – he gestured, and Gorman went to see – 'gives a good view of Miss Mitchell's front door. There was no one on the drive, and if there was a strange car out there it must have been parked out of sight. I watched for another minute, but everything had gone quiet so I drew the curtain again and returned to the television.'

He hesitated then. He needed to know something and didn't want to ask for fear of what the answer might be. But Colonel Aykhurst had never allowed fear to keep him from doing his duty, so he drew a deep breath and asked. 'If I had done something then, could I have saved her?'

Dave Gorman regarded the old man with compassion. 'I don't know for sure, not yet. But I doubt it. If everything went quiet, it's probably because Miss Mitchell had already been attacked. Even if you'd called us – and why would you? Because of a bit of an argument next door? – and even if we'd responded immediately, which we might not have done, the damage was already done.'

'But she was still on her feet. She slammed the door.'

Gorman was intrigued. 'What makes you think that was her?'

'If it had been her visitor slamming the front door as he left, I'd have seen him. And if it was an internal door, wouldn't that be her – leaving the room but not of course leaving the house?'

DS Presley paused in his note-taking. 'If it was a door slamming. Her computer had been smashed. Could that have been what you heard?'

Colonel Aykhurst gave it some thought. 'Possibly,' he said at length. 'So at that point Miss Mitchell was already . . .?'

'Beyond any help you could have given her,' nodded Gorman. 'It seems likely. But you're not to blame for not being psychic. If I'd heard an argument next door that ended with a slammed door, I'd have gone back to watching the news as well.'

They talked a little longer. The colonel was able to fill in some details about Gillian Mitchell's life and work, the kind of person she had been, her normal routine when she was at home rather than away working. Nothing he said cast any great light on what had happened, but then Gorman didn't expect it to. At this point, you just gathered the information. You only worked out what was relevant later.

Driving back to Meadowvale – Park Crescent was on the smarter side of town, the Highfield Road side – Tom Presley said, 'He seemed pretty on the ball, for an old guy.'

Gorman shrugged. 'You know what they say about old soldiers.'

But Presley didn't. 'What?'

'Old soldiers never die, they only march away.' He knew that wasn't quite right, but it satisfied him more than if it had been.

SIXTEEN

Patience was as happy to see Saturday as Saturday was to see Patience. She sat under the long table at Rambles With Books, squeezed up against his legs, occasionally licking his knee through a rent in his jeans. (Ash had noticed the torn jeans as well. He'd been puzzled how someone who could afford a sports car couldn't afford new jeans. The idea that they might have been sold that way, *and for more than if they hadn't been ripped*, simply never occurred to him.)

By the time Ash had finished his account of the stalking, the youth looked pretty much how he himself felt: anxious, outraged, confused. And one more thing: indignant. He said angrily, 'And you thought it was me.'

'Of course not,' Ash demurred.

'Yes you did. You wanted to know how long I'd been back in Norbold. You even asked if I'd left stuff on the doorstep, and had I been in the house before today! Jesus, Gabriel – you think I'd do that to Hazel? Creep into her house at night without any warning? Try to frighten her?'

'No!' Then, more honestly: 'Well – for a moment. For a moment I couldn't believe it was just a coincidence. That, after so long, you turned up where I expected to find him.'

'And then?'

Ash smiled. 'And then I was so bloody glad to see you I didn't know whether to kiss you or yell at you. I decided you'd probably prefer the latter.'

'I thought for a minute you were going to thump me.'

'*I* thought for a minute I was going to thump you.'

They talked for a little while of things that had happened since they were all last together. Then Saturday returned to the subject that, right now, mattered most to both of them. 'So what are we going to do about Hazel's stalker? She's not going to play at squires and shepherdesses forever. We need to make it safe for her to come home, because it won't be long before that's what she does, safe or not.'

Ash was well aware of the fact. 'Detective Chief Inspector Gorman – oh yes: that's another recent development – is on the case, but there isn't much for him to work with. Plus, he has a murder on his hands.' He meant Trucker Watts, didn't yet know about Gillian Mitchell. 'Meadowvale CID isn't any bigger than it was before you left, so he has to prioritise.'

'He's left Hazel to deal with this alone?'

'Of course not. If she had any idea who's behind it, he'd be on top of him like a ton of bricks. But she doesn't.'

'I suppose you're sure about that?'

Ash frowned. 'What do you mean?'

Saturday rolled his eyes. 'You've known her as long as I have. She doesn't like other people fighting her battles. Is there any chance she *does* know who it is, but wants to deal with him herself?'

That was something else that hadn't occurred to Ash. He considered it now. 'I don't think so. I can't imagine her leaving town if she knew who he was.'

'I suppose not. Then it's down to you and me.'

'It is?'

'If Hazel's in Cambridgeshire, and the Keystone Cops are investigating a murder, either you and me have to find this creep or he'll still be on the loose when Hazel comes home. That would not be a good thing.'

'What do you suggest?'

Saturday thought about it. 'We make it look as if she's come home already. I'll move back in for a few days, put the lights on and off, sleep in Hazel's room. Hell, I can wear some of her clothes – hoodies, sweaters and the like. Any idea where I can get a blonde wig? Someone watching from the street will see what he's expecting to see. After the light goes out late at night, maybe he'll have another go at getting into the house.'

Ash hesitated. 'Last time . . .'

'Last time someone broke into that house,' retorted Saturday, 'I wasn't ready for him. I really was asleep. And I still put the bastard in the hospital. Don't worry about me, Gabriel, I can look after myself.'

It was a tempting offer. For whatever reason, Ash and Patience spending their nights under a quilt on the sitting-room sofa wasn't having the desired result. Perhaps they'd been spotted; perhaps the stalker wanted to see evidence that his quarry was within reach before making another attempt. With the best will in the world, Ash in a blonde wig was never going to be mistaken for a twenty-eight-year-old policewoman. There wasn't enough rope in Norbold to suspend disbelief *that* far. But Saturday? He was younger than Hazel, and thinner than Hazel, and her sweaters would fit him only where they touched. But as long as the curtains were half-drawn so he was never visible for more than a second or two, it might just be convincing enough.

'All right,' said Ash. 'But I'll be downstairs. Shout, and I'll be there in ten seconds. And Patience will be there in five.'

'You *will* be downstairs,' agreed Saturday, 'until bedtime. Then you and Patience will leave, by the front door, loudly saying goodnight. After that, anyone who's watching will believe Hazel's alone in the house. When the bedroom light goes off, he'll think she's asleep.'

He saw Ash's misgivings and grinned. 'I'll have you on speed-dial. As soon as I hear something, I'll call you. You can be back here in not much longer than it'll take him to climb the stairs.'

Ash didn't like it. He saw all sorts of ways it could go wrong. He thought Saturday could get hurt. As a plan, the only thing in its favour was that it wouldn't result in Hazel getting hurt, and if they didn't do something soon that would again be a real possibility.

He said quietly, 'Before, when you left—'

'I know,' Saturday interrupted, 'it was a cop-out. I should have had the guts to stay.'

'When you left,' Ash said again, 'and Hazel was falling apart in front of me, I told her you'd be back when we needed you. Thank you for proving me right.'

Hazel had been back at Byrfield for two days, and already the rhythm of a country estate was re-establishing itself in her soul.

As country estates go, it was not First Division. Pete Byrfield worked Home Farm; there were two tenant farms and a handful of smallholdings; and most of the cottages in Burford village were owned by the estate and occupied by current or retired estate workers. On paper it added up to a valuable holding; in practice, most of the assets were tied up, most of the rents were peppercorn, and the income generated was adequate rather than generous. Like farmers up and down the country, Pete Byrfield lived rather more modestly than might have been expected by anyone with knowledge of his assets.

He was mending his wellington boots with a bicycle-tyre repair kit in the kitchen which had once employed a staff of six when Hazel came in from feeding Viv's retired hunter.

(Retired horses are the bane of the land-owning classes. So many of them contrive, early in middle age, to acquire an injury which precludes further work but does not stop them living long and happy lives, cared for by owners who are too sentimental to do the sensible thing and eat them.)

He looked up with a smile. 'Viv says his tack still fits. You should take him out while you're here.'

Hazel eyed him with disbelief. 'Pete, I haven't been on a horse since I was sixteen! If I take up riding again, it'll be on a fat lazy cob, not your crazy sister's crazy hunter!'

'Viv isn't crazy,' protested Byrfield. 'She's just . . . determined.'

'That's what people used to say,' nodded Hazel. 'They used to say, "Look at that determined woman jumping that double-oxer when there's a perfectly good gate through the hedge. Determination runs in that family," they used to say.'

'I suspect they still say it,' said Byrfield ruefully. 'The English like having an aristocracy. It saves them having to hurl insults at one another.'

Hazel was curious. 'Is that how you see yourself? As an aristocrat?'

It was an honest question, asked of one friend by another, and it deserved an honest answer. 'Yes,' said Byrfield slowly, 'I suppose I do. Is that politically incorrect? But I am what I was born to be: the 28th incumbent of a peerage dating back to the Battle of Bosworth. I can't pretend to be something else, any more than Maud here' – the black Labrador at his feet looked up with a smile – 'can pretend to be a poodle. And it would be undignified, and rather patronising, to try.'

'Do you worry about your dignity?'

'I worry more about being patronising.'

Hazel had levered herself up onto the kitchen table, which was as sturdy as the house and possibly as old, and was watching him, her head tip-tilted to one side, as if he was a puzzle to solve. 'It doesn't . . . embarrass you sometimes? That you live like this' – her glance circled the kitchen – 'when so many people have so little?'

Byrfield met her gaze head-on. 'Should I be embarrassed?'

'I don't know. I think some people would be.'

He considered. 'Being embarrassed would suggest I had something to be ashamed of. I don't think I have. This family' – Hazel understood why he put it that way, was one of the few people who would have done – 'has worked this land, for their benefit but also that of their employees, for over five hundred years. It would be unrealistic to suppose there were no bad earls in that time. I imagine some duff Bests would fall out of your family tree if you shook it hard enough. But most of them seem to have done a reasonable job of keeping the land productive and the people working it fed. I take no credit for that, but I don't think it's anything to apologise for either.

'I think I can justify what I have by using it well, and making sure the Byrfield family aren't the only ones to enjoy its success. What's the alternative? Break it up, and give an acre each to five thousand people living on welfare? The land would go to rack and ruin, and the families it supports now, on the farms and in the village, would end up on the dole. Give it to the National Trust? The National Trust is a much bigger landowner than I am, and probably wouldn't be very interested in what is essentially a working farm with an old but hardly important house. It isn't grand enough or pretty enough or special enough to attract sufficient visitors to pay its way. It only makes sense as a working estate, which means somebody has to run it. Why *shouldn't* that be me? I'm qualified, I'm capable, and I already live here.'

Hazel regarded him fondly. 'You're a decent man, Pete Byrfield, even if you are an aristocrat. Byrfield is lucky to have you.'

The 28th earl smiled gravely in return. 'I'm glad you think so. I care what you think, you know.'

That surprised her. 'You shouldn't. If you're happy with your choices, you shouldn't care what other people think.'

'You're not other people.'

She gave that some thought. 'OK, maybe you should care *a little bit* what your friends think.'

He said, 'I wish . . .' And stopped there.

Hazel raised an eyebrow. 'What?'

'I wish I'd known you better when we were younger. I never realised what a fount of good sense, human kindness and endless support was living in the gatehouse.'

Hazel laughed out loud. 'I wasn't a very interesting teenager! I was very conventional, I think. Work hard at school, get to university, get a good job . . . I'm horribly afraid I was a bore. And I thought *you* were stuck-up.'

'I expect I was,' said Byrfield sadly.

'I don't think so. I think it was just the class thing getting in the way. I thought you talked funny. I thought you went to college for the champagne parties, had girlfriends called Cassandra and Imogen, and would never do a proper day's work in your life.'

'It was an *agricultural* college,' he pointed out. 'More beer than champagne. And most of the girls I knew were farmers' daughters. Except for Tracy Olroyd, who was born on a council estate in Barnsley but knew from infancy that what she wanted to do was breed sheep. She manages a hill farm in north Yorkshire now, with a thousand Herdwicks under her crook.'

'You've kept in touch, then?'

'Not really. You always intend to, don't you, but then life gets in the way. You say you'll organise a reunion – but the cattle men can't manage spring and the arable men can't manage autumn, and the sheep people are constantly trying to keep their stock from committing suicide. Dropping dead from no appreciable cause is the average sheep's highest goal in life.'

Hazel chuckled. 'You should have kept in touch with Tracy, at least. She might have bred more than sheep for you.'

Byrfield rolled his eyes. 'Don't you start! I get enough of that from my mother. "You're thirty-two, it's time you were doing your duty by Byrfield, if anything happens to you it's going to Cousin Rodney, and his wife's a Methodist!"' He'd captured the dowager countess's carping tones to perfection. 'What she really means is, if anything happens to me she'd have to move into a service flat in Knightsbridge. Poor soul.'

Privately, Hazel was thinking Poor Knightsbridge. 'But

maybe she has a point. With five and a half centuries of history resting on your . . . er . . . shoulders, maybe you should be looking to the future.'

The 28th earl shook his head firmly. 'It's not a good enough reason to marry. My father did what was required of him. He was unhappily married for thirty years, when the woman he *would* have been happy with lived just down the road. I'm not making the same mistake. If Byrfield ends up with Rodney's family, fine – it won't be the first time it's jumped a groove. If I'm destined to die a shrivelled-up old bachelor, so be it. Whoever it goes to, I'll do my best to leave them a going concern, a farm business on a sound financial footing. But I'm not being put to a filly with the right blood-lines just to keep my mother off my back.'

The adhesive had done its job. He dipped the toe of his boot into a pan of water and no bubbles escaped. '*Anyway*,' he said, determinedly changing the subject, 'what are we going to do about this stalker of yours?'

Hazel shrugged. 'Dave Gorman will track him down, sooner or later. Every time he makes an approach – puts something on the doorstep, takes a picture – he risks leaving something behind that will identify him. Sooner or later he'll make a mistake, and then we'll have him.'

'He was in your house. You can't afford to play long bowls with someone who's already broken into your house.'

'We're doing everything we can,' she insisted. 'Don't get this out of proportion, Pete. It's unpleasant, not least because it's making me look sideways at everyone I know, but he's probably more to be pitied than feared. He's a sad, inadequate man who hasn't any real friends and so doesn't know the difference. I think we're all in danger of over-reacting – me as much as anyone. Hearing him in the house *did* freak me out,' she admitted. 'But the moment he thought he was going to be challenged, he ran away. That's worth remembering.'

'He ran away from a fast-approaching police car,' Byrfield reminded her. 'That doesn't mean he'd have run away if *you'd* confronted him.'

Hazel shrugged negligently. 'This is a man who's too scared to come up to me, introduce himself and ask if I'd meet him for a coffee sometime. If I can't knock the spots off someone like that, I've no business calling myself a police officer.'

It was clear from his expression that Byrfield remained troubled. She gave his arm a friendly clap. 'The average farmer deals with much more dangerous situations every day. Bulls, slurry pits, heavy machinery and God knows what else. Maybe I should whisk you off to safety in Norbold instead of hiding out down here.'

'It isn't the bulls that get you,' muttered Pete Byrfield darkly. 'Everyone knows to be wary round them. It's the cows that come in for milking twice a day, that take nuts from your hand and a scratch between the ears, that you get careless about. Don't get careless around this man, Hazel. Despise him all you like, but don't underestimate him.'

'Will this do?' asked Saturday, holding up the claret sweater. 'It's nice and girly.'

'It'll do fine,' said Ash, with a shortness Saturday had no way of understanding.

Neither of them knew where to acquire a wig at short notice, but they tied one of Hazel's head-scarves pirate-style around Saturday's brow and hoped that, from the point of view of someone in a parked car or an entry across the street, the flicker of colour and movement behind the imperfectly drawn curtains would be convincing enough.

They watched television in the sitting room, a succession of sports programmes which interested neither of them. Ash made coffee. They played cards for pennies. Saturday won. Saturday made coffee. By eleven o'clock, even the prospect of catching the stalker wasn't enough to keep boredom at bay, and both were struggling to stay awake. Patience wasn't even trying: she was curled like a croissant on the sofa at Ash's side, softly snoring.

Ash woke her, hauled himself to his feet and reached for his coat. He fixed Saturday with a penetrating look. 'Are you sure you want to do this? I can stay. Frankie's at home with the boys.'

'I'll be fine,' insisted Saturday. 'Chances are, nothing will happen. But if anything *does* happen, you'll be the second to know.'

'If you think you hear something, call me *before* you go to make sure.'

'I certainly will.' The youth batted his eyelashes. 'A girl can't be too careful.'

Ash grinned and headed for the door.

On the threshold, Patience beside him, he half-turned and called back over his shoulder. 'Goodnight, Hazel. I'll see you tomorrow.' Then he closed the door firmly behind him, checking the lock had caught, and stepped into the street. A moment later the sitting-room light went out; a few seconds after that, the light in the front bedroom came on. The shape of someone moving across the window was visible as a shadow on the curtain.

Still Ash hesitated, shrugging the collar of his coat up round his ears. Patience said, He'll be all right, you know.

'I know,' murmured Ash. 'It's just . . . Oh, I'm being stupid. Nothing will happen. It was a silly idea. It just seemed slightly better than doing nothing.'

They headed round the corner to where Ash had left his car. He opened the front passenger door and Patience jumped in, giving him a long-suffering look as he attached her seatbelt. Then he closed the door and went round to the driver's side.

The figure stepped out of deep shadow, the weapon in his hand already swinging. All Ash knew was a sharp warning bark from his dog, and then pain exploded behind his ear and lights like a shower of meteors flashed across in front of his eyes, leaving red trails that faded slowly to black.

By that time he was on his knees by the front wheel of his car, his senses reeling. The hand he had raised automatically to the pain in his head met the cool slickness of blood, and a desperate part of his fading consciousness realised that he was under attack. He tried to get back on his feet, but all the strength had leached out of him; he only canted sideways, quite slowly, until his cheek met the crumbling tarmac that kept the potholes from running into one another.

Someone was standing over him. He couldn't see who, and – given the state of the street lighting in Alfred Street – probably wouldn't have been able to even without the concussion. But he heard the voice, and he heard the hatred in the voice.

'Stay away from her, you dirty beggar. You're old enough to be her father!'

That's when the boots came in. They came in hard, and they came in fast, and they kept coming long after Ash had stopped trying to fend them off.

There are many things that a dog can do, even the ones that can't talk. But none of them can unfasten a seatbelt and open a car door. So Patience could do nothing, *nothing*, nothing at all, except watch the man she loved beaten to bloody trash in a dirty gutter. Watch, and howl like a soul in torment.

Eventually her howling brought lights on up and down the street. And the man stopped what he was doing and backed away into the shadows again; then he ran away.

SEVENTEEN

'Where is he?' demanded Hazel. 'I want to see him. I want to see him *now*!'

Saturday, Dave Gorman and indeed Ash himself had all known better than to tell her what had happened, knowing exactly what her reaction would be. But Mrs Burden next door, brimming with shock and excitement and uninhibited by too much in the way of insight, had called her mobile at eight o'clock the next morning to tell her that that strange boy who used to lodge with her was back, and that nice Mr Ash had been carted away in an ambulance with the lights and the sirens going and everything.

Pete Byrfield brought her back to Norbold. Her father had wanted to, but Byrfield's car was faster.

Saturday met them in the foyer of Norbold Royal Infirmary. He'd lost the headscarf but was still wearing the pink sweater.

He raised both hands as if to ward off blows. 'He's going to be all right. He looks like shit, but they've done X-rays and there's nothing broken – well, nothing that won't mend. Ribs, mostly; and a hairline fracture behind his right ear. They're going to keep him in for a couple of days, until they're happy about the concussion, but honest, Hazel, he's going to be fine.'

She regarded him with barely contained fury. 'Take me there.'

For a moment, when she opened the door of the side ward, she thought Saturday had brought her to the wrong room. Nothing about the man in the bed seemed familiar. Half his face was hidden by bandages, the other half swollen beyond recognition. He even looked too small to be Ash, too flat under the white sheet, shrunken.

Then slowly, painfully, he opened his good eye, and something that might have been a wry smile spread what might, among the sutures and the bloody scabs, have been his mouth. 'You're not supposed to be here,' he whispered.

'Gabriel – neither are you! This wasn't the deal. I didn't go to Byrfield so that the guy who's been stalking me could beat the crap out of you instead.'

'To be fair,' mumbled Ash, 'that wasn't part of the plan.'

'Plan?' echoed Hazel. 'You two muppets hatched a plan? And it went pear-shaped? Whoever would have guessed?'

'Sarcasm,' Ash said carefully through broken lips, 'doesn't become you.'

By now she could tell that, despite outward appearances, Saturday had been right. Ash would mend. A lot of the fear, and a lot of the anger, drained away, leaving her weak at the knees. She groped for a chair and sat down. 'What happened?'

Ash shook his head, fractionally, without lifting it from the pillow. 'I don't know. We were at your house. About eleven o'clock I went out to my car, and somebody blind-sided me. Knocked me down and put the boot in.'

'Did you see him? Can you describe him? Would you know him if you saw him again?'

'Not a chance,' said Ash apologetically. 'I didn't see him at all before he hit me, and afterwards I couldn't see much of anything for the fireworks going off in my head. The camera saw nothing because we were round the corner in Alfred Street.'

'Did he say anything?'

There was a momentary hesitation. Then: 'I don't remember,' Ash lied.

Finally Hazel turned back to Saturday. She managed half a smile. 'I don't believe I've said hello yet. When did you get back?'

He'd been ready for another verbal pummelling. He still looked and sounded wary. 'Yesterday. I let myself into the house – I hope you don't mind.'

'Why wouldn't you,' sighed Hazel, 'everyone else seems to. Are you back to stay?'

'No,' he said honestly. 'But I'll stay until this business is sorted out.'

'Good,' she nodded. 'We can keep one another safe.'

Pete Byrfield, who'd dropped her at the main entrance then gone to park his car, had joined them in time to hear this last exchange. 'You're not thinking of staying in the house after this?' He sounded appalled.

She flashed him a brittle smile. 'You've seen what happens when I leave Ratman and Bobbin to handle things on their own. Anyway, this is a police matter now.' She turned back to Saturday. 'Has Dave Gorman been?'

'He was here an hour ago. Gabriel wasn't able to tell him anything very helpful. But he spent a bit of time with the doctor, going over the X-rays. I don't know what that was about.'

'I'll ask him.' Hazel stood up. For a moment she regarded Ash, his eye drooping closed again with weariness. Then she bent over him and, picking out a spot on his forehead that was neither bandaged nor bloody, kissed it. 'You: sleep. I'll be back later.'

Gorman and DS Presley were back at Meadowvale, closeted with the FME, going over Ash's X-rays, using the winter sunshine through Gorman's office window as a light box. It was the one of his skull that interested them, together with a photograph of the wound taken before it was stapled. There were two other X-rays and two other photographs tacked up on the window. Dave Gorman knew already that the marks of the sticky tape would be a bugger to remove.

He turned to Dr Fitzgerald. 'What do you think?'

Walter Fitzgerald gave an elaborate shrug. When he wasn't

wearing a protective suit, straining at the zip, he favoured tweeds that were altogether more flattering to his expanding waistline. As he observed ruefully at least once a week, being an FME was a job for a younger, fitter man. Still, he hadn't been defeated by a crime scene yet. It's amazing what even a stout middle-aged doctor can do to reach an interesting corpse.

'Could be,' he said. 'But I couldn't put my hand on my heart and say it was.'

Gorman peered closer, his eyes travelling from one X-ray to the next to the next, from one photograph to the others. 'They look pretty similar.'

'Head wounds tend to. The scalp is under a degree of tension – when anything happens to split it, it tends to gape like this.'

'What about the X-rays? What do they show?'

'Well,' said Fitzgerald, 'you're not really comparing like with like. Two of these' – he gestured with his pen – 'were hit hard enough to kill them. Your friend Ash wasn't. Naturally, there's much less damage to his skull.'

'Can you say *anything* about what caused that damage?'

'Something blunt rather than something sharp. Something about two-point-five centimetres across. If you look closely, you can see where it impacted. There' – he pointed with his pen – 'with the line of the fracture radiating from it.'

'Could it have been a wheel-brace?' asked Presley.

'It could have been a wheel-brace,' said the FME judiciously. 'It could have been a wrench, or a hammer, or any number of other things. Find me a weapon and I'll tell you if it could have done the damage. It's a bit hard to do it the other way round.'

'Was Ash lucky?' Seeing the FME's eyebrows climb, Gorman elaborated. 'I mean, whoever did this, did they mean to kill him? Was he just lucky that he lived to tell the tale, or was it never intended to be a fatal blow?'

'Tell me what constitutes a fatal blow,' said Fitzgerald, 'and I'll tell you if this was meant to be one. Any head injury can be fatal. Almost any head injury is survivable.' But he leaned closer to the window again, studying the evidence. 'If you'll settle for an educated guess, I'd say it was GBH rather than attempted murder. I think the blow to the head was to put him on the floor. That the purpose of the attack was probably the beating.'

Gorman was nodding slowly. 'I think so too. So if these three incidents are connected . . .'

'I didn't say they were,' Fitzgerald reminded him.

'. . . Then the question is, who has a major grudge against Trucker Watts and Gillian Mitchell, but rather less of a grudge against Gabriel Ash?'

'That's not a medical question,' said the FME. 'That's a policeman question. I shall leave you to ponder it alone.'

As he left Gorman's office, Hazel came in. She would have knocked if the door hadn't been held for her, but she probably wouldn't have waited very long for an invitation to enter. 'So whose bright idea was it to let the Chuckle Brothers play at being detectives?'

Gorman knew the combativeness was down to shock. All the same, he didn't like being treated like an errant schoolboy in front of his sergeant. 'Don't look at me,' he said sharply. 'The first I knew was when half Alfred Street dialled 999. I didn't even know Saturday was back in town.'

'Neither did I.' She dragged a weary hand across her face. 'I never got round to asking him why. I'll get the details later. He says he's going to stay until this matter's cleared up.'

She saw the row of X-rays on the window then. 'What's all this about?'

'Those on the left are Trucker Watts's. Those on the right are a woman called Gillian Mitchell, found dead in her house in Park Crescent yesterday morning. The middle ones are Gabriel's.'

'You think they're connected?'

'That's what we're trying to figure out.'

'But that would mean' – Hazel felt herself pale – 'that the guy stalking me is the guy who killed Trucker and this woman in Park Crescent. Which is crazy.'

'Why is it crazy? We know stalkers can be deeply dangerous people.'

'I suppose. But why would anyone who hated Trucker enough to kill him want to stalk me? Or kill this woman, or kick the bejazus out of Gabriel? It doesn't make any sense!'

'It never makes sense until we have all the pieces,' said Gorman. 'When we know who did any one of these things, we'll be able to figure out if he did the others and, if he did, why. In the meantime . . .'

'No,' said Hazel.

'You don't know what I was going to say.'

'Wanna bet?'

Gorman breathed heavily at her. 'Whatever's going on, if we have one perpetrator or three, we know you're a target. Go back to Cambridgeshire. Stay away from Norbold until we're sure you're safe.'

'I tried that,' said Hazel tersely. 'And now Gabriel's in the hospital, and there are pictures of his head on your window. I'm not going anywhere. Saturday's going to stay so I won't be alone in the house. And I will be careful, and you can do as many drive-bys as you can fit in. But I'm not going into hiding while my friends fight my battles for me.'

'Anyway,' she added as an afterthought, 'it's one perpetrator or four.'

Gorman frowned. He looked as if he was peering out from under a cliff. 'Sorry?'

'You said the crimes could be the work of one person or three. But it could be four. Trucker, the Mitchell woman, Gabriel, and my stalker. We don't actually know it was the man Gabriel and Saturday were waiting for who floored Gabriel.'

'Well – yes, we do,' said Gorman, surprised. 'From what he said to Gabriel.'

Hazel narrowed her eyes. 'What did he say to Gabriel?'

EIGHTEEN

She was still angry when she got home. She'd begged a lift with the area car. Byrfield had left a couple of hours earlier, having failed to persuade her to return to Cambridgeshire with him.

'Hazel, we should talk,' he'd said imploringly. 'Please come back with me. You're not safe here, and anything you could do can equally well be done by someone else.'

She'd brushed him off. 'We will talk. When we get this business wrapped up.'

'That could be weeks! Maybe longer.'

'Pete, right now I can't think any further ahead than that. I need to know that everyone I care about is safe, and there's nobody waiting in dark alleys for any of us. I'm sorry I can't be more helpful than that. Go back to Byrfield, see to your cows. I'll call you as soon as there's anything to say.'

'I could stay,' he'd offered. 'I'm not the only one who can run the milking parlour at Home Farm.'

But Hazel had shaken her head. 'There's nothing you can do here. Saturday's going to be at the house, and when I'm not there I'll be at work. Go home. I will call you.'

Anxious and unhappy, finally he had done as she said.

It was midday before she got back to Railway Street. She had her key in the door when someone hailed her – 'Miss Best!' – and she looked round to see Benny Price picking his way through the roadworks towards her.

So she swallowed her temper and replied with a dutiful smile. 'Hello, Benny. How's the work coming along?'

He rocked an ambivalent hand. 'These things take time, you know. But I hope you'll be able to park in front of your own front door next week.' He lowered his voice. 'Never mind that. I've been looking out for you. Do you know there's someone in your house?'

Hazel had cast a quick, searchlight glance up at the house before the likely explanation had occurred to her. 'Did you see him? Describe him.'

'Late teens, maybe early twenties. Fair hair that hasn't seen a barber in a while. About my height, but' – he gave a wry grin – 'only half as far round. Dressed a bit flash – long leather coat, and trainers that probably cost more than a good pair of shoes. I think he was driving the yellow sports car that's parked round the corner.'

This was the first Hazel had heard of a yellow sports car, but otherwise the description was spot on. 'It's all right, Benny,

I know him. He used to live with me. He's working down in London now, but he's here for a visit.' Which was all the detail that a casual acquaintance, even a thoughtful and observant one, required.

If Mr Price was surprised he managed not to show it. 'That's all right, then. It was just, with everything that's been going on . . .'

'I appreciate it, Benny,' she said, and let herself into the house.

As soon as the door had closed behind her she raised her voice up the stairs. 'Saturday, get your backside down here now and . . .'

He wasn't upstairs. The living-room door opened and they were both there, Saturday and Patience, both eyeing her with trepidation.

She marched towards them, put one finger in the middle of Saturday's chest and pushed him back into the room by sheer force of purpose. Patience ducked round the back of the sofa.

'And don't think I didn't notice you, either,' snapped Hazel. 'What's she doing here?'

'She was here with Gabriel, before he got mugged. I left her here when I went to the hospital with him. I haven't got round to taking her home yet.'

'Fine.' Hazel pushed a little harder with her finger and Saturday sat down abruptly on the sofa. 'Now, tell me what happened. *Everything* that happened.' So he did.

When he'd finished, she was satisfied that she'd heard the truth and nothing but the truth; she still wasn't convinced she'd heard the whole truth. 'You went in the ambulance with Gabriel?' The youth nodded. 'Was he conscious?'

'No. His breathing was awful. I thought he was going to die.'

Hazel's anger began to subside. 'So he didn't say anything to you?'

'Nothing. Why?'

'Because by the time he was making enough sense to be interviewed, he told Dave Gorman . . .' There she hesitated. She'd been angry with Saturday because she thought he'd kept this lacerating detail from her deliberately. It seemed he hadn't.

But what if he had? What if Ash had? Hazel's stalker had beat him unconscious out of jealousy for their friendship, and Ash had decided to spare her that knowledge out of kindness. So why was she angry? Understanding that it was just another form of adrenalin reaction, like shaking or bursting into tears, helped her finally to lay it to rest.

'He told DCI Gorman that the man who knocked him down said he was too old for me.'

'Ah,' said Saturday carefully.

'That wasn't a casual mugging. That was the man who's been stalking me.'

'We were right about one thing. We thought he'd come back.'

'The point is,' Hazel said heavily, 'that once again someone I care about has taken a hammering for me. Last time it was you, this time it's Gabriel. What the hell is wrong with me, Saturday? What am I doing so wrong, that being my friend is only slightly less dangerous than being a lion-tamer or a deep-sea diver? Why am I so toxic to everyone who gets close to me?'

Saturday stared at her, appalled. 'Hazel, you're not! None of this is your fault. All you've ever done is try to help people when they needed help, and be a friend when they needed a friend. Everything I have today I owe to you. You took a chance on me when no one else would. *I* thought you were crazy, taking a chance on me. I thought you'd regret it. Well, maybe you did, but I'll be grateful as long as I live.

'And I'm pretty sure that if you ask Gabriel, he feels the same way. Even today. Before you took him under your wing, he was Norbold's resident crazy man, wandering round the town mumbling to his dog because he thought his wife and his children had been murdered. Look at him now. He has his sons. He has his shop. People respect him. OK, maybe they still think he's a bit weird, but they don't cross the road any more when they see him coming. Your friendship did that for him. Toxic? That is so far from the mark it would be funny if it wasn't so tragic!'

Hazel blinked. This wasn't the first time the boy – but he

was a young man now – had stunned her with both the contents of his mind and the fluency with which he could express them, the laconic monosyllabic street-talk shed like casting off last season's clothes. But she'd forgotten. In the thirteen months he'd been away she'd forgotten the unexpected depths she'd discovered in him, and only remembered that he'd been very young and very vulnerable, and very bad at doing the washing-up.

She was distracted by a sudden sensation of cool dampness on the back of her hand, and when she looked down, Patience was licking it. Their eyes met, and after a moment the dog looked away, embarrassed.

'I've never known her do that before,' said Hazel, wondering. 'You'd almost think she knew what we were saying.'

Which would be patently absurd, observed the lurcher mildly; but because Ash was fast asleep in Norbold Royal Infirmary, nobody heard her.

The remains of Gillian Mitchell's computer were sent via Scotland Yard to a laboratory in London, from where DS Presley received a surprisingly prompt report. He took it into the DCI's office next door.

'Do you want the good news or the bad news?'

Gorman lowered his brow. 'I'm hoping the good news is that there isn't any bad news.'

'Not exactly,' said Presley. 'The good news is that whoever smashed it didn't know much about computers, and really only damaged the case. The hard disk was intact, and all the information on it has been retrieved.'

That wasn't at all what Gorman had been expecting. 'Well – good. *Was* there some bad news?'

'The bad news is, the computer was six years old.'

Gorman waited. But that seemed to be the whole of it. 'So?'

'Have you any idea how many documents a journalist can create in six years?'

There were reports. There were features. There were letters to accompany reports and features. There were letters to friends.

'Who the hell writes letters to friends these days?' demanded Gorman.

'Apparently writers do,' said Presley.

There were ideas for articles. There were lists of contacts. There were records for HM Revenue & Customs. There was a whole file of letters complaining about the speed of her broadband connection.

There were photographs. Some of them were plainly personal, some professional. Some were identified only by gnomic tags like 'LH @ SPP, 19/7' and could have been anything at all. Some she had apparently taken herself, others she had downloaded from a multiplicity of sources.

'Six years, hm?' said Dave Gorman levelly.

'And in all that time she never found the Recycle Bin.'

'Writers,' said Gorman, and both men rolled their eyes. 'OK. I take it we can now access all this material?' Presley nodded. 'Then someone had better start working through it. Someone young, who isn't going to see early retirement as a tempting alternative.'

An unworthy thought occurred to both of them at the same time.

'Would Maybourne lend her to us?'

'She might,' said Gorman. 'It would solve the problem of what to do with Hazel now she's back in town and we still haven't caught her stalker. She wants to get into CID? – well, this is what we do in CID.'

'At least until we've got enough seniority to make other people do it for us,' muttered Presley.

'IT's Hazel's thing. She's probably the best person for the job anyway. And sitting up here away from the general public, working her way through six years' worth of a journalist's life, even Hazel couldn't get into much trouble. And she might come up with something useful. I'm going to ask Maybourne if I can borrow her. And you . . .'

Presley saw immediately what was coming, took a sharp step backwards. 'Oh no. Not a chance.'

Gorman frowned. 'What was that you were saying about seniority, and the power it gives us to order other people around?'

'But the best kind of leadership,' responded Presley, inspired by sheer desperation, 'is leading from the front.

Not asking your team to do anything you wouldn't do yourself. Showing junior officers how to defuse potentially explosive situations.'

The DCI gave in with a bad grace. 'Oh, all right. I'll talk to Maybourne, and then I'll talk to Hazel.'

NINETEEN

Superintendent Maybourne, who had not become Norbold's senior police officer by having her name pulled out of a hat, saw immediately the advantages of Detective Chief Inspector Gorman's request. With Gabriel Ash in hospital, nothing would induce Hazel to return to Cambridgeshire; and if she was going to be in Norbold, the safest place for her was at a computer in the upper reaches of Meadowvale Police Station. She agreed to a temporary attachment to CID while Gorman was still warming up his argument.

More surprisingly, Hazel herself raised no objection. Indeed, she seemed to see the proposal as a good career move, and Saturday morning found her out of uniform and closeted with Gillian Mitchell's computer files.

DS Presley was right: IT was her thing. She'd taught the subject at high school level before joining the police, and she knew what Tom Presley did not: that computers aren't clever, they just do very simple things very quickly, and the secret to making them work for you lies in how you formulate your instructions. Hazel would only open the files one after another and read their contents page by page, which is what Presley would have done, if she couldn't find what she was looking for in a fraction of the time by searching the entire drive for a list of key words.

After two hours of this, she had preliminary findings to share.

'This is not a comprehensive list of everything Gillian Mitchell wrote on her computer,' she explained, pausing until Gorman nodded his understanding. 'I haven't finished. I'll go down deeper, unpeeling the memory like an onion, and there'll be other connections I haven't stumbled on yet. But what I've got so far is worth you having a look at right now.'

'Yes?' hazarded Gorman. 'Good . . .'

Hazel smiled tolerantly. He was not really a twenty-first-century policeman. He was more at home with notebooks than iPads, with breaking down doors than dismantling security protocols, and with villains he could wrestle with rather than those he had to out-think. That didn't stop him being an effective investigator, it just meant that when it came to data manipulation he needed the explanations to be kept simple. So she didn't try to impress him with her skill but went straight to the headline.

'Gillian Mitchell knew Leo Harte.'

Dave Gorman's eyebrows shot up into his hairline. Admittedly, they hadn't far to go, and once there they blended in perfectly. But Hazel would treasure his astonishment for the rest of her life. 'Did she, by God!'

'She had a file full of facts, figures and dates, charting his career from teenage hustler to serious white-collar criminal. Hard to know how much of this would stand up in court, but if even a quarter of it was verifiable he was going to spend the next fifteen years behind bars.'

'She was writing an article about him?' Gorman whistled, deeply impressed. 'That took guts.'

'I think she was writing a book. There's an outline there, a couple of chapters roughed out – and then it all stops.'

'Well, yes,' said Gorman. 'It would, wouldn't it?'

'*Before* she was killed, I mean,' said Hazel patiently. 'The last time she worked on it was four months ago.'

Gorman wasn't sure what that meant, so he left it where it was for the moment. 'What *was* she working on in the last weeks of her life? I suppose, as a freelance journalist, she had to sell stuff to pay the bills. She might have put her book on hold while she earned enough to pay the rates.'

Hazel nodded. 'I thought that too. And there are some bits and pieces that she wrote more recently, together with invoices for payment from the papers that took them. But none of them is of much consequence, either professionally or financially.

She sold a piece on school outings being cancelled because teachers can't drive the minibuses. That might have paid the groceries, it wouldn't have paid the rates. She was halfway through an article on the Air Transport Auxiliary girls delivering Spitfires – nostalgia piece, nothing new in it, nothing to make even *Aviation Today* hold the front page. They're pot-boilers. And for this she stopped work on a book that could bring a major crime figure to justice? Never mind the public interest, an exposé like that would have put her at the top table among serious investigative journalists. She'd never have had to write pot-boilers again.'

Gorman shrugged. 'Writer's block?'

'I don't think professional writers can afford to be blocked for four months at a time,' said Hazel. 'Something changed. Something happened to make her put aside the most important thing she had to work on, and never go back to it.'

Gorman's policeman's radar was beginning to ping. 'Harte found out what she was doing. And he got to her.'

'If he got to her four months ago, and scared her so much that she dropped a project this important to her, why would he come back and kill her now?'

'To make sure? Maybe he thought she wasn't scared enough to leave her book unwritten forever.'

Hazel wasn't persuaded. 'This was an intelligent, articulate woman, a journalist who was used to dealing with difficult and sometimes dangerous people. If Harte threatened her, she might have caved – but she had enough experience to realise that wasn't the smartest thing to do. She could have either rushed something into print – as a newspaper article if the book would take too long – or come to us. Either way, we'd have known what she was doing, and what Harte was doing. After that, however much he felt like braining her, actually doing it would have been very stupid indeed. And I don't think he's a stupid man.'

'He could have been a very angry man by then. Too angry to be thinking clearly.'

'But why would he be angry if she'd buckled under? She *didn't* print her story, and she didn't come to us for help. And by now Harte must have been reasonably confident that she wasn't going to. It makes no sense, Dave. Either he should have brained her four months ago, or he shouldn't have brained her at all.'

'It can't be a coincidence,' Gorman stated flatly. 'That she was getting ready to expose Harte, but somebody else took a wheel-brace to her head.' After a moment he added, 'Was there anything else in her files? Anyone else who might have had a reason to want her dead?'

'I haven't found anything else yet. That doesn't mean there isn't anything there. If you want to know everything that was on her computer, it'll take time. When I found this, I thought you'd want to see it right away.'

'What was the last thing she wrote before she died?'

Hazel consulted her notes. 'I don't think she was killed for this. It's a feel-good story about a deaf girl and her assistance dog. The last file she opened was about some mediaeval monk.'

'I think we can rule him out of our inquiries,' said Gorman, exasperated. 'OK, Hazel – well, keep looking. There must be something in there somewhere. At least, whoever killed her had reason to believe there was something in there, or why try to destroy it?'

'What will you do about Leo Harte?'

'I don't know,' said Dave Gorman honestly.

The DCI was right: there *had* to be something significant on Gillian Mitchell's computer. Hazel remained at her borrowed desk in the CID offices until the cleaner turned up and glared at her. Then she went home.

It was over a year since she'd last come home to the little terraced house in Railway Street and found the lights on. For a second, as she turned the corner, the hairs rose on the back of her neck. Then she remembered Saturday, and her heart swelled. He'd said he would stay until she was safe, and clearly he'd meant it. She was immensely glad.

He'd also lit the fire and bought fish and chips for their supper. They had dried out a little in the oven, but food that she hadn't had to prepare herself was infinitely welcome. Hazel kicked off her shoes, pushed Patience to one end of the sofa and slumped against the cushions, plate in one hand, fork in the other. They ate in a companionable silence.

But the hot meal and the hot coffee that came with it repelled the weariness that had crept up on her, mostly unnoticed, while she was searching the computer. Saturday glanced up from the ritual of squeezing the last of his chips into a brown bread sandwich to find her watching him.

'What?'

'Tell me about London.'

He thought for a moment. 'Well, it's this big place on a river. The Queen lives there. There's a big castle, and . . .'

'Tell me,' Hazel said levelly, 'about your life in London. Where do you live?'

'I have a flat. In Docklands.'

'That isn't cheap.'

'No,' he agreed, 'it isn't.'

'And the car. That wasn't cheap.'

'No.'

'I don't even know how you got insurance for a car like that at your age. Saturday – tell me what you're doing is legal.'

'It *is* legal,' he assured her gravely. 'I work for a consultancy. Big companies call us in to test their security systems. Cyber security – you know, computers?' Hazel nodded, expressionless. 'The flat and the car – and the insurance – aren't actually mine. They're part of my remuneration package. If I left tomorrow, someone else would be using them by the end of the week.'

That sounded feasible. Hazel would have been more worried if he'd acquired that kind of capital since leaving Norbold with not much more than he stood up in. 'How did you get the job?'

'I answered an ad.'

'And they weren't bothered that your last job was stacking shelves?'

'That wasn't the sort of question they asked.'

They regarded one another in silence for a while. Then Hazel asked what she most wanted to know. 'Why did you leave like that? Without a word. Without a postcard to say you were safe. Nothing. Not then, and not since.'

'You know why,' said Saturday, his voice low.

'I thought you did it to punish me.'

His heart-shaped face, beginning to broaden as he moved from adolescence into manhood, was astonished. 'What for?'

'I thought you blamed me for what Oliver Ford did to you. God knows I blamed myself.'

One of his hands – his agile hands with their long swift fingers – found one of hers on top of the coffee table. 'Hazel. Everything I have now, I owe to you. Everything I have, everything I am. *That's* what you're responsible for. Nothing else.'

Which is what Ash had told her, again and again, so often that she had almost, *almost*, come to believe it. But if she had really and truly believed it, why did hearing Saturday say the same thing feel like . . . like . . . Like she'd been wearing a lead vest for so long she hardly noticed it, except that hearing him say that was like taking the vest off and suddenly realising how heavy it had been. Like she was able to breathe properly for the first time in thirteen months.

'You should have sent a postcard,' she said.

'I know I should,' said Saturday.

TWENTY

She wanted to be at work by eight on Monday morning, so Hazel left the house at a quarter to. There was still a hole in the road where she liked to park, so she walked quickly round the corner – the rain had more than a hint of sleet in it – straight into what might have been described as a man-mountain if he'd been six inches taller.

John Carson had been the shortest boy in his year at school. It hadn't stopped him being a demon on the football field. He'd been the shortest recruit in his intake when he joined the Army. It hadn't stopped him wiping the floor with anyone who commented on the fact, or becoming the go-to guy when there was something tough, dirty and important to do.

It was now some years since his return to civvy street, but he still looked like a soldier. His well-made suits barely disguised the bulk not of middle-age spread but muscle, hard, densely packed, ready for action.

This morning he was standing beside Hazel's new car with an open umbrella. 'Morning, miss.'

Hazel recognised him immediately – not from the previous occasion when she'd caught only a fleeting glimpse of him, but from the photographs on Gorman's desk. She bounced back – the sleet seeming more attractive than any shelter she might have to share with him – and straightened up, making herself look as big and strong and unafraid as possible. She was in fact taller than Carson. But one out of three ain't great.

'What do you want?'

'I don't want anything, miss,' he said mildly. 'My employer' – he glanced past her – 'wonders if you could spare him a quick word.'

The third thing people noticed about John Carson, after his lack of inches and excess of muscles, was that he spoke like a civilised man. People who knew who and what he was, and what he did and who he did it for, expected him to talk like a thug, and he didn't. His might have been a bog-standard inner-city state education, but – like everything else – he'd learned how to make it work for him. He spoke with a generic East End accent. But what he said was careful and courteous.

Hazel darted a quick look across the road, where a long pale-grey saloon was taking up most of the kerb. There was someone in the back seat. She didn't have to be able to see him to know who it was. 'I don't think so,' she said shortly.

Carson didn't move, except that he extended the umbrella a little in her direction. 'Please, miss. We won't detain you long.'

'You won't detain me at all,' retorted Hazel. 'Lay a finger on me and you'll be parting with your belt and your shoelaces before the hour's out.'

Carson liked that. He grinned. Then Hazel heard the car door open and close, and Leo Harte joined them under the umbrella. 'We'd have been so much more comfortable in my car,' he said reproachfully.

Hazel made an effort to breathe herself calm. She was in a residential street where most of the inhabitants had yet to leave for work – if she started shouting, people would come. Admittedly, some of them would take one look at John Carson and leave again, but someone would either help or summon help. Safe is a comparative term. But she didn't think she was in any immediate danger.

'What is it you want?'

This wasn't the first time she had met Leo Harte, but it was the first time she'd met him knowing who he was, and the first time therefore that she'd taken the trouble to study him. He was a younger man than she had supposed. He might have been Ash's age or a little more, around his mid-forties. She supposed he was good-looking, although her mother had impressed on her the rule that handsome is as handsome does and that put Leo Harte at something of a disadvantage. He reminded her of a fox – not just his colouring, which was more russet than red, but the cunning in his expression, the sly amusement in his eye. A sophisticated urban fox, the master of his environment, confident in his ability either to bite or to run very fast, and to know instantly which would serve him best.

'When we met the other day,' he began, 'I didn't know who you were.'

'And now you do?'

'Yes,' he said. 'Which is to say, I know you by reputation.'

Hazel caught his eye and held it. 'What a coincidence.'

Harte smiled briefly. It was like someone had flicked a light-switch on and then off. 'You're working on Gillian Mitchell's computer.'

'Now, how would you know a thing like that?' She kept her tone even because she didn't want him to know that he'd rattled her. But she was disturbed. It wasn't public information. The only way he should have known that was if he had contacts inside Meadowvale, and that would be very bad news indeed.

Harte shrugged. 'The only thing that leaks worse than a police station is a colander. Speaking of which' – he switched his gaze to John Carson – 'are you actually *trying* to drip rainwater down the back of my neck?'

'Sorry, Mr Harte,' said Carson, dutifully adjusting the angle of his umbrella.

'That's all right, Mr Carson,' said Leo Harte. 'So by now, Miss Best, you will be aware that Miss Mitchell started to write a book about me.'

'That's right. And then she stopped. What happened? Did you frighten her off?'

'Ah.' It was a mere breath of a sigh. 'You didn't know Gillian Mitchell, did you? If you had, you wouldn't be considering that as a possibility. She did not react well to threats. I am not a timid man, Miss Best, but I would only have risked frightening her off by phone, from a long way away and preferably behind a blast wall.' He did the smile again. 'I have heard similar things said of you, Miss Best.'

Hazel didn't rise to that. 'Are you telling me that you didn't threaten her? That she got some juicy stuff on you, stuff that even a well-paid brief might have struggled to explain, but on mature reflection she decided not to write the book after all? What – seduced by your charms, was she?'

Harte's eyes were an unusual shade somewhere between blue and green. But that wasn't what startled Hazel. It was the look in them that she glimpsed before he looked away. The sorrow – no, the grief. Hurt and grief.

'She *was*?'

Harte didn't deign to answer. 'I engineered this meeting,' he said stiffly, 'for two reasons. To tell you, and through you Detective Chief Inspector Gorman, that if you think I had anything to do with Gillian Mitchell's death you are mistaken, and while you're trying to prove something which isn't true you are not looking for the person who actually killed her.

'And secondly, to offer any help I can give, any information that may come my way, that will assist in apprehending the actual murderer. I know there are rumours spreading. I know that Gillian Mitchell and Trucker Watts appear to have been killed in the same way, and that I am one of the few acquaintances they had in common. Couple that with the strange misapprehension in police circles that I am involved in illegal activities, and it is sadly inevitable that I should be considered a suspect.

'I'm telling you now, as clearly as I can, that would be a mistake. Not because I can't deal with unfounded allegations – I'm sure that, as my social secretary, Mr Carson here can provide you with an exact account of my whereabouts at any material time – but because, while you're busy barking up the wrong tree, the cat is sneaking away into the undergrowth and covering his tracks. None of us wants that – not you, and certainly not me.'

As the initial surge of alarm subsided – for though she knew this was a dangerous man, Hazel didn't feel that he was a danger to her, at least not here and now – she recognised that Harte had inadvertently afforded her an opportunity she could hardly have hoped for: the chance to probe his involvement, face to face, in the absence of his highly paid solicitor and without any tapes running. Nor could he object to conditions he had himself created. He didn't have to answer her questions. But if he wanted her to believe what he'd already said, he might find it hard to walk away.

She said, 'What were you doing at Maggie Watts's house last week?'

The thoughts that had flashed through Hazel's mind flashed through Leo Harte's, and he reached the same conclusion: that refusing to answer would look as if he had something to hide. 'I went to offer my condolences. I wanted to assure her that, even though I hadn't been able to offer Trucker a job, I bore him no ill will. And I wanted to be sure that she had enough money to manage.'

'You mean, you bribed her not to tell us that Trucker had been to see you.'

Harte gave a wintry smile. 'Why on earth would I want to do that, Miss Best?'

Hazel shrugged. 'It was an unfortunate coincidence that you were one of the last people to see him alive. In view of this misapprehension in police circles, I mean.'

'And the last person to see someone alive is the first person to see him dead? Not this time, Miss Best.' He nodded at John Carson and turned back to his car. 'I'd be grateful if you'd relay this conversation to Detective Chief Inspector Gorman.'

'Of course I shall,' said Hazel, left standing out in the rain. 'He'll be most interested. Whether he'll be convinced is something else.'

Leo Harte lowered his window a couple of inches. 'It was good to meet you, Miss Best. I feel sure we'll see one another again.'

Hazel bridled. 'Is that meant to be a threat?'

Harte looked momentarily nonplussed. 'No.' Then he smiled. 'I was just trying to seduce you with my charm.'

'Five minutes.' DCI Gorman was only just not shouting. 'You've been back in town five minutes, and already you've conducted an unregulated interview with a prime suspect in a murder case!'

'It wasn't my idea,' Hazel objected. 'He cornered me. I was just trying to get something in return.'

'*Was* he threatening you?'

She shook her head. 'I don't think so. I mean, he's a bit intimidating even when he's just standing there breathing in and out, but I don't think he meant me any harm. He wanted to send you a message without going through official channels.'

'The message that he had nothing to do with this. Did you believe him?'

Hazel retreated behind the wooden expression they taught her in Basic Training. 'It's not my job to believe or disbelieve, only to gather evidence and then to test it.'

'Yeah, yeah. But did you *believe* him?'

Hazel was cornered again. 'On the whole, I think I did. If he was responsible for Trucker's death, he just might have gone to pay blood-money to his mother. But I don't think he took a wheel-brace to Gillian Mitchell's head. I think he wants you to find out who did. I think – I *think* – they were an item.'

Gorman's eyebrows did their disappearing trick again. 'Gillian Mitchell and Leo Harte? The investigative journalist and the crime boss? Pull the other one, it has bells on.'

'I know it seems unlikely. But he didn't tell me that. I threw it out as bait. But his expression . . . Dave, I think I caught a fish.'

She paused for a moment, marshalling her thoughts. 'It might explain some of the things we don't understand. Like why, having started this book and got together some incendiary material, she suddenly stopped writing it four months before she died. Her research brought her into contact with Harte. He knew how much of a danger she represented. Maybe he intended to scare her off, or maybe he hoped to seduce her, shut her up that way. But events overtook them. The more they saw of each other, the more they found they really liked one another.

'And then, Gillian hadn't been commissioned to write about Harte, it was a personal project – she could put it aside without letting anyone down or having to answer any awkward questions. She just stopped writing the book and moved on to other stories. The assistance dog, the Spitfire girls and the mad monk.'

'We need to know for sure. Try to find something in her files. A letter, maybe, to a friend or relative, talking about him. We'll access her e-mail account, see if there's anything there. And social media.'

'By "we",' guessed Hazel, 'I suppose you mean me.'

He had the grace to look uncomfortable. 'You're so much better with this electronic stuff than I am – and even I'm better than Tom Presley. And if I ask Scotland Yard for help, they'll end up taking over.'

'You get the authority, I'll do the donkey-work,' said Hazel. She grinned, impishly. 'Five minutes I've been in CID, and already you can't manage without me.'

TWENTY-ONE

Gillian Mitchell had been a professional journalist: she knew that words launched into cyberspace were there forever, travelling to places their creator had never foreseen, and had been far too smart to be indiscreet about her personal relationships. All her posts were essentially advertisements for her writing, and when they found the file with her passwords in it there was little personal correspondence in her e-mail account.

'She doesn't seem to have had much of a life beyond work,' said Hazel sadly. 'I think she was quite a lonely person.'

She was propped on her sofa at home, her laptop on her knee. She'd copied the Mitchell files onto an external hard drive so she could keep chiselling away at them without annoying the office cleaners.

Saturday had just got back from visiting Ash at the hospital. There was sleet trapped in his hair. 'Lonely, or just solitary? They're not the same thing.'

'I suppose not.' But to Hazel, an essentially gregarious woman who enjoyed the company of other people, for whom a cloistered life held no appeal, they seemed almost the same.

'If she was a journalist, she probably met as many people as she wanted to through her work. Maybe she couldn't wait to see the back of them all and be alone with her own thoughts,' suggested Saturday.

'Perhaps . . .' Hazel sounded unconvinced. 'Or maybe it's the downside of the digital revolution. We spend our days communicating, but we're not actually *talking* to *anyone*. We're just throwing words out there. Well, not me so much, policing is rather more hands-on than most jobs, but that's pretty much what Gillian was doing. She e-mailed newspapers with ideas for articles; they e-mailed back and agreed; she did her research on-line; as often as not she interviewed people by e-mail too. She could have gone days without actually talking to anyone. That's not good for people. It turns them in on themselves.'

Saturday shrugged. 'It seems to have worked for her. She was successful. She didn't buy a house in Park Crescent without being good at her job.'

'She *was* successful,' acknowledged Hazel, 'but *that's* not always the same as being happy. She had plenty of followers, but the closest thing to a friend she seems to have had was Colonel Aykhurst next door, and they didn't use first names. She was an intelligent woman, successful and still young, but she was isolated.

'And then she met Leo Harte. And Leo Harte is a bad man, but he is a practised charmer. When he learned what she was planning, charm might have been the first gun he pulled. It can be as lethal as the other kind, and you can't be done for having it without a licence. And an intelligent, articulate, isolated woman who was still young but aware of getting older might have been the very one to fall for it. To fall for *him*.'

'You think that's all it was? He buttered her up because it was cheaper than buying her off and safer than pushing her under a train?'

Hazel looked up from her screen. 'Actually, no. I think that's probably how it started. He realised she was a threat to him and set out to neutralise her. But then . . . Maybe he fell for his own promo. Maybe he told her they were soul-mates, and started believing it himself. If that isn't love, it's something pretty close to it. Maybe something as close as a practised charmer is going to get.'

'Yeah, right,' drawled Saturday. 'And there's fairy gold at the end of a rainbow, and if you're frowning when the wind changes you'll stay like that forever.'

Hazel laughed. 'There is no romance in your soul! But I was watching him when he spoke about her. He wasn't relieved that a problem had been solved. He was hurting. He wanted to know what had happened to her. Improbable as it sounds, I think they were in love. She loved him enough to give up her book. And he loved her enough to break the habit of a lifetime and offer to help the police.'

'Or he just wanted to convince you that it wasn't him who killed her.'

It was an alternative Hazel couldn't safely dismiss. She knew what she'd seen. There remained the possibility that she'd seen what she was meant to. 'Then let's look at what we know for sure. Gillian Mitchell was a freelance journalist. She was self-employed, she worked alone, she lived alone, she travelled quite a bit. She probably found it hard to make new friends, or see much of her old ones. Which is borne out by her letter files and e-mail account. Lots about work, not much about her personal life.'

'That makes her fall for a crook?'

'Maybe it makes her more vulnerable to an unexpectedly pleasant encounter than someone with more of a support network. She started writing this book because she was a journalist and she'd come across a story that needed telling. About this successful Birmingham entrepreneur who *didn't* get where he was by blood, sweat and tears – or at least, not his own.

'She asked him for an interview.' Hazel had the e-mails in front of her. 'Which was a brave thing to do, but I suppose she thought she had a professional obligation to let him tell his side of the story. He agreed – because he wanted to know how much she knew, and how much she could prove. Well, they did the interview, and they seem to have parted on good terms – gratitude expressed on both sides, Harte sends flowers the next day – then the following week they meet again. Twice. And twice the next week. And after that, Gillian Mitchell stops working on her book.'

'Because Harte asks her to?'

'Not in writing. But then, you wouldn't expect him to.'

'So he warned her off.'

'I don't think so. Judging by the e-mails, they go on meeting. Meals out, the Birmingham Philharmonic, a day at the races. Then in one of them – yes, this one – he says they'll be late back and suggests she brings her toothbrush, and she says she might.'

'She doesn't sound scared of him,' admitted Saturday. 'Maybe she thought Harte was her last shot at a meal-ticket.'

'Saturday!' Hazel was appalled and amused in equal measures. 'Gillian Mitchell was a successful professional woman. She didn't need a meal-ticket.'

'She was no spring chicken, either,' he retorted. 'How old was she?'

'Forty-three.'

'Second half of her career, then. Maybe she was wanting to slow down a bit. Ease up on the travelling and the deadlines. Maybe that's why she was trying to switch from newspapers to books.'

'That's possible,' conceded Hazel.

'So maybe she was tempted by the idea of being a

kept woman.' He must have heard the expression in his grandparents' house: no one of Saturday's generation used it. 'Correct me if I'm wrong, but I don't think women of forty-three get as many offers as girls of twenty-three. Harte might have looked like her last best chance.'

'You're wrong about older women. The offers are there, it's just that we get more particular about which ones we take.'

He grinned at that. 'Well, whether she was thinking with her heart or her head, she seems to have seen Leo Harte as a gamble worth taking. You'd expect a professional journalist to be a bit more cynical.'

'I think they went way past where professionalism was any help to them. Not just her – Harte as well. I think they both threw caution to the wind. They must have thought that what they had was worth the risks they were taking.'

There was a pause then. Hazel returned to her files, thinking the conversation was over. But it wasn't quite. At length Saturday said, 'You're going to need a very long spoon.'

Hazel looked up, puzzled. 'What?'

'It's what people say, isn't it? If you're going to sup with the devil, take a long spoon. Well, Leo Harte might be holding umbrellas over you right now, because he wants something from you. What about when you find out who killed Gillian? Gorman's going to want to arrest him and put him in front of a jury. But if this is personal, Harte might prefer a more direct approach. He's offering to help you now because he means to use you later. Take a long spoon. Take a very long spoon.'

Hazel collected Ash from the hospital the following morning. Then she collected Patience from Railway Street, and drove them both to Highfield Road.

Frankie had gathered every cushion in the house and piled them in his armchair in the study; and looked out a spare quilt for over his knees in case the room got cold. When she went away to make the lunch, Ash whispered, 'She makes me feel like Methuselah's grandpa.'

'I'm not sure how to break this to you, Gabriel,' murmured Hazel. 'But right now you *look* like Methuselah's grandpa.'

It was true. The concussion had resolved, the strapped ribs

were knitting, even his bruises were fading from Technicolor to watercolour. But he moved like an old man. If someone had offered him an arm, or a stick, he would have accepted with gratitude.

'It was the steel toe-caps that did the damage,' he said.

Hazel winced. Then she frowned. 'You had time to study his footwear?'

'I hadn't time to be sure it wasn't a truck rolling over me. The doctor in A&E reckoned he could tell.'

'You know, we're starting to get a picture of this guy,' Hazel said thoughtfully. 'Steel toe-caps suggest he works in heavy industry, or maybe a garage or workshop. That would fit with the wheel-brace or wrench or whatever he hits people with.'

Ash was staring at her. 'Who?'

For a moment she thought he was being incredibly dense. 'The guy who's behind all this, of course,' she said. Then she remembered that he hadn't seen the three sets of X-rays taped to Gorman's window, and she hadn't meant to discuss the implications with him, at least not yet.

'All what? Hazel, the guy who's been stalking you left flowers and wine, and kicked seven bells out of someone he thought was a rival. Apart from this' – he touched the side of his head cautiously – 'there's no suggestion that he's ever hit anyone with anything. The wheel-brace belongs to the other guy: the one who murdered Trucker, and possibly the journalist.'

'Yes, of course,' said Hazel, flustered. 'I've been working on Gillian Mitchell's files. I got confused for a moment.'

'Yes?' He peered at her. 'Hazel – have you some reason for thinking it's the same man?'

'No,' she lied, shaking her head. 'Really. It was just . . . two things buzzing round in my head at the same time . . . they collided. It doesn't mean anything.'

Ash disagreed. 'It might mean something. It might mean your unconscious mind has spotted points of similarity between the three cases while your conscious mind is still weighing the evidence.'

Already she was wishing she'd been honest with him. She

needed his input. Ash was very good at making connections. It was his field of expertise. Sooner or later – probably sooner – he would figure out that she knew more than she was telling him, and the reason for her reticence was that she didn't want him worrying about what she might do next. She said carefully, 'How would I know?'

He thought for a moment. 'You have Gillian Mitchell's computer files? Letters, documents, e-mails?' Hazel nodded. 'See if anyone left unexpected presents for her in the weeks before . . .'

You wouldn't think it was possible to pronounce a full stop. But it is, and therefore it's easy to tell the difference between a sentence which is complete and one which has been, for whatever reason, truncated. Hazel recognised that he had meant to say something more; and a moment later she knew what it would have been. 'Before she was killed.' A chill ran down her back like – yes, like rainwater dripping from an umbrella.

Ash nodded sombrely. 'Yes. Before she was killed.'

Hazel swallowed. 'It's a bit of a leap, isn't it? From flowers on the doorstep to beating someone's head in with a wheel-brace?'

'It would be,' said Ash, 'if he took the direct route. But stalkers don't. They move by increments; their intentions, and the risk they pose, change a step at a time. Your man took a big step when he entered your house. He may not have meant to harm you. He may have told himself he was only checking that you were safe, or that the house was secure, or he wanted to watch over you while you slept. But his behaviour is diverging from what is normally considered acceptable. We have an in-built inhibitor that warns us when we're in danger of stepping over some kind of a line: either his is becoming less and less effective, or he's finding it easier to ignore. Kicking the living daylights out of me was another step along the same road.

'He's become obsessed with you. It isn't rational. By definition, stalkers are not rational people. He thinks he has a relationship with you: you might think of him as a casual acquaintance, though it's entirely possible you wouldn't recognise him if you met. And before long that's going to start annoying him. All these things he's done for you, and you look through him when you pass in the street.

'Once he starts getting angry, that same faulty inhibitor will let him think he's entitled to punish you for rejecting him. I don't know if he's done this before, but he may have done. I don't know if he's hurt anyone before, but there was nothing amateurish about the way he ambushed me. If your instincts are telling you that the man who's stalking you is the same man who murdered Gillian Mitchell, and probably Trucker Watts as well, I think you should listen to them.'

He was frightening her, all the more so because she had more than instinct to go on. There were those X-rays. They proved nothing; but two experienced observers had noted the similarities. 'And do what?' she demanded. 'I'm already being as careful as I can be. Saturday's going to stay at Railway Street until the danger passes. Apart from that, Gabriel, what can I do? The ball's in his court. The ball's always going to be in his court.'

'You could go back to Byrfield. You'd be safe there.'

She knew he was right. *He* knew she wasn't going to do it. 'Run away again? Wait to see which of my friends he picks off next? Or are we *all* going to head down to Byrfield? I know it's a big house, but even Pete might get a bit fed up if half of Norbold descends on him.

'You want to know what my instinct's telling me? That the only place this is going to be resolved is right here. If I go somewhere else, it'll be waiting for me when I get back. *He'll* be waiting for me. I don't like it any more than you do, but I think – I *think* – the only way we're going to catch this man is by drawing him out.

'Somehow he's got the idea that I can offer him something worth risking his liberty for. We can use that. And better sooner than later, while he's still feeling protective, before he starts getting angry with me. He probably poses less of a threat to me today than he will in a month's time. When we've got him, when we know who he is, we'll know if there's anything to connect him to the murders.'

'Hazel – you're not thinking of setting a trap for him?' Alarm was rolling up the flatness in Ash's voice like a rug.

'No, of course not.' But even as she said it, she knew it was another lie.

TWENTY-TWO

'How do I set a trap for him?'

Hazel had left the computer screen for the recommended ten-minute break, having sat staring at it for rather longer than the recommended fifty minutes, and taken coffee through to Dave Gorman's office. It said everything about his new role that, just for a moment, she wasn't sure he was there, hunched behind the Alpine paperwork.

'That's easy,' said Gorman immediately, reaching for the waxed cup through a kind of mountain pass between crime reports on the one hand and annual reviews on the other. 'You don't.'

'Why not?'

'You know why not. It's entrapment. It would get the case thrown out of court, you thrown out of the police and me thrown to the wolves.'

'So I just have to wait until he tries to jump my bones again?'

'Of course you don't,' said Gorman. 'Or to put it slightly differently, yes. Or here's a thought: you could go back to Cambridgeshire and finish your holiday.'

'We talked about that,' Hazel said shortly. 'It wouldn't solve anything, just spin it out. Besides . . .'

'Besides what?'

'Oh – nothing. I'm sorry, chief, but I'm not going anywhere. I can come in here and work, or I can stay at home and listen for footsteps on the stairs. There isn't a third option.'

'Fine. Because sitting by an open window with a Colt 45 hidden under your negligee certainly isn't one.'

Hazel considered. But it was no use, she was the wrong generation. 'What's a negligee?'

'Beats me,' admitted Gorman. 'I think you sleep in them, but I never had one.'

When she got home, without a word Saturday handed her the post. Among the bills and fliers was a stiff brown envelope.

Hazel glanced at him. 'Did you open it?'

'Of course I didn't open it,' he retorted sharply. 'I don't go round opening other people's post! What do you take me for?'

'Sorry,' she countered, 'just for a minute I thought you were my friend Saturday who hacks into people's bank accounts for a living.'

It wasn't perfectly accurate, but it was too close for him to argue. 'Point taken,' he murmured. 'Do you want me to open it?'

Hazel shook her head. 'No, I'll open it. See what little treat he's got in store for me this time. Wait a minute while I get some gloves.'

Again she opened it at the bottom, although the flap of the first envelope had failed to yield any traces of DNA so probably this one wouldn't either. It was, as they both expected, a photograph. Hazel pulled it out carefully.

Saturday heard the sharp intake of breath and looked at her in concern. Her face had frozen, lips parted in shock, eyes wide. 'Hazel?' But as he twisted to see the reason, she snapped back into action and crumpled the photograph violently, tossing it towards the fire.

'No!' He dived after it, retrieving it – or most of it – at the cost of singed fingertips. 'What are you doing? That's evidence.'

She sucked in a deep breath. 'Yes. Have you seen what it's evidence of?'

It wasn't top quality. It was taken with a cheap phone, after dark, in a street with not enough municipal lighting. Only the wet pavements bouncing the flash around made any sense of the image it recorded.

'Jesus!' whistled Saturday.

It was Ash. It had been taken well on into the attack, after he'd stopped trying to defend himself. If he wasn't already unconscious he was the next thing to it; which was why his

assailant could spare a hand to take happy snaps. With his
other hand he was holding Ash's head off the road by a fistful
of his hair, rat-tailed, the rain mingling with blood from his
split scalp. There was another gaping gash across his cheek-
bone. By the time Hazel saw it in the hospital, it had been
reduced to a thin scabby line by a row of neat stitches which
gave almost no indication of what the A&E staff had had to
deal with. His eyes were unresponsive, almost closed, thin
white crescents under the bruised lids. His mouth was torn,
and mired from the dirt running in the gutter.

'You're right,' Hazel said unsteadily, 'I shouldn't burn it.
But I'm sure as hell not putting it in his bloody album! I'll
e-mail a copy to Dave Gorman, see what he makes of it.'

Her hands were shaking. Saturday quietly took over, taking
the crumpled photograph, smoothing it out, scanning it onto
her laptop. At the second time of trying, Hazel pulled up the
DCI's address, and Saturday wrote a brief explanation and
attached the image to it.

'I need a drink.' Hazel was in no danger of becoming an
alcoholic – she didn't like the taste enough – but she kept a
bottle of whisky for emergencies, and this was one.

'I'll stick with coffee,' said Saturday, unusually diplomatic.
'In case we have to go down to the police station.' So Hazel
put the bottle back and made coffee for two.

Saturday put the laptop aside as she came back from the
kitchen. 'How are you getting on with your homework?' He
meant Gillian Mitchell's files, a hefty block of data currently
occupying much of Hazel's hard drive. They needed something
to talk about other than the sight of their friend beaten to
bloody rags in the street.

'It's slow,' she said, pulling herself together. 'And most of
it's pretty boring. There must be people who want to read
articles about cod stocks around Iceland and the role of aid
organisations in Yemen, but I'm not one of them. And I have
to. Since I don't know what it is I'm looking for I can't
afford to skip.'

'You think the reason for what happened to Gillian Mitchell
is a story she wrote, or one she was working on?'

Hazel shrugged. 'Her work is what brought her into contact

with Leo Harte. If she met someone even more disreputable, who didn't take a shine to her, that's probably how.'

'I don't think she was murdered by an Icelandic cod-fisherman.'

'Neither do I. But she took her job seriously. Her work was supported by a lot of research – names, places, dates. It's possible that one of these references puts somebody somewhere he shouldn't have been, and it was going to cost him money or reputation or both if a newspaper showed that he was.'

'If someone killed her to stop a story appearing, it had to be one she was still writing. There'd be no point killing her after it was in print and the damage was done.'

Hazel widened her eyes at him. 'So you think I should start with the most recent files and work backwards? Oh wait – that's what I thought, too.'

Saturday grinned. 'If you don't want my help, you just have to say so.'

'Of course I want your help. Who knows, the very next thing you suggest, I mightn't have figured out for myself two days ago.'

'OK. Well, my next suggestion is that you can probably exclude Brother Jam from your inquiries.'

Hazel frowned. 'Who?'

'The mad monk. He may have been the terror of the cloisters seven hundred years ago, but I don't think he's responsible for Trucker, for Gillian Mitchell or' – his gaze slid sideways to the crumpled photograph on the coffee table – 'that.'

Hazel laughed out loud. '*James*! Brother *James*. When did you last get your eyes tested?'

'I have twenty/twenty vision,' said Saturday with dignity, picking up the computer again, 'and it definitely says Jam here.'

'Then it's a typo,' chuckled Hazel. 'Whoever heard of someone in holy orders being named after a fruit preserve?'

When the coffee had steadied her hands, she went to return the photograph to its cardboard sleeve. Her grunt of surprise made Saturday look up. 'What?'

'There's something else in here.'

'More of the same?' His voice was harsh.

Hazel shook her head. 'It's scenery of some kind.' Her voice lifted in unreasoning hope. 'Hell's bells, Saturday, I think he's sent us his holiday snaps by accident!'

Breakthroughs in criminal detection come as a result of happy accidents more often than detectives like to admit. But that would have represented a new nadir of stupidity in a field largely – though not exclusively – populated by stupid people, and when Hazel carefully took it out and examined it, there was nothing to identify the photographer. No one grinning in a Kiss Me Quick hat, no car with the number-plate showing, not even a signpost to indicate where it was taken.

It showed a heavily wooded little glen and a waterfall pouring white foam over a stone ledge into a mossy pool. It wasn't the kind of beauty spot tourists travel halfway round the world to see. It was the kind to visit with your kids and a picnic if the sun happens to be shining and there's nothing worth watching on the television.

'Is that somewhere local, do you suppose?' But she was asking the wrong person. Saturday's interest in the natural world had never gone much beyond how cold it was likely to get at night and whether there would be more rain than an ancient parka could cope with. 'And wherever it is, why does he want me to have it?'

'It's an invitation,' said Saturday.

'What?'

'You're meant to read it alongside the other one. He came to your house. He found Gabriel leaving, late at night. He . . . marked his disapproval, and took a photograph to show you. The second picture is to say that he won't be coming back here – that it's your turn to come to him. That's where you'll find him – in that wood, by that waterfall.'

Hazel considered. It was a bold interpretation of not many facts, but the more she thought about it, the more she felt he could be right. She couldn't think what else it *could* mean. 'He might want me to come to him, but he can't seriously think I'm going to.'

Saturday shrugged thin shoulders. 'Who knows what he thinks? This is a deeply disturbed person. You start understanding his thought processes, it's time to question your own sanity.'

Hazel was peering deeper and deeper into the photograph, as if by concentrating she might pass through into that other reality, look around her and see more than the photograph showed. 'Do you suppose he lives there? In a cabin in the woods?'

'Me Tarzan, you Hazel? Of course he doesn't live there. It's a rendezvous. Somewhere quiet where he thinks the two of you won't be disturbed. But he's pretty sure you can find it if you put your mind to it.'

'Why would I want to?'

'Because of the other photograph,' said Saturday.

And actually, he was right. If Hazel had recognised the spot, she would have gone there. To put an end to this before anyone else got hurt. She would have organised back-up, of course, and then she would have gone. Except . . .

'If he doesn't live there, how will he know that I've solved his puzzle and I'm on my way?'

Saturday thought the explanation was obvious. Reluctantly, he put it into words. 'He's watching you. He's going to *be* watching you. He'll know if you go there, and he'll know if you go alone. Unless you're alone, he won't show.'

Hazel shivered. 'Well, it's all a bit immaterial since I don't know where it is he wants to meet me. And I wouldn't go alone if I did.'

'I could come.'

The offer was meant kindly and Hazel was grateful for it. But she wouldn't have dreamed of taking him up on it. 'If this comes to anything, it's outdoor specialists we'll need – woodsmen, trackers, maybe dog handlers. People who can search rough country without getting lost or falling down ravines. You're a good friend, Saturday, but you're not really pioneer material.

'Plus, when we find this man we'll need enough people to arrest him safely. I couldn't do that on my own, and you and I couldn't do it together. That might be what he wants, but he's not going to get it. I'll talk to Dave Gorman tomorrow, see if we can figure out where this waterfall is. But I'm going nowhere near it unless I've got five burly coppers squeezed into a Black Maria right behind me.'

TWENTY-THREE

D CI Gorman didn't recognise the waterfall, but then he didn't claim to be much of a pioneer either. He liked the feel of concrete under his feet. He e-mailed a copy of the photograph to the nearest office of the Rivers Agency, but they didn't recognise it either. Perhaps because the water-course was too minor to be on their radar; perhaps because it was on private land.

'Aren't most watercourses on private land?'

'Apparently, some land is more private than others.'

'So what are we looking for?' asked Hazel, peering at the picture again. 'A country estate, something like that?'

Gorman shrugged. 'Maybe. Or a bit of farmland that's too rough to be cultivated. I don't know how you'd set about finding it without something more to go on.'

Hazel looked at him askance. 'How *I'd* set about finding it?'

The DCI scowled. 'That was a rhetorical *you*. The Queen says *one* – where I come from we say *you*. You, second person singular, Constable Hazel Best, are *not* to go looking for it on your own. If you see a picture postcard of it in the newsagent's window, you will tell me and I will organise a reconnaissance.'

'Yes, sir,' Hazel said obediently.

Gorman never quite trusted her when she was agreeing with him.

Good instincts were part of what had earned him a measure of professional success. As soon as she came off duty, Hazel headed round to the council offices.

Norbold was not a spa town. It was not a seaside resort. Neither John Constable nor William Wordsworth had felt moved to immortalise its charms, and almost none of the tourists who flocked to Stratford made the comparatively short trip from there to Norbold. It had never, therefore, had much use for a Tourist Information Office. But hope springs eternal, and the town council had prepared for the possibility that one day an American president would find he had forebears in the district, or a Norbold lad would make it big in Hollywood, or – more likely – some major disaster would attract the world's press, by setting up a desk in the Town Hall foyer with scenic views and Things to Do in Norbold pamphlets. These were, necessarily, brief pamphlets and a scant half-dozen photographs.

Nevertheless, Hazel studied them carefully. The old corn mill in Miller's Lane, its dereliction rendered almost picturesque by the setting sun, might once have been water-powered: could there still be a water-course in the trees behind it? Might the stream in her photograph be feeding the local canal? The trees overhanging the waterfall were native broadleaves rather than commercial conifers, so it probably wasn't forestry land; but there were several large estates in the area, any of which might have a wild and inaccessible corner such as this tucked away from common view.

Nothing she saw was of any help, so Hazel moved over to the desk to enlist the services of the receptionist. It was a short conversation. The receptionist was unfamiliar with the scene Hazel showed her, and wasn't sure who might do better. 'Have you tried the Rivers Agency?'

Hazel nodded. 'They said it wasn't one of theirs.'

'Oh dear.' She was a middle-aged woman who took her job seriously and didn't like not being able to answer a question about Norbold's scenic attractions. There weren't so many of them as to require a lifetime's study. But she had no information to contribute. 'It's quite a pretty scene, isn't it?'

'Yes, it is.' Hazel couldn't see how much further that got them.

'Would it be worth talking to someone at the Art Club? I can give you a number for their secretary.'

Hazel was impressed. 'Good idea. Yes, please – I'll try them.'

'And how about the Ornithological Society? They'll go anywhere in search of a Lesser Spotted Godwit.'

Hazel scribbled down names and numbers, and thanked the

receptionist. 'You've done better than me and my DCI put together.' The woman simpered with pleasure.

The chairman of the Art Club called her husband in from the garden and they pored over the photograph together, but ultimately without success. 'I thought for a minute . . .' murmured the chairman; 'but no. I'm sorry, Constable Best, I don't think I've ever been there, and I can't remember seeing a painting of it. I suppose it is a local scene, is it?'

Hazel shrugged helplessly. 'Your guess is as good as mine. It may even be a hoax – not local, and nothing to do with the case we're investigating.' But actually she didn't believe that. The photograph accompanying it made this one significant. Whoever had beaten Ash had wanted her to know about this place, and thought she was capable of finding it. Otherwise, why bother?

The secretary of the birdwatchers' association was distracted by a blur in one corner of the photograph that might possibly have been a tree creeper. The waterfall only interested him in so far as it might attract dippers. He didn't think he'd ever seen it himself – though he admitted he was better at remembering what he'd seen than where he'd seen them. 'You don't take in much of the scenery if you're looking for a Dartford warbler.'

Seeing her out, however, he had one helpful suggestion. 'Have you tried the Woodsmen?'

Hazel shook her head. 'Who are they?'

'Pretty much what the name says – tree huggers. They camp out and plant saplings and carve walking sticks out of fallen branches – that kind of thing. Somebody told me they give the trees names and sing to them. All a bit New Age for me. I mean, I'm all in favour of trees – where are the birds going to nest without them? – but giving them names is just plain silly.'

'Where would I find a Woodsman to talk to?'

The ornithologist shrugged negligently. 'Beats me. I don't know any personally.'

Hazel hung onto her patience. 'All right. Then who was it told you about them?'

'A fellow birdwatcher, of course,' he said, as if she should have known. 'Chap from the council. Works department. Name of . . .'

'Benny,' she said, arriving home in time to find the road crew filling in the last of the hole outside her door. 'The very man I'm looking for.'

Benny Price didn't know whether to be pleased or alarmed. 'I am?'

'I want to contact someone from the local branch – chapter, whatever – of the Woodsmen. A twitcher I asked thought you knew something about them.'

'Not really,' said Benny regretfully. 'Not for a long time. I used to do a bit of bush-craft when I was young. You know, living off the land, taking nothing you can't carry on your back, leaving nothing but footprints. There were half a dozen of us, all young lads from the town. It was a chap from the Woodsmen got us started – showed us how to make a fire, how to keep it safe, what plants we could eat, even how to trap and skin a rabbit.

'We managed to catch a rabbit once.' He smiled fondly, run over by the traffic in Memory Lane. 'We looked at one another, and we looked at the rabbit; and we stroked the rabbit; and then we let the rabbit go, hiked back into town and bought fish and chips.'

Hazel chuckled. 'Do you know if there are any Woodsmen around still?'

Benny thought about it. 'I expect there are, but I don't know any. The chap I'm talking about must have gone to the great Campfire in the Sky by now.'

'You don't remember his name?' But Benny Price shook his head. 'What about the other lads you mentioned?'

Benny rolled his eyes. 'It's twenty years ago! Some of them I haven't seen since. Jacko Warren joined the Army – I never heard where he ended up. Miggsy went to London – did The Knowledge and bought himself a black cab. I saw Ginger in town a couple of years ago, doing the weekend shop. He's married with five children. Five children,' he repeated in tones of awe. 'But if you're wondering if I'd know how to contact any of them, I'm afraid the answer's no.'

'They probably couldn't be much help anyway,' said Hazel. 'It's not that I'm desperate to find a Woodsman per se, I'm just trying to identify a bit of woodland from a picture. You're a tw . . .' She reconsidered the frowned-on term just in time. "Bird-watcher, aren't you? I don't suppose you recognise the place.' She showed him the photograph.

Benny Price shook his head regretfully. 'I'm sorry, Miss Best. It doesn't ring any bells.'

'Maybe I should post it on Facebook and see if anyone can identify it.'

Benny looked shocked. 'Don't do that, Miss Best! You've no idea who'd contact you. There are some real weirdos on social media sites.'

Hazel tried not to smile. 'So I've been told, Benny. So I've been told.'

She searched Gillian Mitchell's files for any reference to flowers, wine or chocolates. There were many. The woman wrote for a living, using the same computer for the last six years: there probably wasn't a word in the Oxford English Dictionary that she hadn't employed time and again. Hazel sighed and resigned herself to checking them all in turn; but the longer it took, the more convinced she became that no unexpected presents had appeared on the murdered woman's doorstep.

Which was reassuring. Perhaps what had looked like a connection between her stalker and the murders – and it had only ever been a tenuous one, considered but by no means accepted by a tired and worried DCI with no other leads to focus on – was nothing more than a coincidence. Everyone who'd ever been hit over the head with something hard could probably show a wound similar to Ash's.

Saturday was sprawled on the sofa, reading last week's *Norbold News*, amused by the reporter's attempts to describe Trucker Watts in terms that were suitably respectful to a murder victim. Saturday had been loitering on the edge of Trucker's gang when Hazel and Ash first met him. He hadn't had much good to say of Trucker when he was alive, but dying at the hands of somebody even more unpleasant had vested his memory with a tint of rose.

'You can say what you like about Trucker,' he began.

Hazel waited, but nothing followed. 'But?' she prompted.

'No, that was it,' said Saturday. 'You can say what you like about Trucker. The poor bastard can't do anything about it any more.'

Hazel pushed the laptop in his direction. 'OK, Hackmeister. You're the one with the expensive skills. I'm going to have a shower – you winkle Gillian Mitchell's killer out of her files. I want three viable leads by the time I've dried my hair.'

'Only three?' he asked sardonically.

In fact, opting for a long soak in the bath instead, she was hoping for at least five viable leads by the time she went downstairs again, wrapped in her dressing-gown and with her hair turbaned in a towel. 'Well? Solved the mystery, have you?'

'It was the monk what did it,' said Saturday, deadpan.

'The mediaeval monk?' Hazel's scepticism would have pickled gherkins. 'Brother James, the mad monk, who's been dead for seven hundred years, killed two people in Norbold in the last month and may have been leaving pressies on my doorstep?'

'Ah, well,' said Saturday complacently. 'There are some unwarranted assumptions in there. As you probably noticed, these are notes rather than a finished article, so she doesn't spell everything out. She's just reminding herself of what she knows – bullet-points rather than details. But nowhere does she state that these are historic events. She uses the present tense throughout. She makes no reference to the mediaeval period, or any other timeframe. I think she was talking about current events.'

'You're serious?' But Saturday had lied to her enough in the past that Hazel thought she could tell that he wasn't lying now. She edged behind the sofa to look over his shoulder at the screen. 'There really are mad monks still around?' But there was a problem. 'Even if there are, Norbold doesn't have a monastery.'

'And that's another of those unwarranted assumptions,' said Saturday breezily. 'Nowhere does she say he's a monk.'

'She calls him Brother James. What are you suggesting – that they're members of the same trades union?'

'In fact,' said Saturday, 'she calls him Brother Jam. It's not a typo – she wrote it that way three different times. It could be his name, it could be a nickname, it could be his initials, but it isn't a mistake.'

Hazel reached down to scroll through the notes. It was the first time she'd read them properly. She'd dismissed the file as irrelevant when she'd first opened it and thought it was a baroque history piece. 'No, it isn't,' she conceded. 'All right, so if he isn't a monk, who is he?'

'I came up with four possible reasons for her to refer to him as Brother, some more likely than others. One, he really *is* a monk. Seems a shade unlikely, but there are such people and I bet they're at least as likely to turn homicidal maniac as, for instance, bus drivers and dairy farmers.'

'"If hate killed men, Brother Lawrence, God's blood, would not mine kill you!"' Hazel murmured.

Saturday swivelled to look at her. 'What?'

'Sorry – a bit of half-remembered poetry welling up from the fountains of youth. I'm sure you're right: if a dog-collar can't always stop people going over to the dark side, I don't suppose a cowl can either. On the other hand, if he really is a monk, he shouldn't be too hard to find. There aren't *that* many of them – and very few called Jam. Jam?' She still didn't quite believe it.

'Jam,' confirmed Saturday. He highlighted the text in all three places.

'You thought of four reasons she might call him Brother. What were the others?'

'He could be an evangelist rather than a monk. They call one another Brother and Sister, don't they? The ones you see in films do, anyhow.'

'I suppose it's possible. So, come to that, is the trades unionist.'

Saturday nodded. 'He was number three. Number four is a bit of a long shot . . .'

'Those weren't?' marvelled Hazel.

The young man ignored her. '. . . But suppose she's telling us exactly who he is? She calls him Brother Jam because he is, in fact . . .'

Hazel's eyes flared wide. 'Her brother? Gillian Mitchell was murdered by her brother? Her actual brother?'

TWENTY-FOUR

'Let me get this right,' said DCI Gorman. 'You're saying Gillian Mitchell was murdered by her brother.'

'Of course I'm not saying that,' said Hazel tartly. 'I don't even know if she had a brother. Even if she had, I've no idea if he's the sort of man to end an argument with a wheel-brace. I'm just saying, it's a possibility we should look into. Most murder victims know their killers. Many are related to their killers. This wouldn't be the first time that a family squabble ended up in the Coroner's Court.'

'Is that what she was writing about? A family squabble? She was hoping to sell an article about how she fell out with her brother?' He sounded deeply unconvinced.

Hazel had printed out the contents of the folder Gillian Mitchell had labelled 'Brother Jam'. At some point Gorman would need to read all the material it contained; for the immediate purposes, however, it would be quicker if she summarised it.

'I don't think she was writing this for public consumption. I think it was how she ordered her thoughts about something that bothered her. Thinking on the page – it's a writer thing. Police officers bounce ideas off one another to see if they have legs: writers fix their thoughts by putting them down on paper. Or, these days, on a screen.

'And then, she seems to have used the file as a journal. She jotted things down as they happened, important things and trivial things alike. As far as Jam goes, I think she was keeping a record that she could refer back to later, to give her a bit of perspective on things. She was concerned about his behaviour, and leaving herself notes about it was a way of judging if she was making a mountain out of a molehill or if he really was becoming increasingly odd.'

'Odd in what way?'

'She started the folder six months ago, after he threw a newspaper at her. He disagreed with what she'd written about the political situation in Greece.'

Gorman stared. 'He knew about the political situation in Greece? He *cared* about the political situation in Greece?'

'Apparently. I think that was what worried her – more than the argument, more than having a newspaper thrown at her. She was a journalist, she'd probably had worse things thrown at her.'

'Haven't we all?' muttered Gorman darkly.

'But he was her brother, they were both middle-aged, and it was an abnormal reaction to reading something he disagreed with. I don't think it was the first odd thing he'd done: I think it was the one that prompted her to start taking notes. She wanted to remind herself exactly what had happened, so she didn't either blow it out of proportion or convince herself it was nothing to worry about. She was concerned: not so much for her safety as for his well-being. His mental well-being.'

'What happened next?'

'More arguments. Also, he told her he'd argued with people at work – that they didn't respect him. When she asked him to explain, either he couldn't or wouldn't. He wanted her to write an article about workplace harassment, and sulked when she told him to fight his own battles.

'He had a girlfriend. Gillian never met her, but her brother seemed to value the relationship. When the woman ended it, Jam – I'm sorry, I don't know what else to call him – blamed that on his colleagues too. He believed they'd poisoned her against him, convinced her she could do better elsewhere.'

'Did Gillian think that was what happened?'

Hazel shook her head. 'She thought he was avoiding the truth – that it was his own increasingly random behaviour that wrecked the relationship.'

'Did she tell him that?'

'If she did, there's no record of it here. But she *did* confront him after the place where he worked burned down.'

Gorman's eyebrows shot up into his hairline again. 'He torched the place?'

'Gillian didn't know that. She considered it a possibility. She asked him about it, and he denied it. She had no evidence that he'd done anything wrong, only his growing tendency to over-react to perceived slights and setbacks. She didn't think it was enough to accuse anyone of arson, let alone her own brother.'

'Bad decision,' growled Gorman. 'If she had . . .'

'She'd be alive today? Well, maybe. Maybe we'd have found enough evidence for the CPS to bring charges. The other possibility is that we'd have thought she was a histrionic woman who'd fallen out with her brother and was now blaming him for every unsolved crime since the Whitechapel murders.'

'We wouldn't have done that,' he said, outraged, 'would we? If she'd come to us, we'd have taken her concerns seriously. There's a distinct progression there, from episodes of rage to possible arson to a potential murder. Ah . . .'

'Well, quite,' nodded Hazel. 'There was no way she could anticipate *that* when she was writing these notes. All she had was a lot of unease and a bit of speculation and not very much concrete at all.'

DCI Gorman leaned back in his chair. The realities of policing had been his constant companions since he was twenty years old. He knew that chances to apprehend criminals were missed all the time because there wasn't the manpower to investigate every report of suspicious behaviour; that hindsight was a wonderful thing; that his job would be very much easier if time ran backwards, so that the fact of a crime in December could be used as grounds for arresting someone when he was contemplating it in October.

He sighed. 'Jam is a pretty funny name for anyone's brother. A couple who called their daughter Gillian seem unlikely to have got that imaginative with their son.'

Hazel agreed. 'So it's a nickname. Maybe he was christened James, and Jam was a baby name that stuck. Or maybe it's his initials – J. A. Mitchell. That would work. If we get her birth certificate, we can find out what other children lived in

the same house at the next census. That should tell us who
Jam is.'

'Not bad,' conceded Gorman. 'Now, if I only knew someone
who was really good at electronic data-retrieval . . .'

Gillian Mitchell had no brothers. She had one sister, Muriel,
who had died in infancy. Her parents, Martin and Betty, had
continued to live in their rented house in Coventry Road for
another fifteen years; both were now deceased. Gillian bought
the house in Park Crescent in 2012, at the peak of her earning
ability. She had always lived there alone. So far as Colonel
Aykhurst or any of the neighbours were aware, she had no
surviving family and did not know any monks, evangelists or
trades unionists.

While Hazel was working the data, Gorman turned his
attention to the workplace fire, the only event referenced in the
Brother Jam file that was capable of verification. When he
found that, he'd know where Jam had been working and
managers or other staff would be able to give him a proper
name. Most people have a fairly keen sense of oddness in those
around them. Some have so keen a sense of it that they think
almost everyone they know qualifies, but if three or four people
who used to work at the torched business came up with the
same name, even if they weren't able to explain their reasoning,
Gorman would have a prime suspect.

He put Tom Presley onto it. 'There can't have been that
many suspicious fires in factories or businesses in Norbold in
the last six months. Talk to the Fire & Rescue people. They
usually know if a fire's been started deliberately, even if we
can't nail anyone for it.'

But DS Presley's trip to the fire station on the ring road was
discouraging. 'They couldn't come up with a single suspicious
fire in the last six months that involved a business big enough
to employ both the arsonist and the workmates who didn't like
him. There was a fire in a hay barn out past Sedgewick in the
spring, but it turned out to be the farmer's teenage sons and
their friends smoking roll-ups behind the bales. The only other
possibility was when Fashionistas in Arkwright Street burned
down midway through the summer sales. There was a strong

suspicion that Alberto Beattie had torched his own shop for the insurance, but we couldn't prove it.'

The sergeant looked up from his notes. 'He did, though. I was at school with Bert Beattie, he always was a lying git. Anyway, all his employees were female – two women, three girls. Nobody's Brother Jam.'

Gorman scowled. 'I suppose the fact that Gillian Mitchell lived in Norbold is no guarantee that the guy she's talking about worked here too. He could have worked in Birmingham – Coventry – Wolverhampton . . . Any damn place, actually. They obviously got together sometimes, but we're in the middle of the bloody country: you're never more than a train ride away from anyone. That's why they call us the Midlands.'

Tom Presley blew his cheeks out. 'You want me to look for suspicious fires in business premises elsewhere in the Division? Within a hundred miles of Norbold? Further afield?'

But Gorman shook his head. 'There'll be too many, we'd never work our way through them. I was assuming that, whoever this Jam guy is, he was living locally. But of course, he doesn't have to be. Hell, he could have flown in from the other side of the world in order to throw things at Gillian Mitchell and then beat her head in! We're going to have to find him first. Then check where he was working six months ago and see if there were any unexplained fires there.'

He considered a little longer. Then he said: 'What about Hazel?'

Presley rolled his eyes. 'God, I know!'

The DCI radiated disapproval. 'I *mean*, how much danger do we think she's in?'

'From me, quite a bit,' grumbled Presley. 'From the stalker, rather less – unless she eats all the chocolate, drinks all the wine and has a heart attack. From Gillian Mitchell's Brother Jam? None at all, I wouldn't think.'

'You don't think it's the same man?'

'I don't see any reason to think it is. Someone hit Rambles with a blunt instrument. Well, we've all *wanted* to do that, one time or another. Was it the same blunt instrument that was used to kill Mitchell and Trucker Watts? – there's no evidence that it was, and the fact that they're dead and he isn't suggests that it wasn't. What do you think? Your instincts are further up the pay-scale than mine.'

They had worked together for a number of years, and Presley had earned a certain amount of leeway. Gorman had no wish to surround himself with yes-men – when he asked for opinions, he didn't want to hear only his own, tactfully rephrased, coming back to him – but to people who didn't know him, Tom Presley came over as a bit of a dinosaur: a throw-back to policing the way it used to be done, before the Police & Criminal Evidence Act. And actually, to people who did know him, too.

Gorman said, 'Coincidences make me uneasy.'

Presley sniffed. 'Does it even amount to a coincidence? Stick your head in at the Royal's A&E on a Saturday night and ask how many people they've treated for being hit round the head with a blunt instrument. Dozens? Scores? It's what people do when they're drunk or angry or feel threatened: they grab something hard and heavy, and swing it.

'We don't know why Mitchell and Watts were killed, but we *do* know it was a deliberate act in both cases. We don't have a murder weapon, so the perp took it away with him. If he also took it to the scene – which seems likely: there are no brass candlesticks missing from Park Crescent, and I don't imagine there ever were any behind the skips at the shopping centre – then both attacks were premeditated. He didn't get carried away: he meant to kill, in both cases.'

'The attack on Gabriel Ash may have been premeditated.'

'Maybe,' conceded Presley. 'But the intent was different. The guy who ambushed him could have killed him if he'd wanted – he had him on the ground, too stunned to fight back, with the first blow. But he didn't keep hitting him over the head with his blunt instrument. He kicked the shit out of him instead. He wanted to hurt him, and he wanted to warn him off. Apparently, out of some kind of bizarre obsession with Hazel Best. What can that possibly have to do with Watts and Mitchell?'

Gorman was nodding slowly. He couldn't argue with any of the points his sergeant had made. That didn't mean he agreed with his conclusion. 'Still, I'd be happier if she'd stayed in Cambridgeshire.'

'Me too,' said Tom Presley fervently.

TWENTY-FIVE

Coventry Road was on Hazel's way home from Meadowvale. Well, not *exactly* on her way home, but it only meant a short detour. She wasn't sure what taking a look at Gillian Mitchell's childhood home would tell her, but she had nothing better to do; and if the house told her nothing, there was always the possibility that the neighbours might tell her more.

It was a modest house – two up and two down, halfway along a late Victorian brick-built terrace, rendered only slightly posher than Hazel's house in Railway Street by the postage-stamp front garden between the door and the pavement. It was modest now, and would have been modest when the Mitchell family lived there. Gillian's father worked in the china factory; the only occupation ascribed to her mother in the 1981 census was 'housewife'.

There was nothing to distinguish them from a thousand other families in Norbold, gainfully employed but without the means to climb the socio-economic ladder, except this: they produced a daughter with the talent, the intelligence and the ambition to make a career for herself. Gillian Mitchell had gone from this modest little house and the A-stream at the local comprehensive to writing for national newspapers. She had gone from Coventry Road to Park Crescent. Any way you looked at it, that was a success story.

And it ended when someone beat her head in with a wheel-brace. There was still no evidence as to who that was, although observations she left on her computer pointed the finger of suspicion at someone she referred to as Brother Jam. There was no official record of her having a brother. But not everything goes into the official records. Sometimes a nosy neighbour knows more than the state.

So after a cursory glance at the house – whoever lived there now could not have known the Mitchell family – Hazel looked for someone to talk to. It had been dark since soon after four, but there were lights in most of the houses, and across the road someone was parking his car in a driveway so short the bumper overhung the pavement.

Hazel hailed him with a smile and showed her warrant card. He was too young to be much help, so she asked if he knew who'd lived in this part of Coventry Road for longest. He directed her to Mrs Mackey, four doors along.

Mrs Mackey was certainly old enough to remember the Mitchells. She was almost old enough to remember the houses going up, and everyone who had ever lived in them. 'Yes? What?' she demanded.

Hazel gave the warrant card another airing. 'I'm looking for someone who remembers the Mitchell family, who used to live at Number 34.'

'Why?'

Slightly taken aback, Hazel resorted to the stock policeman's answer: 'Just routine inquiries. Did you know them at all?'

'I knew her,' said the old woman.

'Her?'

'Mrs Mitchell. Betty. Listen, if you want to talk you'll have to come in. My feet are giving me gyp.'

Hazel followed Mrs Mackey into her front room, where the old woman promptly took the best chair and raised her legs onto a footstool. 'That's better. You can sit there.' She pointed. 'Now, what do you want to know?'

'I'm trying to find relatives of Gillian Mitchell, the journalist. I suppose you heard that she'd died?'

'I heard that she'd got her head beat in,' said Mrs Mackey with obscure satisfaction. 'I'm not surprised. No good ever comes of it.'

'Of what?'

'Telling people things. Newspapers, television – they're always *telling* you things. Things you don't need to know. Things you're better *not* knowing. No good ever came of it, nor ever will.'

Hazel knew better than to enter into that discussion. 'How many children did Betty Mitchell have? Do you remember?'

'Two. But one died as a baby.'

'That would be' – Hazel consulted her notebook – 'Muriel?'

Mrs Mackey nodded. 'So Gillian was raised as an only child.'

'That's right.'

'Someone told me she had a brother.' It was the whitest of white lies.

Mrs Mackey shook her head firmly. 'They never had another. Betty wouldn't. She couldn't bear the idea of losing another baby. Took it to heart something dreadful, she did.' She sniffed. 'A bit unnecessary, if you ask me. My generation, we expected to lose some of them. Sickly babies, babies that came too soon, babies with problems – they slipped into the world and they slipped out again. You blew your nose and hoped for better luck next time.'

To Hazel, raised in safer times, it sounded terribly callous. For all her lifetime, infant mortality had been a rare disaster: even she, with no great desire for motherhood, could not imagine being able to dismiss it as the luck of the draw, the way Mrs Mackey seemed to. 'But the Mitchells didn't want to run the risk?'

Mrs Mackey gave her an arch look. 'Now, that's not what I said. I said *Betty* wasn't up for having another one. They didn't exactly see eye-to-eye on it.'

'Mr Mitchell would have liked another child?'

'That's what Betty said. *On at her*, she said. He was *on at her* to give it another go. But she wouldn't. She said she wouldn't, and she never changed her mind. He thought it was a phase she was going through. You know – grieving. He gave her time to get over it. And then he *got on at her* again. Well, he was still a young man, wasn't he? If he'd wanted to live like a monk for the rest of his life he'd never have got married.'

Hazel thought that the old woman was saying slightly less than she knew, and expected Hazel to hear slightly more than she was saying. 'Mrs Mackey – are you telling me Martin Mitchell had an affair?'

'An affair? Well, I suppose you could call it that. If it's still an affair after ten years and more.'

'He had a mistress?' Hazel wasn't sure what word a woman of Mrs Mackey's vintage would use.

'A bit on the side,' she said judiciously. 'Betty told me. She didn't know who she was, only that she lived over towards Wittering. She found bus tickets in his pockets. She asked him, and he admitted as much.'

'Could they have had children? Martin Mitchell and the woman over Wittering way?'

'Could have, dear. Betty didn't know. Didn't *want* to know. I think she felt that, since he wasn't getting what he wanted at home, she shouldn't blame the man for looking elsewhere.'

'So they didn't break up over it?'

Mrs Mackey shook her head. 'They were fond of one another in spite of everything. He died four or five years ago. Betty nursed him through his last illness, then she quietly gave up on life as well. Spent six months in a home, then she died. Small funerals for both of them. Betty, Gillian and me at his; just Gillian and me at hers. If the woman over Wittering way was still on the scene, she didn't show her face at Martin's funeral.'

Hazel pondered the information on the way home. Martin Mitchell had wanted more children – or perhaps (Hazel was a realist) he'd just wanted more sex. Either way, when his wife rebuffed him he found a woman out Wittering way. Mrs Mackey reckoned they were involved with one another for more than a decade, in spite of his continuing affection for his wife, so there must have been something binding them together. Perhaps it really was children he wanted, and she gave them to him. Perhaps one of them was a son.

If Betty Mitchell knew about her husband's second family, perhaps Gillian did too, at the time or later. If she knew she had a brother, and the area where he lived, she could have sought him out. Or perhaps he found her. Martin would have been proud of her achievements, shown the newspapers with her by-lines to his other children. It might have been easier for Jam to find her than for Gillian to find him.

Jam? What the hell kind of a name was Jam? Hazel hoped it wasn't Gillian's pet-name for him because that couldn't help her find him. James . . . or J. A. Mitchell . . . or . . . But then she thought, would his surname be Mitchell? Martin and the woman out Wittering way weren't married, and his continuing commitment to Betty and Gillian suggested he never contemplated marrying her. So wouldn't any child of theirs carry its mother's surname? This was, after all, some forty years ago. People were a lot more coy about offspring born out of wedlock at that time. Now it was a commonplace: then, it was something to be discreet about.

So maybe Hazel knew something about the woman out Wittering way after all. Maybe she knew that her surname began with an M.

Unless she christened the poor benighted infant Jamboree.

With thoughts like this going round in her head like carousel horses, faster and faster but always ending up in the same place, it was no wonder that Hazel found herself not in Railway Street but turning into Highfield Road.

Ash was looking better. A week on, the cuts had knit, the bruises faded, even the cracked ribs were less painful than they had been. Hazel found him supervising the boys' homework at the kitchen table. With the bookshop closed for the moment he had no accounts to occupy him, so he was sewing discord in his sons' heads by explaining the way he'd been taught to do long division, three decades earlier.

'Teachers hate you doing that,' Hazel confided when the boys had grabbed the opportunity afforded by her arrival to escape.

'Doing what? I'm helping them.'

'No, you're confusing them. The teachers teach the way they were taught to teach, and that's how the children learn and how their exams will be marked. If you offer them an alternative, even if it works just as well, they're going to lose track of which process belongs in which system. Like children brought up in bilingual households speaking a combination of languages.'

Ash sniffed. Hazel thought he was a little offended. She changed the subject. 'So how are you feeling? You're moving a bit more freely.'

'I'm on the mend,' he agreed. 'I think I'll open the shop tomorrow.'

'Why not open it for half the day? You might find you've had enough by lunchtime.'

He nodded ruefully. 'I don't seem to bounce the way I did fifteen years ago.'

'Who does? I remember the first time I cross-countried one of the Byrfields' ponies. I fell off at the first jump. I fell off at the second. I didn't fall off at the third, but I was so busy congratulating myself that I fell in the ditch at the fourth. And I don't remember any of it hurting. I know I got back on each time, and I finished the course. They gave me a special rosette, for sticking at it. I bet, if I looked hard enough, I could still find that rosette.'

Ash gave a dutiful smile. He had never understood the urge of otherwise intelligent people to trust their safety to an animal with the brainpower of a two-year-old child, and the same tendency to throw its teddy out of the pram. 'I'm sorry you didn't get to spend long at Byrfield. Your father would have liked having you there for Christmas. There's still time, you know. If you wanted to go back.'

'We've talked about this, Gabriel,' she reminded him firmly. 'I will go back, but not while this lunatic is still at large. Besides, Christmas isn't just about family. It's about friends too.'

'Pete Byrfield is your friend.'

'Yes, he is,' she agreed. Pensively, she caught her lip between her teeth. 'They all are. Well – except for the countess, who always looks at me as if she'd like to put me through the dog wash.'

Ash was puzzled. 'What's a dog wash?'

'It's like a car wash, but for dogs. And since she looks at everyone else that way too, I don't take it personally.'

'Who else was there? Pete's sisters?'

'Viv was busy in London, but Posy came over one afternoon. We got the old photo albums out.' A sudden sickness rose through her at the thought of the pictures in the stiffened brown envelopes. She hadn't told Ash about the one of him – she'd thought it was something he could do without seeing while the pain it memorialised was still raw – but she was feeling guilty about that, knew she'd have to find the right time to update him. She didn't want him to learn about it – or worse, be shown it – by Tom Presley, who was a decent detective but had all the tact of a rutting rhinoceros.

She hurried on. 'And David dropped in briefly on his way to dig up something in Durham that was so archaeologically important that the local planners thought it was a good spot for a supermarket.'

'I suppose Byrfield, rather than Norbold, is where your roots are,' said Ash, a shade wistfully.

Hazel shrugged. 'I'm lucky. I have roots there *and* here. People I care about in both places.'

Ash smiled. 'Saturday's done well for himself, hasn't he? Even without our support and guidance. It seems the streets of London really are paved with gold.'

'Saturday's a survivor. All he needed was a chance. We gave him a breathing space, so he could take advantage of whatever other chances came his way.'

'You'll miss him when he goes back.'

The hypersensitive might have detected a fractional pause before she answered. 'I shan't miss him leaving dirty dishes in the sink. I mean, how much trouble *is* it to wash them and put them away?'

'I think the posh flat in Docklands came with a dishwasher.'

'Yes? Well, the poky little house in Railway Street didn't. Not an electric one, and not a human one either.'

There was a lull in the conversation then. This was neither uncommon nor, usually, significant. They knew one another well enough to be comfortable with silence when they ran out of things to say. There was, however, something slightly charged about this silence that told Hazel that Ash was struggling less with finding something to say and more with finding a way to say it. Finally running out of patience she said quietly, 'Gabriel, what's troubling you?'

He started to say, 'Nothing . . .' but saw in her face it wouldn't do. He sighed. 'Actually, I was about to ask you the same thing. You've seemed . . . strained . . . ever since you got back from Cambridgeshire. Did something happen?'

'Of course something happened!' she retorted fiercely. 'My

best friend got kicked to a bloody pulp, and if it wasn't my fault, it still wouldn't have happened if he'd never met me! Strained? I'm so bloody angry I could bite the heads off ferrets!'

Ash looked surprised. When it came to country pursuits, he deferred to her greater experience. He'd never heard of anyone doing that, but he wouldn't have been entirely surprised. 'I mean, apart from that. Did something happen at Byrfield?'

'Not really,' she said, unconvincingly.

Ash thought for a moment, then rephrased it. '*What* happened at Byrfield?'

Hazel wasn't ready to tell him, not quite. 'What makes you think something happened?'

Her prevarication might have annoyed him, except that he knew that she wasn't obfuscating deliberately, or slyly, or because she wanted to tease him. She was, he felt certain, struggling to understand or come to terms with some development, and she wasn't sure if discussing it with someone else – even, or perhaps particularly, with him – would be a help or a hindrance.

'Well,' he said gently, 'I was a little surprised that Pete went back home as soon as he did. I know – he had cows waiting for him. He also has a stockman, and various other employees. I got the impression that the two of you needed, or at least wanted, some time apart. Did you argue?'

'Pete doesn't argue,' Hazel said, a shade sadly. 'It's like drawing teeth, getting him to disagree with anything you say.'

'That's a problem?'

'No, of course not. He's a really nice guy. He's kind, he's thoughtful and he's good company. He's one of those people you can rely on: always dependable, always the same. There's no question of catching him in a good mood. He's *always* in a good mood.'

'And is *that* a problem?'

'There isn't a problem,' she retorted. 'At least, I didn't think there was. I thought he was someone who'd be my friend forever. Regardless of what the world threw at us, regardless of where we ended up or who with, I thought Pete Byrfield was someone I could always count on to be my friend.'

'And then?' asked Ash.

Hazel took a deep, not entirely steady breath. She looked straight at him, and her smile was as bright, and as brittle, as glass. 'And then he proposed to me.' She burst into tears.

TWENTY-SIX

Gabriel Ash didn't know what to say. He didn't know what to feel. But he knew what to do. He put his arms around her and held her against his aching ribs. 'Well, that's . . . wonderful,' he managed eventually.

'Is it?' Hazel had stopped crying, and was dabbing ineffectually at his shirt-front with her handkerchief.

'Isn't it?'

'Pete's my friend!'

'I think you're allowed to marry friends,' Ash said carefully. 'In fact, I think it's positively encouraged.'

'I don't want to be a countess!'

Ash considered. 'Isn't that rather snobbish?'

Her eyes widened in surprise. 'How do you figure that?'

'It's a bit like saying you don't want to be a dustman's wife. If you love him, it shouldn't matter what he does for a living.'

'Being an earl isn't a career! It's not what he does, it's what he is. What his family have been since the fifteenth century.'

'And? Are you suggesting your family don't go back to the fifteenth century?'

Hazel hadn't thought of it that way. 'I suppose they do. But who knows who or what they were.'

'But why does that matter? If they were farriers, or farmers, or millers, or . . .' Ingenuity almost failed him. 'Or poachers. Why would it matter? They must have been good at something. Good enough to be called Best.'

That drew a watery smile from her. 'My mother's family were called Payne. She used to say that Dad was the Best she could do, and she was a Payne to him.'

Ash grinned bravely. The shock was passing. Of all the

things that might have happened today, this was the most unexpected. That didn't make it a bad thing. From Hazel's point of view, it was hard to see a downside. And he wasn't entitled to a point of view, not on this. He treasured her friendship, but he had nothing beyond that to offer her. He was still a married man. He had made no move towards divorcing his wife, despite the damage she had done him. He shied away even from contemplating it.

Hazel knew that – it was a given between them. They had never seen one another as potential life partners. Even without the complication of Cathy, Ash believed he had nothing to give that was worth the baggage he brought. He was fourteen years Hazel's senior, he had a history of mental health issues, he hadn't worked for seven years – unless you counted the bookshop which, on a good week, broke even. He had two young sons who occupied much of his time and energy, and he thought – he *thought* – he owned a talking dog. If he put a postcard in the convenience store window, eligible young women would be queueing round the block, wouldn't they?

And Hazel had the chance of an earl. And not just any old earl, but one she'd known and liked for years. The 28th earl of Byrford, Peregrine to his mother, Pip to his sisters, Pete to everyone else, was a good, kind, generous man and Ash would – should – ought to be delighted at the prospect of seeing Hazel settled with him.

She ought to be delighted. Why wasn't she?

Ash took half a step back and ducked his head to peer into her face. Hazel was tall; he was taller. 'Come on, Hazel – talk to your Uncle Gabriel. What's the problem? Anyone who knows the pair of you will see this as a good idea. Why don't you?' A sudden thought dipped one brow over its deep-set eye. 'You *can't* be feeling nostalgic about Oliver Ford?'

There was real anger in the look she flashed him. 'Of course not.'

'Then . . . is there someone else?' He didn't think so; but perhaps he wouldn't have known. They hadn't been as close as they once were. Real life – her work, his sons, even the bookshop – took up too much time.

'No . . .' she said slowly. 'It's just, this isn't how I saw my future shaping up.'

'Being married?'

'I always thought my career would come first. That marriage, if it happened at all, could wait.'

Ash looked for a tactful way of saying this, failed to find one. 'Maybe marriage shouldn't wait too long. You're twenty-eight. If you mean to have children – and I imagine Pete would like to produce an heir – you probably shouldn't put it off too much longer.'

'Lots of women have babies in their forties,' Hazel retorted.

'But the odds turn against you.'

'You don't get a guarantee at any age! *I* don't know if I can have children. I don't know if Pete can. The chance to replicate yourself is not the only reason to get married. I'm not sure it's the best one.'

'It isn't,' agreed Ash. 'Most couples seem to feel it's the icing on the cake.'

'Yes? Well, I'm still trying to decide if I even want the cake! If I wouldn't just as soon have a ham-and-pickle sandwich.'

They stared at one another, and Hazel's eyes were hot and Ash's were troubled; and gradually a sense of the absurd dawned on both of them. Hazel giggled, and Ash gave a rueful little laugh, hugged her and put her down. 'So what did you tell Pete?'

'That I'd need to think about it. That he'd knocked me for six. That I had no idea that was anywhere in his mind, and if he wanted a sensible answer he'd need to leave me to think about it calmly for a while.'

'That's why he went back to Byrfield.'

'Well – that, and an in-calf heifer with bloat,' Hazel said honestly.

'I'm glad you told me,' said Ash, walking her to her car, hissing in his teeth as the front steps found the weakness in his cracked ribs.

'*I'm* glad I told you. I don't know why I didn't tell you before. It's not exactly a guilty secret, is it?'

'Of course not,' he said, smiling; and as he lifted one hand in a cautious wave, it wasn't just his ribs that were breaking.

* * *

The next day Hazel worked her feet a little further under the CID table.

It occurred to her that there was someone who might know about Gillian Mitchell's half-brother and who might tell her when he would tell no one else, and he was only a short trip up the motorway in Birmingham.

DCI Gorman heard her out, but it was obvious from his expression – he must have been a terrible poker player – that he didn't like it. 'Don't be fooled by the fact that he has nice manners. Leo Harte is a deeply dangerous man.'

Hazel believed him. But she didn't think he was a danger to her. 'Just this once, we're on the same side. We want the same thing – to find Gillian Mitchell's killer. If he can help, I think he will.'

'We'll go together,' said Gorman.

Hazel didn't like disappointing him – strictly speaking, she wasn't in a position to disappoint him – but she knew intuitively that it would be a mistake. 'I don't think he'll talk in front of you. I don't think he'll talk to anyone as freely as he'll talk to me. You're a senior CID officer: you ask to speak to him, the first thing he'll do is call his solicitor. I'm a uniformed constable, and a woman, currently seconded to CID but likely to be seeing small children across busy roads this time next week: he'd be ashamed to admit he couldn't deal with me himself. Also, we've talked about Gillian Mitchell before. There's no reason for him to clam up now.'

Gorman scowled. 'I don't like you getting close to this man.'

'I'm not getting close to him. But we have a common cause. I know – I'm sure – that his interest in this case is deeply personal. Leo Harte wouldn't give tuppence to save Norbold from a serial killer, except that one of the victims was a woman he cared about. He wants the man who killed her to pay for it. He'll help us if he can, and he'll be more open with me than he would be with you or anyone else.'

The more Gorman thought about it, the more he had to concede that she was probably right. He pulled the address off the file for her. 'But you phone me before you go in, and you phone me again the moment you come out. You have half an hour. After that, I'm sending in the cavalry.'

John Carson remembered her, remembered what his employer had said. 'Miss Best, isn't it? Are you looking for Mr Harte? I'll ask if he's free.' He was, and Carson showed her up.

Harte's office was a dizzying height above the Bull Ring. Hazel wasn't used to skyscrapers: the tallest building in Norbold was still the Victorian ceramics factory. There were no tower blocks even in the Flying Horse estate: not enough people wanted to live there.

Harte half-rose behind his desk to greet her. 'There's something I can help you with?' He sounded wary – of course he sounded wary, anyone in his position needed to be wary in the presence of even a very junior police officer – but more than that he sounded hopeful.

'It's a bit of a long shot,' she admitted, taking the chair he indicted. 'But I know you and Gillian Mitchell spent time together. I know she cared for you – enough to change her mind about the exposé she'd intended to write—'

Harte leaned forward sharply, ready to protest, but Hazel waved him back with more self-possession than she actually possessed. 'This is your office, Mr Harte, you know there are no bugs here. Unless you think I'm wearing a wire, in which case' – she spread her arms – 'you're welcome to frisk me.'

Leo Harte gave a tiny cautious smile. 'May I take a rain-check?'

So Hazel continued setting out her stall. 'And I believe you cared about her. I think, in all the circumstances – what she was, what you are – that must have involved a considerable amount of trust. And I'm just wondering if that trust extended to her telling you about her family.'

Now Harte looked puzzled. 'She didn't have a family.'

'She wasn't found under a cabbage-leaf, Mr Harte. Of course she had a family. She had the usual quota of parents, she had a sister who died in infancy, and she may have had a half-brother. Did she ever talk about him?'

She could see Harte trying to remember. 'I don't think so. You have to understand, Miss Best, we weren't an old married couple with nothing better to do than grumble about our relatives when we got together. A half-brother? What's his name?'

Hazel spread her hands again, this time helplessly. 'We don't know. She refers to him as Jam – but whether that's short for something, or initials, or just a nickname, your guess is as good as mine. She was worried about him. She thought he was mentally unstable, and becoming unpredictable. I think she was a little afraid of him.'

Leo Harte's face had gone very still. 'You think *he* . . .' He had to stop a moment to recover his composure. 'You think he was the one who killed her?'

'I really don't know. But it's someone in her life that we haven't been able to find and talk to, and until we have we can't rule out the possibility. Did she never mention him? Or his mother? She lived out Wittering way, apparently.' Then, remembering that he wasn't a local: 'A few miles the far side of Norbold.'

Again she saw him trying to remember. But then, regretfully, he shook his head. 'I don't believe Gillian ever mentioned him. She certainly never told me she was afraid of him. *That* I would remember. That, I would have done something about.'

Hazel believed him. And also that he would have helped her if he could. There was nothing to be gained by questioning him further. She stood up. 'All right. I did say it was a long shot. Thank you for seeing me, Mr Harte.'

A final thought occurred to her. 'One more thing. The first time we met, outside Maggie Watts's house. Why were you really there?'

That took Harte by surprise. 'I told you. Expressing my condolences.'

'Why? You hardly knew Trucker. You never did give him that job he wanted, did you?'

'No. But . . .' Sandy eyebrows gave a kind of facial shrug. 'There were rumours going round. The rumour that reached you: that Watts's death had something to do with me. I knew there was no truth in it, and I didn't want his mother thinking that maybe there was. I think she believed me.'

Truth or not, Hazel thought, Maggie Watts would have been wise to believe Leo Harte. 'And?'

'And what?'

'And what else?'

He looked faintly embarrassed; and also as if he hadn't felt that particular emotion for years. 'I left her some money. She hadn't a lot when Watts was alive – she'll have even less now.'

'You tried to bribe her?'

Now he looked astonished. 'Whatever could Maggie Watts have that I could *possibly* want? Whatever could she know that I could want keeping quiet?'

Hazel knew better than to trust him. But she was largely persuaded. 'Out of the goodness of your heart, then.'

Leo Harte smiled. 'Don't tell people, will you?'

'No, Mr Harte,' she said solemnly, 'your secret is safe with me. And, I'm sorry for your loss.'

Leo Harte dipped his turquoise eyes in acknowledgement. 'The relationship between Gillian and me wasn't public knowledge. We both felt that discretion was the better part of valour. I didn't want her to suffer professionally because of me – didn't want people who would have been willing to talk to her refusing to do so for fear of what she might pass on to me. Because she never did that – never talked about her work except in the most general terms. If I wanted to know what she was working on, I had to buy the paper like everyone else.'

His smile was sorrowful. 'So it's only very close friends who know I'm grieving for her. No sympathy cards, no compassionate handshakes. In truth, there's not much anyone can say at a time like this, but just trying helps. When they don't know there's anything *to* say, it feels as if we're all ignoring what's happened. As if she lived, and died horribly and far too soon, and nobody cares very much.

'It's been good talking to you about Gillian, Miss Best. Thank you for coming here; and thank you for your efforts to get justice for her. Please feel free to contact me again if there's any help I can offer. Take this.' He slid a small, infinitely discreet business card across his desk.

Once outside the building she called Gorman, as she'd promised. He sounded slightly surprised that she'd emerged none the worse for the encounter, less so that she'd learned nothing useful from it.

*   *   *

When she got home, Hazel had the house to herself. Saturday's yellow sports car was missing from the street outside – she didn't think he'd have swapped it for a maroon hatchback, which was in any event on the other side of the road – and there was no reply to her hail. She shrugged out of her warm coat and went upstairs to run a bath. She'd got out of the way of sharing her bathroom: now it felt like a luxury, to wallow and steam and know no one was going to be tapping on the door in increasing urgency.

It was too late to get dressed again: she pulled on her pyjamas, wrapped a fluffy dressing-gown over the top and went downstairs to make herself some supper. Hot chocolate, toast and marmalade, on a tray on the bedside table while she leafed through a magazine – the ultimate indulgence. Whether it was that, or the bath, or telling Ash what she'd started to feel guilty about keeping from him, or simply because she was tired, she slept better than she had for days.

Her first intimation that all was not well came the next morning when she found the kitchen in the same state that she'd left it the previous night. Saturday had the same effect on a room that a tsunami has on a coastal village: it was impossible not to notice that he had passed through. Still Hazel felt obliged to check. Her own car was in the street – the workmen having finally departed – but no yellow sportster. She called his name, twice, without response. And when she went to look in his room, he wasn't there and the bed hadn't been slept in.

She told herself there was nothing sinister about a young man staying out on a Friday night. Perhaps he had met up with old friends; perhaps he'd got lucky. He wouldn't have brought a girl back to her house. With his new-found riches, he could have taken a suite at The Lord Warden if he'd wanted to. The only thing that puzzled her was that, given his temporary acting position as her bodyguard, he hadn't thought to let her know.

So maybe he had. She checked her phone for voice mail, without success. So maybe he'd left her a note somewhere.

It took her another ten minutes to find it, mixed in with a pile of double-glazing adverts and offers for credit cards she didn't need and a stiffened brown envelope and a bill from the electricity supplier. The stupid boy must have taken the post in while he was looking for somewhere to leave his note that she couldn't miss it.

He'd written: 'Something I want to check out. See you teatime – Saturday.'

In Railway Street, the post arrived around eleven o'clock. He hadn't got back for tea at six; he hadn't got back for supper. He'd been missing for twenty-one hours.

A stiffened brown envelope . . . Hazel grabbed for it, tore it apart without regard for any fingerprints or DNA it might be preserving. There was, as she expected, a photograph inside. It was a photograph of Saturday parking his yellow car in the street outside her house.

She phoned DCI Gorman, gabbling so much in her anxiety that it took him precious moments to grasp what she was talking about.

'He's got Saturday!'

Like most of the population, Dave Gorman tended to think of Saturday as a day of the week, so the sentence made no sense to him. 'Hazel? He who? What's he got to do on Saturday?'

She was shaking her head vigorously, oblivious of the fact that he couldn't see her. '*Him.* My stalker. He's sent me another picture.'

'What of?'

'Saturday!'

'What?'

Hazel forced herself to slow down and use words that allowed no misunderstanding. 'My lodger, Saturday. He's missing. He's *been* missing since mid-morning yesterday. He went to check something out and didn't come back. And the man who sent me a photograph of Gabriel's shop, and then another photograph of Gabriel's face after he'd beaten him senseless, has sent me one of Saturday. He's got him, Dave. Saturday found something significant, and now the bastard's got hold of him.'

'Unless . . .' Something even worse occurred to her.

Gorman was right with her now, sharing her sense of urgency. 'Unless what?'

'Unless he's already dead, and we just haven't found him yet.'

TWENTY-SEVEN

I t was Friday, the crack of dawn as it is measured by teen-agers, and Saturday was still curled in the warm cave of his duvet, half asleep and half awake, contemplating the possi-bility of padding downstairs and making himself a baked-bean sandwich, when a diffident knock at the front door impinged on his comfort. He considered ignoring it. It wouldn't be Hazel – she had her own key, and kept a spare secreted in the back yard for emergencies – and no one else knew he was here. Except Ash, and he probably wasn't up to paying visits yet. No one would shout at him if he just went back to sleep . . .

The knocker sounded again, a little more doggedly. Saturday cranked one eye open enough to read the clock. Ten forty-five. The postman, maybe, with something too big to push through the letterbox? If Hazel was waiting for a delivery, she'd know he couldn't be bothered to take it in. Reluctantly, hissing as his bare feet hit the cold lino, he headed downstairs. Lacking a dressing-gown, he pulled on his leather coat as he went.

It wasn't the postman. It was a middle-aged man in an anorak and a bobble hat, carrying a shopping bag and holding a book in front of him rather like a shield. He seemed taken aback at the sight of Saturday. 'Is Miss Best at home, please?'

Saturday shook his head. His hair looked more than ever like a badly made haystack. 'She's at work.'

The man in the anorak nodded, embarrassed. 'Of course. I was thinking she was still on nights, but her shift changed last week, didn't it? I'm sorry, I'll come back later.' He went to turn away.

Saturday said, 'Do you want me to give her a message?'

The visitor hesitated. 'Yes – perhaps, if you wouldn't mind. You could tell her Mr Price called. Mr Price from the council – she knows who I am.' He gave a shy smile and gestured at the patchwork of tarmac beside the kerb. 'I was overseeing her roadworks.'

'OK, I'll tell her,' said Saturday. 'Do you want to leave the book?'

'Er . . .' Mr Price hadn't thought that far. He switched the book into his right hand, which meant switching his shopping bag onto his left arm. 'I probably shouldn't. It's not actually mine – I borrowed it from the Town Hall library.' Thinking some further explanation was necessary he added, 'I think I've found the waterfall she was looking for. Well, maybe . . . It's not exactly the same, but then the book's forty years old. I thought she'd want to see it, anyway.'

'Of course she will,' said Saturday kindly. 'You'll probably catch her at the police station if you want to talk to her. Or I could phone her.'

'No, don't do that,' said Mr Price, faintly horrified. 'Not when she's working. I'm sure it'll wait. I'll pop back this evening.' He gave a fleeting little scowl. 'Of course, it'll be dark by then. If she wants to go and look, it'll have to be tomorrow. Unless she's working this weekend.' He nodded, the decision made. 'Thank you, young man. If you'll tell her I called, and I'll come back this evening.'

Saturday's own mental processes, sluggish from the night that his body insisted had hardly ended, were beginning to catch up. He knew about the waterfall, and Hazel's attempts to identify a spot she was sure was important. Tonight and tomorrow were too far away if the man sending her photographs posed as much of a danger to her as he had to Gabriel Ash.

'Wait,' he said. 'Look, why don't you show me? Then I can check it out for her. If there's anything there, I can tell her. If not, it'll save wasting her time.'

Mr Price looked doubtful. Then he shrugged, and followed Saturday into the little sitting room at the front of the house. 'All right. There may be nothing in it. But I came across this picture' – he turned straight to it, aided by a bookmark bearing the legend 'Poets do it in rhyming couplets' – 'and I thought it might be the place she was asking me about. I've never been there myself, but it must have been a bit of a local beauty-spot forty years ago.' He laid the open book on the coffee table.

Hazel hadn't wanted to keep the album she'd been sent in her sitting room, as if it was something to be proud of. She'd put it in the cupboard under the sink. Saturday went into the kitchen and took it out. Then he took out the photograph of the waterfall. He didn't think Hazel would want him sharing the other images with Mr Price or anyone else.

He put the photograph Hazel had been sent beside that printed in the book. They studied them together, with much frowning and sucking of cheeks. Finally Price straightened up. 'Well, I'm sure I don't know. It could be the same place. It's a lot more overgrown in that one' – the new photograph – 'but maybe that's to be expected. And then, *this* one' – in the book – 'was taken in summer, with all the trees in full leaf and less water in the stream. Of course it would look different, forty years later and in December.'

Saturday too was struggling to find any diagnostic feature. It could be the same place; it might not be. He turned his attention to the accompanying text on the book's opposite page. 'Lubbuck's Gully. At least they weren't setting up unrealistic expectations with the name.'

Mr Price smiled thinly. 'The Lubbuck estate was broken up in the Seventies. The usual thing – too many death duties to pay. Some of it was incorporated into Forestry Commission woodland, some of it was sold to adjoining farms.'

As well as the book he'd brought a map – an Ordnance Survey walkers' map with sites of interest in and around Norbold marked on it. There weren't many of them. Price sketched a rough circle with his thumb. 'The thin blue lines are water-courses. To get a decent waterfall, you'd probably need one coming off a fairly steep hillside. Like this one' – he pointed again – 'or this. That whole area is probably pretty overgrown. It's too rough to farm, too steep for forestry.'

Saturday was staring. 'You can tell all that from looking at a map?'

'I used to do a bit of bush-craft,' said Benny Price modestly.

'How do I get there?'

Benny pointed again. 'I know that track. They use it to extract timber – it's stoned and not too rough. You could drive to within half a mile. After that you'd have to walk.' He looked down at Saturday's bare feet and smiled. 'Unless you've got some proper boots, you might be better leaving it to Hazel.'

If it wasn't meant as a challenge, Saturday responded to it as one. 'Half a mile? I've walked half a mile in wet trainers more times than I care to remember. What about you? Will you show me the way?'

He didn't think Mr Price was expecting that. 'I left my car at home.'

'*I* have a car. Give me five minutes to put some clothes on, and we'll go check it out. Yes?'

'Er . . .'

'Do you have to go back to work?'

'No. But . . .'

'Mr Price, you've already gone to a lot of trouble to help Hazel. I'm sure she'll be grateful. She'll be even more impressed if we can tell her we've identified the place in the photograph. Or even that we went there and there was nothing to see. Right now she needs a bit of help. We can be there and back in an hour. How about it?'

Benny Price drew a deep breath. 'Oh, all right.'

As they left the house, the postman was poised to knock. 'You need a bigger letterbox,' he muttered darkly.

'No, just smaller mail,' said Saturday airily. But he took the assorted fliers and envelopes, and took them back inside.

That was when it occurred to him he should leave a note, in case Hazel dropped in at lunchtime and missed him. He scribbled something on a scrap of paper and propped it up on top of the post on the kitchen table.

'Are we going, then?' called Benny Price from the door. He sounded as though he was already having second thoughts.

The chilly gust of air that came in with his voice blew the note onto the kitchen floor. Saturday picked it up and weighed it in place with some of the post. Hazel would find it when she sorted through her mail. 'I'm coming now.'

Benny regarded the yellow sports car with misgivings. Saturday saw him weighing up the relative sizes of himself, his book, his map, his shopping bag and the passenger seat. Saturday took the bag. 'I'll put this in the boot, shall I? Good grief,' he said then, 'are you tooling up for a siege?'

Benny frowned. He wasn't very good at levity. 'Asda were doing buy-one-get-one-free on tinned goods. It was a good

time to stock up.' He gave a shy smile. 'So I treated myself
with what I saved.'

Saturday couldn't imagine what a middle-aged man who
worked for the council and used to do a bit of bush-craft would
consider a treat. A solar-powered torch? Tungsten-tipped tent
pegs for use on rocky outcrops?

'New tools. I'm a bit of a carpenter on the side. Nothing
fancy – rustic garden furniture, that kind of thing. But I can't
pass a hardware shop without seeing what they've got. It's not
the saw that weighs so much,' he added by way of explanation,
'as some of the other stuff.'

The car's engine came to life with a throaty roar. 'You want
to tell me where to go?'

Benny looked at him in surprise. Saturday sighed. 'You've
got the map. I don't do maps – I do sat-nav. You need to tell
me which way to go.'

'Oh – yes,' said Benny Price.

Hazel wasn't going to tell Ash that Saturday was missing. He
wasn't strong enough to do anything but worry, and she could
worry just fine by herself. But Gorman called him. 'I need
you to go round to Hazel's house and make sure she doesn't
leave.'

His tone brooked no argument, and Ash offered none. 'I'll
be there in ten minutes. What's happened?'

'Hazel will fill you in when you get there. Gabriel – don't
let her leave. Whatever happens, however much she wants to,
don't let her out of your sight.'

While Ash was reading Saturday's note, Hazel said, 'I'm
going next door. Mrs Burden may have seen something.'

Ash looked up doubtfully, Gorman's injunction ringing in
his ears. But she didn't have her coat on, and he could see
her car keys hanging in their usual place on the back of the
kitchen door, and he decided it would be absurd to insist on
accompanying her the couple of metres from her front step to
Mrs Burden's. 'Come straight back.'

It was too cold to talk outside: Mrs Burden asked her in.
She was cleaning the house. Experience told her that if she
did it as soon as Alec went out in the morning, it would stay

done until he got home in the evening. Doing it with him there was like herding cats.

Hazel explained briefly that she'd mislaid her lodger and was becoming concerned, and that he probably left the house about eleven o'clock the previous morning. 'I don't suppose you saw him go?'

'I heard the car,' said Mrs Burden helpfully. 'Yes, around mid-morning.'

Hazel had hoped for more. But Mrs Burden wasn't a fully fledged nosy neighbour who would drop whatever she was doing in order to investigate a knock on somebody else's door. 'Do you know if he was alone?'

'I didn't see, dear. But there was someone at the door ten or fifteen minutes earlier. When I was letting the cat out.'

Hazel's instincts sharpened. 'Who?'

'I don't know his name. But you might – I saw you talking to him while they were working on the road.'

'One of the workmen?' Memory focused, presented her with a picture. 'Mr Price, the man from the council?'

'A slightly tubby gentleman, not particularly tall, maybe about forty? Wearing an anorak and carrying a shopping bag.'

Hazel didn't know about the bag, but otherwise the description fitted. 'And Saturday answered the door?' Mrs Burden nodded. 'I don't suppose you heard what they said.'

Mrs Burden sniffed, ready to take offence. 'I'm sure I don't go round listening to other people's conversations. Nobody can accuse me of going round listening to other people's conversations.'

'Of course not, Mrs B.' Hazel tempered her sense of urgency with the need to keep the other woman on-side. 'But these are small houses – voices carry. Especially men's voices, don't you find? I just thought you might have caught a few words. If Saturday headed out soon afterwards, it might be because of something Mr Price said to him.'

'Well,' said Mrs Burden, mollified. 'He was looking for you, of course. The council man. Your young friend offered to take a message. I don't know if that's what they did – I went back inside. I heard nothing more until I heard the car leaving ten or fifteen minutes later.'

There was nothing more to be learned from her. Hazel thanked her and returned home.

The simplest way to find out what Benny Price had said to Saturday was to ask him. Hazel phoned the council works department. But Benny had finished for the weekend.

She asked for his home address and phone-number. Very properly, the council clerk at the other end of the line declined to give them.

'I am a police officer,' Hazel reminded her, 'and this could be quite urgent.'

'And of course we'll co-operate with police inquiries,' the clerk assured her. 'But I need to be sure you really are who you say you are. I can't take your word for it over the phone.'

Hazel breathed heavily, but actually she couldn't argue with that. 'Fine. Me and my warrant card will be with you in five minutes.'

Ash had promised DCI Gorman that he wouldn't let her out of his sight. Actually, he'd promised that he wouldn't let her leave the house, but he didn't think this was what Gorman had been worried about – that she might go as far as the council offices on Jubilee Road. 'I'll come with you.'

They took Hazel's nice new car. She spread a blanket on the back seat and Patience, rolling her toffee-coloured eyes, sat on it.

The clerk inspected Hazel's warrant card and apologised; but in fact she had nothing to apologise for. 'You're right to be cautious,' said Hazel, scribbling down the information she'd been given. 'People shouldn't believe everything they're told.'

'I hope Mr Price isn't in any kind of trouble.'

'Good Lord, no,' said Hazel, surprised. 'He was trying to contact me. I think he left a message with my friend – but my friend's now gone missing, and if I knew what the message was I might know where to look for him.' She frowned. 'Where exactly is Studley Row?'

'It's that terrace of agricultural labourers' cottages off Wittering Road,' the clerk explained. 'A couple of miles out of town. They were built for the old parish council back in the nineteenth century.'

Hazel nodded. 'I'll try phoning him first. But if I can't get hold of him, I'll take a run out.'

She called from the car park. It was a mobile number, which slightly surprised Hazel. She'd had Benny Price down as the last man in England to hold onto his landline, with the possible exception of Gabriel Ash. But the call went straight to voice mail. She left a message, asking him to call her back. But with no confidence that he'd get it in the immediate future, she started the car again and turned towards Wittering.

'Aren't we going home?' asked Ash.

'I need to talk to Benny Price,' said Hazel doggedly. 'As far as I know, he's the last person who spoke to Saturday before he disappeared. It may be a coincidence, but he must have had some reason for calling at my house. I asked him about the picture of the waterfall: if he remembered something, maybe he came round to tell me. And since I was at work, Saturday may have decided to check it out himself. It's only a couple of miles, Gabriel. If Benny isn't at home, we'll be back in ten minutes.'

'And if he is at home?'

She knew what he was asking. 'That'll depend on what he tells us.'

'Dave Gorman will have my guts for garters if I let anything happen to you.'

'What's going to happen to me?' she scoffed. 'I just want a word with a member of the council works department! If he has anything useful to say, I'll call Dave.'

'And let him take it from there,' insisted Ash.

The slight hesitation may have been significant. 'And let him take it from there.'

TWENTY-EIGHT

There are a number of ways, given modern technology, of locating a missing vehicle. Unfortunately, most of them depend on having information that DCI Gorman lacked. He didn't know the make, model or registration number of Saturday's car, only that it was yellow. He didn't know the name of the registered owners, only that it was the outfit Saturday had been working for. Though he assumed Saturday had a phone, he didn't know the number or the network – the youth had turned up out of the blue and hadn't, to the best of his knowledge, called anyone since he arrived. With enough time to find the yellow sportster on security cameras as it passed through Norbold, he could eventually get a readable plate and everything that would follow from that. And indeed, he set DCs Friend and Patton to collecting CCTV footage for just such a purpose. But time was an issue. They might get lucky and find a clear shot on the first clip they examined. Or they could stare and stare until their eyes burned and still find nothing helpful. And while they were staring, an eighteen-year-old boy could be dying in a ditch.

'I want a helicopter,' Gorman told Superintendent Maybourne. 'The only useful information we have about that car right now is that it's bright yellow – and a bright yellow car will be visible from the air in places it wouldn't be visible on the ground from five metres away.'

Grace Maybourne paled. 'You do know how much those things cost every hour?'

Gorman didn't know and didn't care. 'Hazel's stalker broke into her house when she was asleep. Then he kicked the shit out of Gabriel Ash. Now the kid who's moved back in with Hazel has gone missing. He said he'd be back within a couple of hours, twenty-four hours ago. We don't know where he went – but we do know that the man who stalked Hazel and attacked Ash took a photograph of him outside Hazel's house. Whether or not this is the same guy who murdered Gillian Mitchell and Trucker Watts, if he has Saturday the kid's in danger. We have to find him. And I need a helicopter to do it.'

Superintendent Maybourne offered no further argument. 'I'll make the call.'

As luck would have it the force's helicopter, based halfway across the county, had been on a training exercise at the Clover Hill dam, only a few minutes' flying time from Norbold. Two further factors improved the chances of success. It was a bright morning, the sun streaming down from what passed for its zenith this close to the winter solstice; and the trees were largely bare, allowing an almost uninterrupted view to ground level.

Still, neither DCI Gorman nor DS Presley underestimated the scale of the task. 'On the bright side,' said Presley, 'if he'd been in a crash we'd know about it by now.'

'The same probably applies if he'd had his head beaten in,' said Gorman. 'Trucker and the woman, and Ash, were all found where they were attacked. Whoever was responsible didn't go to much trouble to hide them.'

'Maybe the kid's fine, he's just gone back to London,' suggested Presley. 'He did it before, didn't he? He has no real ties here any more. Maybe he just got bored and buggered off again.'

'He left that note. He said he'd be back for tea.'

'I think you can get tea in London, too.'

But Gorman had seen more of Saturday than Presley had, knew that he did have ties in Norbold – that his regard for Hazel had drawn him back, and the same thing would have prevented him from abandoning her now. He shook his head. 'Something's happened to him. Not a word from him, not a call, not a text, for damn near twenty-four hours. How many eighteen-year-olds do you know who stay out of touch that long?'

'He was out of touch for over a year,' Presley pointed out. 'Compared with that, twenty-four hours is nothing. It's too soon to assume the worst.'

'I hope you're right,' said Gorman grimly. 'But I think you're wrong.'

Studley Row was constructed in the mid-Victorian period, when people were flocking to the new industrial centres of the Midlands to fill the thousands of jobs being created there. The only way to keep agricultural workers on the farms that needed them was to provide them, for the first time, with decent accommodation. When new, the dozen houses each had two bedrooms, a sitting room, a kitchen with plumbed-in

water, a convenient outhouse and a garden running to a fifth
of an acre, an area judged adequate for a family to grow
enough food to live on and perhaps keep a pig or a couple
of goats.

The pigs were long gone, the outhouses replaced by fully
functioning bathrooms; the gardens had been turned over
mostly to flowers, and in many cases the cottages extended to
include a third bedroom and another room downstairs. What
had never been provided, and was only missed on cold wet
windy nights by residents carrying a week's worth of shopping, was a roadway along the front of the houses. There was
a footpath, and a parking area at the end of the terrace.

Hazel saw Ash weighing up the distance from the car park
to the furthest-but-one cottage. 'You stay here,' she said. 'I
shan't be a minute. Even if he's there, it won't take him long
to tell me what he told Saturday.'

'I promised Dave Gorman . . .'

'. . . That you wouldn't let me out of your sight. Well, sit
up straight and you'll be able to see me all the way to the
front door. If anyone tries to jump my bones between here
and there, set Patience on him.'

On the back seat, Patience contrived to look both prim and
smug.

There were roses round the door and a rustic bench
under the front window. Hazel thought Benny Price might
have made the bench himself: it had a homespun quality, sturdy
and dependable rather than refined, and it afforded pleasing
views over a shallow valley dotted with sheep to the woods
cloaking the rising ground on the far side.

But Benny wasn't enjoying the view today. There was no
reply to Hazel's knock; and when she tried his phone again,
she couldn't hear it ringing nor did he answer.

She wrote him a note and pushed it through his polished
brass letterbox: 'Need to speak to you urgently. Please call
me as soon as you get this – Hazel Best.' She wrote down her
number. Then she walked back to the car.

'No luck?' asked Ash.

Hazel shook her head. 'There's no one in. I left a note.'

Concerned as he was for Saturday, Ash was almost relieved.

He'd been afraid that Price would tell Hazel something that would encourage her to continue the search, and that he wouldn't be able to persuade her to pass that information on to Dave Gorman and go home. 'Back to Norbold, then?'

'Can we give it ten minutes? In case he comes back.'

'Of course.'

In fact they gave it half an hour, but Benny did not return. Hazel tried a couple of the other cottages, but even when someone answered the door, all she learned was that Mr Price had gone out early, in his Land Rover, and if he'd gone for a hike up the Malvern Hills he could be away all day. A big hiker, was Mr Price. He had the boots for it.

'OK then – home,' said Hazel, disconsolate. She started the car.

But as they drove back towards Norbold, an elderly jeep passed them heading in the opposite direction. There was just time to recognise the driver and Hazel braked sharply. 'That's him.'

Benny must have recognised her too, because the jeep pulled over, waiting. Hazel got out, trotted up the hill and leaned in at the driver's door.

Even by sitting up straight, all Ash could see was Hazel resting an arm on the sill of the open window and occasionally nodding. The conversation continued for some minutes. Then she nodded again, and came back. 'Gabriel, can you drive?'

If he was offended, he tried not to let it show. 'I've always thought so. I never claimed to be Lewis Hamilton or Jenson Zip, but I think I'm reasonably competent . . .'

Hazel was rolling her eyes. 'I mean, right now, with your ribs strapped up. Are you safe to drive?'

Embarrassed by the misunderstanding, he dipped his gaze. 'Yes, of course.'

'Then will you take my car home? Benny's going to take me to the place he took Saturday yesterday morning. A waterfall in the woods. He thought – well, they both thought – it might be the place in the photograph. Benny found it in a book at the Town Hall. Saturday wanted to check it out, so Benny showed him the way. Then Saturday drove him home. But he may have gone back afterwards. Apparently he wasn't happy with the photographs he took for me. Gabriel, maybe that's what's happened to him. If he went back into those woods alone, and slipped on some moss and broke his ankle . . .'

'Wouldn't he have phoned for help?'

She shrugged. 'If he could get a signal. You know what it's like out of town. Maybe he was lying out there all night, unable to get back to his car. I have to go and look. If he's there, he'll be in a bad way by now.'

'Well, all right,' Ash agreed reluctantly. 'But why not take your car? Mr Price can lead the way.'

Hazel shook her head. 'He says the track into the woods is pretty rough, and I don't want my nice new car getting beaten up. Take it home for me, will you, Gabriel? There are only two seats in the Land Rover, and I'm not sitting in the load-bay in my good clothes and you're not fit to. If we find Saturday, I'll call Dave or an ambulance, or both, and get a lift into town with them. If not, Benny says he'll drive me home.'

Ash wasn't happy, but he couldn't quite say why not. 'You think that's what's happened? Saturday's had an accident up in the woods?'

'I think it's the likeliest explanation, yes. Given that he and Benny were there earlier, playing at detectives.' She lowered her fair brows at him. 'Like some other people I could mention.'

'Superintendent Maybourne's got half Meadowvale out looking for him. Plus' – he cocked an ear for the half-familiar sound – 'I think she's whistled up a helicopter as well. And you think he's sprained his ankle?'

Now Hazel's eyebrows soared. 'You'd rather it was something worse? All right, maybe I over-reacted. You're surprised? With two bodies in the morgue, you among the walking wounded, and someone prowling round my house at night? Even if it is just a sprained ankle, obviously he can't get home by himself or he would have done. We have to find him. It's midwinter, and he's already spent one night outside. He might not survive another one.'

Ash took her point. 'It's just that, precisely because of everything that's happened, do we really believe in a simple accident? What about the photograph of Saturday outside your house?'

Hazel shrugged. 'All it proves is that my stalker had noticed him coming and going. Maybe he didn't like that, any more than he liked you hanging around. But that doesn't mean he did anything about it.'

'He did something about it when he didn't like me . . . visiting.' Ash didn't like the suggestion that he hung around her.

'He knocked you down and kicked you in the ribs. All right, several times. What he did not do is kidnap you.' She paused, considering. 'Look, it's Occam's Razor, isn't it? Simple is more likely to happen than complicated. Common happens more often than rare. And people have accidents a lot more often than they're abducted by homicidal maniacs. Anyway, who'd want to kidnap Saturday? What would they do with him once they'd got him? He's not worth ransoming, and he's not well enough house-trained to keep as a pet.

'Please, Gabriel, just do as I ask. Take the car home. Or stay here, if you prefer, and wait for me. I'll go up to the woods with Benny, he can show me this waterfall, and if Saturday did go back there we'll find him. Whether we do or not, I'll be back in an hour. Yes?'

Ash still didn't like it. If he'd been up to scrambling through a wet wood, he'd have insisted on going with her. He told himself that at least she wasn't going alone, that Benny Price who had the proper boots for hiking could probably look after both of them in a bit of woodland less than three miles from the centre of Norbold. It wasn't exactly the Fawcett expedition. 'Well, all right. But – you know – be careful.'

'I'm always careful,' Hazel said, with more dignity than accuracy. 'And by the way, it's Button.'

Ash frowned. 'What's a button?'

'Jenson Button. Not Zip.'

'I wasn't sure I'd got that right,' admitted Ash.

I could go with her, volunteered Patience as they watched Hazel jog back to the jeep.

But Ash had taken Patience into woods before now. There were too many little furry things living in the undergrowth, and though she could boast an unusual talent, she was still descended from hunting dogs. If she gave Hazel the slip and compounded the offence with an attack of canine selective deafness, he'd never hear the end of it. 'No, we'll stay here. They'll be back in an hour.' He said it as if he believed it.

TWENTY-NINE

Old as it was, Benny Price's Land Rover took the change from tarmac to forestry track without blinking. Hazel was glad she'd left her own car behind. It could probably have coped with the stony surface, but she'd have been picking mud out of the grille for days.

'How far up here did Saturday drive?'

'A bit further than this,' said Benny. 'I told him I didn't mind walking the last mile, but he looked rather horrified.'

Hazel chuckled. 'Saturday's not really mountain-man material. He prefers the urban jungle.' Her fondness for him was a pang beneath her breastbone. 'I hope we find him. I hope he's all right.'

'I'm sure we'll find him,' said Benny. 'Er . . .'

Hazel glanced at him. 'What?'

'It's really none of my business,' Benny demurred.

'But?'

'He seems an unlikely . . . companion . . . for you. I was a little surprised when he answered your door.'

'He's just staying for a few days,' Hazel said off-handedly. 'He used to rent a room from me, before he went to London. I hadn't seen him for ages, then suddenly he turned up again.'

'Then you two aren't . . .?'

Hazel stared at him. 'Me and Saturday? Good grief, no. He's ten years younger than me. What do you take me for, a baby-snatcher? A *desperate* baby-snatcher?'

'I'm sorry, I didn't mean to offend you. It really is none of my business.'

'No, it isn't.' Then, relenting, she added: 'You're not the

first one to wonder. But he's a good kid, and he needed a helping hand, and I was in a position to offer one. That's all it was.'

'It's good to have friends,' said Benny Price wistfully.

'Yes, it is,' said Hazel.

There was a long pause while he worked up to saying what he wanted to. 'I hope you'll always consider me one of yours. That young thug on the train – I know we shouldn't speak ill of the dead, but it's the truth. I thought I was going to die. I *felt* that knife sliding into me. And then you . . . And you did it so easily. With such . . . grace. I thought then, I will *never* meet anyone like that again.'

He was making Hazel uncomfortable. Ingratitude was much easier to deal with than adulation. 'Benny, I told you before, I was only doing my job. What I was trained to do. Trucker *was* a thug, there's no getting away from it. But if there weren't people like Trucker, there wouldn't have to be people like me. I can't say I liked him. But I'm sorry he didn't live long enough to grow up and learn some sense.'

'He doesn't deserve your pity,' muttered Benny Price.

'He didn't deserve what he got, either.'

Among the trees ahead was a sudden flash of yellow. 'That's it,' exclaimed Hazel. 'That's Saturday's car. So he *did* come back here. And he never left.'

She thought it had run off the track into the wood. But there was a small area of hard standing where the forestry workers could park equipment without blocking the lane. Benny turned down into it and pulled up beside the sports car. Hazel was out and peering through the windows before the jeep was fully stopped. But Saturday was neither inside nor in sight.

'He meant to come straight back,' she said, disappointment a lump in her throat. 'The keys are in the ignition.' She raised her voice in a penetrating hail. 'Saturday! Saturday, where are you?'

But though they both listened hard, there was no answering cry among the trees.

'All right,' said Hazel levelly. 'If the car's here, he can't be far away. We just have to look. But first' – she took her phone out – 'I must let DCI Gorman know where we are.'

'Can you get a signal?'

'Er – no.' She glared at the trees, as if demanding that the culprit own up. 'I'll go back up onto the lane.'

'We should go this way.' Benny was already heading for a path leading down into the wood.

Hazel frowned. 'Usually, you get better reception higher up.'

'The waterfall is this way.'

That made a difference. 'How far?'

'Three hundred yards, maybe. It's rough going, though. Too rough for logging, which is why it's overgrown.'

'Rough I can do,' she said stoutly. 'You lead the way.' She put her phone back in her coat pocket.

The helicopter was equipped with infra-red. The jeep's engine was the biggest heat source in this part of the wood, and when they got out the two figures appeared as bright signatures beside it. The pilot dropped down for a closer look and the observer detected the yellow gleam through the bare branches.

They put a call through to DI Gorman. 'We think we've got the car.' The observer read out the map reference. 'But someone's beaten us to it.'

Dave Gorman frowned at his phone. 'Who?'

'No idea,' admitted the observer cheerfully. 'Infra-red's a wonderful thing but it isn't psychic. Two people in what looks like a Land Rover. They've gone into the woods on foot.'

'I'm about' – Gorman did a quick calculation – 'six minutes away. Can you keep them under surveillance till I get there?'

'As long as nothing blocks our line of sight. Infra-red can't shoot round corners either.'

Gorman let DS Presley drive so he could make some calls. The first failed to connect, which tended to reinforce his suspicion about the identity of one of the bright signatures in the wood. The second was picked up so quickly the phone's owner must have been waiting for it to ring.

'Gabriel? Where are you?'

'Er . . .'

'Please,' said Gorman with chilly emphasis, '*please* tell me you're at Railway Street, and that Hazel is with you.'

'Sorry, Dave, I wish I could,' Ash said quietly. 'We're a

couple of miles up towards Wittering. Someone thought Saturday might have gone into the woods north of the road.'

'And Hazel's with you?'

'Not right now. She went ahead with someone she knows who has a Land Rover. She didn't want to get her paintwork dirty.'

There was a lengthy silence that suggested dirty paintwork might be the least of their problems. 'Then who's "we"?'

'Me and Patience,' mumbled Ash, embarrassed.

Gorman forbore to comment. 'So who is it that Hazel's gone with?'

Ash told him all he knew of Benny Price, but it wasn't much. 'He works for the council,' he finished lamely. 'And he hikes or birdwatches or something. She asked if he could identify the waterfall in the photograph, and he thought maybe he could. He took Saturday up there yesterday morning.'

'And left him there?!!' Gorman's indignation pierced through the slightly patchy reception.

'Of course not. But he might have gone back later.'

'All right,' decided Gorman. 'Stay where you are, Gabriel. I think the helicopter has them spotted – Hazel and her friend, anyway. I don't know about Saturday. It looks like his car's there, but they're not getting a heat signature from it so the engine's cold. I'll have boots on the ground in ten minutes, we'll catch up with them in fifteen. Then you can take her home. And this time, try to keep her there.'

'She won't leave until you find Saturday.'

'She'll do what she's bloody well told,' snarled Gorman, 'if I have to cuff her and sling her in the back of a Black Maria.'

A few minutes later Gorman's car passed Ash on its way up the Wittering road. It didn't stop, but Gorman raised a hand in acknowledgement. Increasingly restless, knowing there was no point in following but too anxious to do nothing, Ash cast around for some contribution he could make while he was waiting. But the best he could come up with, in his current fragile state, was to go over in his mind what they knew, what they thought they knew and what they only thought, and hope that some kind of a revelation would present itself.

In the last couple of years, this kind of exercise had mostly involved playing mental ping-pong with Hazel, bouncing ideas between them until solutions began to take shape. Clearly, that wasn't an option today. He turned to look at Patience. 'I guess you're it.'

Can I sit on the front seat?

'If you'll sit on the blanket, and not shed any hairs.'

He moved into the driving seat, cleared his throat and began. 'Trucker Watts and Gillian Mitchell were murdered in the same way, a few days apart, probably by the same person. To the best of our knowledge they had only one acquaintance in common: Leo Harte. As a target criminal, Leo Harte would seem a promising suspect, except that Hazel believes he was in love with Gillian Mitchell.'

People do kill people they love, said Patience.

'Yes, they do,' Ash agreed slowly. 'And more often they kill people they don't love any more. But Hazel thinks Harte wants to find the killer as much as the police do.'

She could be mistaken.

'Of course she could. So maybe we don't dismiss Mr Harte just yet.' He considered a little longer. 'The other potential suspect is Gillian's brother, or possibly half-brother. Jam.'

Jam?

'Jam,' Ash said again, firmly. 'All right, that's probably not the name on his passport, but it's the only one we have for him so it'll have to do for now. The notes on her laptop suggest Gillian was becoming increasingly worried about his mental state. She thought he'd committed arson somewhere he used to work because his colleagues teased him. He blamed them when his girlfriend left. I think that's what the psychiatric fraternity, of which I have some experience, describe as a paranoid delusion. If Jam decided his sister was being less supportive than she should be, he might have become violent towards her as well.'

And Trucker? Patience remembered the young man well, following a close encounter with the seat of his trousers.

Ash was puzzled. 'Maybe they did know one another. It's hard to think that a professional journalist and Trucker Watts had many acquaintances in common, but if they had one they may have had more. Could Trucker have been one of the workmates Jam was angry with?'

I don't think Trucker was ever anybody's workmate. I shouldn't think he's ever worked.

'Good point. Then perhaps he upset Jam in some other way. This girlfriend who left him – could she have ended up with Trucker? Not likely,' he said then, answering his own question. 'Trucker was twenty years younger than Gillian Mitchell – a different generation. Even if Jam was her younger brother, and his girlfriend was younger than him, that's a big age gap.

'Well, perhaps we don't need to know what Trucker did, only that somehow he drew the wrath of a man losing contact with reality. He caught up with Trucker behind the skips at the shopping centre and beat his head in. Ten days later he did the same to his sister. Because she'd found out about Trucker? She was a journalist, she would have extensive contacts, she may have learned something that made sense in the context of what she already suspected. Or maybe he told her, and then wished he hadn't. He'd expected her to take his side. When he began to suspect she was going to tell the police, he had to protect himself.'

What did *you* do to offend him?

Ash stared at her. 'We don't know that was the same man.'

Hazel thought it was. And Hazel . . .

'. . . Has good instincts,' admitted Ash. 'All right, let's think about that. Hazel's been the subject of a fairly aggressive stalking. It began with nice little presents, and ended up with someone breaking into her house while she was sleeping. That's the person Saturday and I sat up watching for, and that's the person who used me as a football.'

Having first knocked you senseless with a blunt instrument. Such as was used on Trucker and the journalist.

'True. But he didn't kill me, or try to kill me. He was warning me off. He said as much. He was warning me off because . . . because he was jealous. He thought there was something going on between Hazel and me.' He sighed sadly.

And Saturday?

'That's a good question.' Patience looked pleased. 'Where

does Saturday fit into the pattern? *Does* Saturday fit into the pattern?'

Hazel decided not.

'And Hazel has good instincts. But not . . .'

. . . Infallible ones.

'Two possible scenarios. Hazel's right, and Saturday was doing a bit of detecting on his own and had an accident. Couldn't get back to his car, wasn't able to call for help – either because he's hurt too badly or because he couldn't get a signal. In which case she'll find him. She may have found him already.'

Or?

'Or Hazel was right the first time, and he really has been kidnapped. Or at least, led into a trap. Which would fit the pattern, insofar as there *is* a pattern, if the man who was jealous of me was also jealous of him. For the same reason: he didn't like Hazel wasting her time on unworthy companions – me too old, Saturday too young – when she could be with him. He's convinced himself he has some sort of a relationship with her. Some sort of a future with her, if he can just discourage her hangers-on.'

Are we talking about two men here? A murderer and a stalker? Or just one?

'I don't know. If we can't find a connection between Gillian Mitchell and Trucker Watts, or between them and me, how the hell are we going to find one between the three of us *and* Saturday?'

Then he paused. If Hazel had been there, she would have seen his face grow still and his eyes slip out of focus, gazing over the inner landscape of his mind. Perhaps Patience saw it too, because she said nothing to interrupt his thought processes.

After a couple of minutes, Ash came back. 'Hazel is the connection. Apart from Gillian Mitchell, Hazel is or was known to all of us – to Trucker, me, Saturday, and the stalker. And if the stalker is also the killer, *he* was known to Gillian – he was her Brother Jam.'

Which means, Patience said quietly, Saturday probably didn't have an accident.

'Not unless we're very, very lucky.' Ash chewed his lip, thinking still. The mental electricity was probably disrupting broadband speeds all the way back to Norbold. Abruptly he looked up, frowning, and back over his shoulder up the hill they'd driven down. 'If Hazel is the connection, this is the nexus. The place where things come to a point. This is the Wittering road. Gillian Mitchell's father's mistress' – he had never said Bit on the Side, and never would – 'lived out Wittering way. It's all we know about her. We don't even know for sure that she had a son. But if she did, it's entirely possible that he stayed in the same area where he was brought up. He may still live in the same house.'

He started Hazel's car, turned it clumsily – he hoped she was too far away to hear him clash the gears – and drove back towards Studley Row.

'And one name that Jam just might be short for . . .'

. . . Is Benjamin.

THIRTY

Hazel was pretty sure they'd come more than three hundred yards. But then, Benny Price was a hiker – he had the boots to prove it – and though she was a country girl at heart, it was a while since she'd walked far on anything other than pavement.

Sensing she was beginning to flag, Price broke his ground-eating stride where the trail skirted a tumble of boulders and sat down on one. Hazel sank onto another.

'Sorry,' said Price. 'It's rather further than I remember.'

'You're sure we're going the right way?'

'Oh yes. Down there' – he pointed to where the land fell away from the edge of the trail – 'is the stream. If we keep following it, we'll come to the waterfall.'

Hazel managed a grin. 'I bet Saturday was puffing by the time you got here.'

'Not particularly,' said Price, an odd sourness to his tone. 'Of course, he is very young. And he was keen to solve your puzzle.'

'You solved it,' Hazel said generously. 'Neither Saturday nor me, nor all of Meadowvale, would ever have found the place if you hadn't spotted it in that book.'

Benny Price glowed with pleasure. 'You asked for my help. How could I not, after what you did for me?'

Hazel just smiled. 'We'd better keep going. Saturday must be in trouble or he'd have got back to his car before now.'

As Price extended his hand to help her up, it struck her how well he fitted into this environment. When they'd met on the train, she'd seen only a rather short, rather plump middle-aged man carrying a shopping bag. But out here, where his anorak blended into the dark trees, he seemed compact rather than short, sturdy rather than plump, and she felt now the strength of the hand that had carried his shopping. He was also younger than she'd thought, and plainly fitter than she was. Looking back, it explained something which had puzzled her: why someone like Benny Price, however indignant, had thought he could stand up to someone like Trucker Watts. In a fair fight, if he hadn't pulled a knife, Trucker would probably have come second.

They trudged on, Price helping Hazel over the rougher parts. There were fallen trees to negotiate, and places where the track – it was never as grand as a path – disappeared entirely under years of leaf-litter. After the first descent from where they'd left the cars, the way began to climb, not steeply but relentlessly. The trees crowded in, jostling for a better look at the intruders. Every stage of timber was there, from age-hollowed grandfathers broken by their last winter to lanky juveniles shooting out of their clothes in their urgent desire to reach the sun before a rival should steal it. At their feet were the sad remains of those which hadn't had a chance, or hadn't taken it.

More to distract herself from worrying about Saturday than because she wanted to know, Hazel said, 'Have you always lived round here?'

'Oh yes,' said Price. 'I was born in Studley Row. That was my mother's house.'

'Have you any family?'

'Not any more.' He turned to her with a sheepish grin.

'Unless I can catch the eye of some nice girl who likes hiking in the woods and birdwatching, and doesn't mind being seen in a fifteen-year-old Land Rover.'

Hazel smiled back. 'There must be loads. Personally, I'm holding out for a guy who doesn't mind me working nights, who won't faint if I come home with a black eye, and isn't allergic to the hair of my best friend's dog.'

'Constable Best,' Price said lightly, 'I think we're made for one another. Except I'm not sure about the dog.'

'Ah, then I'm afraid we're doomed. The dog's part of the deal. At least, the friend's part of the deal, and he and the dog are joined at the hip. You'd better keep looking.'

Hazel raised her voice, called again; still no reply. Perhaps Saturday wasn't here. Perhaps he was here but couldn't hear her; perhaps he was here but couldn't answer. She gritted her teeth and struggled on. 'What did you find at the waterfall? I never got round to asking you.'

Price shrugged. 'Nothing. Just a waterfall – a couple of metres high, dropping into a rocky pool. Trees all around. Very overgrown: it might have been a beauty spot once, but it's pretty neglected now.'

Hazel's brow creased with bewilderment. 'I don't understand *any* of this. Why would anyone want me to come here? And why would Saturday come back a second time?'

They were largely rhetorical questions, mere thinking aloud, but Price considered them as if she was waiting for an answer. 'You thought at one point that I was leaving little presents on your doorstep. I told you it wasn't me, but – I hope I'm not being indiscreet here – it sounds as if you had a secret admirer. He sent you the photograph of the waterfall? Perhaps he's hoping you'll meet him there.'

Hazel hesitated, wondering how much she should say. But he'd gone well out of his way to help her, and she thought she owed him some kind of explanation. 'Benny, you've been very patient, and I do appreciate it. I can't go into a lot of detail even now – I'm sure you understand why – but you deserve to know what's going on. If only so that you can decide to turn back if it all seems a bit too risky.

'He isn't a secret admirer, he's a stalker. He's been watching me, and he broke into my house, and he beat up one of my friends. There's also the possibility that he was involved in the death of Trucker Watts and a woman called Mitchell.

'I thought, when Saturday went missing, that he'd hurt him too. I think now, having tramped through these woods, it's more likely that he's hurt himself – but I could be wrong. Even if I'm not, if the stalker is watching me, it's entirely possible that he's followed us here. If you want to turn back, I'm sure I can manage the rest of the way on my own.'

Benny Price looked at her as if, just for a moment, he wanted to slap her. 'You think I'd do that? Leave you alone up here? When you could be in danger?'

'It's my job to deal with dangerous and unpredictable people, and I've been taught how to do it. It's your job to oversee roadworks and make sure there are no potholes left behind. I signed up for this kind of thing: you didn't.'

'Miss Best,' he said after a moment, 'I appreciate the suggestion, and I understand why you felt you had to make it, but if I abandoned you I would never be able to look myself in the face again. I promise you, I'm better equipped to take care of myself in this kind of terrain than you probably think. I know, I'm not a teenager any more, and even when I was I knew my limitations. I'm a rambler, not an explorer. But I've spent a lot of time in woodlands: I know how to make this environment work for me. This is what *I* signed up for. I'm not saying I'm a match for a jealous stalker wielding a hammer, but I think both of us together might be. We came here together. We'll leave the same way.'

Hazel was quite touched. 'Thanks, Benny. I hoped that was how you'd feel. But I had to ask.'

He flicked her a fond little smile and returned to the trail, hefting the backpack that had replaced his shopping bag. Hazel couldn't think what he'd felt the need to bring on a woodland walk almost within sight of Norbold, but clearly it had some substance to it. A gas stove and a set of folding saucepans? A collapsible campbed? Something that reinforced his image of himself, out here, where he was no longer Benny Price who worked for the council but Price the adventurer, Price the survivalist, Price who may not have found the source of the Nile but did track down the waterfall in Lubbuck's Gully.

His voice came at her over his shoulder. 'If your admirer – sorry, your stalker – was expecting you to come here yesterday, he must have been sadly disappointed to see me and that young man coming up the trail.'

'God knows how long he's spent up here, waiting. He couldn't know when, or even if, I'd manage to identify the photograph. He couldn't know what I'd do about it if I did.'

'If he's been watching you, he'd know if you left Norbold and drove this way. He'd guess that you'd figured out where the waterfall was, and follow you.'

'But *why*? It's the middle of nowhere! What's so special about a little waterfall that I have to trek through acres of wet forest to look at it? I might have seen all this mud and given up in disgust.'

Price smiled. 'I don't think you're someone who gives up very easily. And now of course you have a reason to keep going. To find your friend.'

'Yes.' She raised her voice, calling Saturday's name yet again; yet again there was silence. 'How much further is it?'

'Not very far at all,' he promised. 'A few minutes. Do you need another rest?'

Hazel shook her head. 'Let's keep moving. If we don't find Saturday in the next few minutes, we're looking in the wrong place.'

'No,' said Benny Price decisively. 'No, I think we're in the right place. I think this is where you needed to come.'

Hazel looked at him slightly askance. 'Benny – is there anything you haven't told me? Something Saturday said, that would explain him coming back here? I can just about imagine a determined stalker luring me here in the hope that I'd come alone, and maybe he'd get to have his wicked way with me. But Saturday came here with you, found nothing, then drove you home. And then he came all the way back, driving his flash car up that stony lane and tramping this apology for a track in his best trainers for a second time. And I can't imagine why.'

'He did say he wasn't happy with the photographs he took for you.'

'You think maybe he decided to take some more?'

Price shrugged and changed the subject. 'How exactly do you define stalking? From a legal point of view.'

'That takes a whole chapter in a law book, and keeps lawyers arguing happily for hours. But *I* define it as someone pestering you with unwanted attention, breaking into your house and beating up your friend.'

Hazel became aware that the sound of the stream had become louder, that it was becoming louder still as they followed it uphill.

'Of course,' said Price, 'it's hard to trust someone when you don't know who they are or what their intentions might be. But surely it's safe to assume that he means you well? That he's drawn to you, and wouldn't want to see you hurt?'

'You'd think so,' grunted Hazel, taking his hand over a broken part of the track. 'And probably that's how it starts out, as misplaced affection awkwardly expressed. Sadly, it isn't always how it finishes. Stalkers *do* hurt their victims, mentally and physically. Sometimes they kill them.'

Price was shocked. 'What possible reason could anyone have for wanting to kill you?'

Hazel barked a laugh. 'You'd be surprised. The point is, stalking is not the act of a rational person. Someone who thinks that breaking into your house is an acceptable part of courtship will get it just as wrong when things don't go his way. If his feelings aren't returned, he can't be trusted to take the rejection gracefully, put it down to experience and move on. He may well come back armed with a wheel-brace.' She frowned, hearing an echo of something Price had said earlier. 'Or a hammer, I suppose. We thought we were looking for a wheel-brace, but it could have been either.'

'We're nearly there,' said Benny Price.

And indeed, the sound of the waterfall was clear now, the stream swollen by winter rains, and a flash of white showed between the crowding branches ahead. Hazel thought it was white water rushing over the stony lintel, tumbling into the rocky bowl below. But it wasn't.

THIRTY-ONE

D CI Gorman was pretty sure he was lost.

He and Presley had followed the instructions called down from the helicopter as best they could. But neither of them had any experience of orienteering, and an increasingly impatient voice from above had kept warning him he was getting further away from the people on the trail instead of closer. Then it reported that the helicopter was running low on fuel – it had, of course, come on from its earlier exercise instead of directly from its base – and would have to leave. A last volley of directions closed with the words, 'Keep that heading and you really can't miss them,' and then the aircraft banked away and the sound of the rotors quickly diminished.

That was ten minutes ago. Now Gorman was surrounded on all sides by trees, he had no idea what direction he was walking in, he'd fallen twice on the muddy trail, and if Tom Presley said, 'I still think we should have taken the left fork back there' *one* more time he was going to get a knuckle sandwich.

Ash left Patience in the car and hurried – insofar as he was capable of haste – to that one of the Studley Row cottages where Hazel had found someone in. She was still in: a woman of about seventy doing her housework in an apron. Her name was Mrs Morris.

Yes, she said, needing no more encouragement to gossip about her neighbour than an attentive ear, Benny Price had grown up in the next-to-end cottage. His mother had had it from her parents; her father was an agricultural labourer at a time when the words meant something. Benny's father? He didn't live with them, but he visited regularly, made sure they had what they needed. What's this his name was? Murdoch? Witchell? Mrs Morris didn't want telling, it would come to her in a minute . . .

'Mitchell?' asked Ash softly.

That was it: Mitchell. Martin Mitchell. He worked in the big ceramics factory in Norbold. Jenny Price mightn't have got a wedding ring out of him, but she had the finest tea set in the whole of Studley Row.

'Did Benny ever talk about his sister?'

That would be a short conversation, cackled Mrs Morris, since he didn't have one.

'Half-sister, then,' said Ash. 'Martin Mitchell's daughter with his wife.'

That rang a bell with Mrs Morris. Yes. Benny hadn't known her when he was growing up. He'd found her on that inter-web thing. She was some kind of a writer. He was very excited when they arranged to meet, told Mrs Morris all about it: where they went for lunch, what they ordered. He showed her newspapers – proper newspapers, London ones, not that Norbold rag – with her name on the articles. They were as thick as thieves for months. Then . . .

'Something changed?' asked Ash.

Mrs Morris thought there'd been a falling out. If she asked after Benny's sister, which – striving to meet her obligations as a nosy neighbour – she not infrequently did, he would grunt and change the subject, or make an excuse and go inside. Only once was he more forthcoming. Mrs Morris thought the disagreement between them had come to a head, leaving him angry and unguarded.

'It was about a girl. Benny had managed to get himself another girlfriend. I never met her, but I could tell he was a bit smitten. I just hoped it would work out better for him this time. He was smitten with the other one too, took it desperate hard when she disappeared.'

The hairs on the back of Ash's neck stood up. 'Literally?'

Mrs Morris squinted at him. 'Don't be so wet. I mean, she stopped coming round. He stopped taking her out. It was over. Pity, really. I *did* meet her, I thought she was a nice enough sort. Miriam, she was called. Bit on the plain side – bit of a mouse. But he was never going to pull a stunner, was he, not Benny, and he seemed pretty satisfied. He thought they were going to get married.'

'What went wrong? Do you know?'

'Benny blamed it on the lads he worked with. Said he took her to the place where he worked – wanting to show her off, you know. But Benny always gets things that little bit wrong, and instead of treating him like the conquering hero, which is what he expected, they made fun of him. Harmless enough, I'm sure, but it got under his skin. They asked Miriam if she'd really thought this through, and told her she could do better. Told her Benny wasn't much of a catch and she ought to set her sights a bit higher. Benny was furious. *Furious.* He hates being treated with anything less than respect.'

'These were men he worked with at the council?'

'Oh no,' said Mrs Morris, 'this was before he was a park warden. He worked for a joiner or something, in Coventry. When the workshop burned down he had to find a new job.'

Ash was confused. 'So why was Benny angry with his sister?'

'That was later. Like I told you, he got another girlfriend. He thought his sister'd be pleased for him, but she seemed to think it was a bad idea. He said she was no better than the men at the workshop, putting him down, trying to spoil things for him. Disrespect – see? He can go on a bit, can Benny, once he's riled. Anyway, *she* said his colleagues weren't the reason Miriam left: that she left him because he'd become obsessive and controlling, and if he made the same mistake with the new one he'd lose her too.

'He was wildly indignant about that, wanted to know what an old spinster like her knew about it anyway. He said she was just jealous, because he had someone and she was going to be an old maid. He said – what was it he said? – he said if she tried to spoil things for him again, he'd put her nose in a sling. I said that wasn't a very nice thing to do, to threaten his sister, and Benny said she started it. She threatened to tell his new girlfriend that he was a weirdo and she should have nothing to do with him. Or words to that effect.'

'Do *you* think he's a weirdo?'

'Probably,' admitted Mrs Morris cheerfully, 'but it doesn't bother me. He's just Benny – I'm used to him and he's used to me. By the time you get to my age, dear, most of the people you've ever known seem a *little* weird.'

Ash considered. 'The new girlfriend. Did he tell you anything about her?'

Mrs Morris gave a gap-toothed leer. 'He said she was a police officer. I mean, really? Benny?'

Ash sucked in as deep a breath as his ribs would allow. He was about to thank her for her candour – a politer word than gossip – and leave, when his brain flagged up a query about something she'd said earlier. 'Benny's a park warden? I thought he was something to do with roadworks. Pipe laying, potholes – that kind of thing.'

'Don't know what would make you think that, dear,' said Mrs Morris dismissively. 'Benny's always been an open-air fanatic. Hiking, camping, that kind of stuff. He knows the woods round here' – she indicated with a gesture, in case Ash might think she meant some other woods – 'like the back of his hand.'

Ash tried to phone Dave Gorman. But his signal was patchy and Gorman's non-existent. Now desperately anxious for Hazel's safety, he was still worrying how to get what he'd discovered to those who needed to know it when one of the squad cars from Meadowvale sailed past the end of the lane, heading up the Wittering road. He'd given chase almost before he'd decided to.

By the time he got there, the hard standing at the top of the stony laneway was full. Saturday's yellow sports car was there, so was Price's Land Rover, and so was Gorman's smart new saloon, an indulgence he'd treated himself to when his promotion came through. There was also a maroon hatchback that Ash didn't recognise. The squad car had squeezed in by shoving its bonnet into a bush, and Ash parked beside it. If anyone wanted to leave in a hurry, there'd be chaos.

DC Emma Friend came over as soon as she saw him. 'We're organising a search of the wood for the missing boy. The chief and Tom Presley have gone ahead, but we've lost communication with them. All these trees.' She made a gesture not unlike Mrs Morris's.

'It's not just Saturday who's in trouble: Hazel is too. The man she's with – Benny Price, the man from the council, who offered to show her the waterfall' – Ash was aware from DC Friend's expression how little sense he was making, but the situation was too urgent to explain more fully – 'I think he's the one who's been stalking her. He's Gillian Mitchell's half-brother, and I think he's the one who killed her.'

If he'd stammered that out to DS Presley, the sergeant would have laughed out loud and then started to explain, carefully, as to a child or an idiot, why he couldn't possibly be right. But Presley remembered Ash in his doolally days, when he was known at Meadowvale as Rambles With Dogs, and Friend had arrived in Norbold more recently and was more aware of the things he and Hazel Best had accomplished.

So she listened, and took in what he was trying to say, and turned back to her colleagues and raised her voice. 'Listen, everyone. It's not just the boy we're looking for now – Hazel could be in trouble too. We need to move off and find her. And the guy she's with? – exercise caution.'

It was as simple as that. No one asked for details: they spread out among the trails leaving the little car park, and no one spoke because they were listening as well as looking. Within a minute they had disappeared entirely among the trees, leaving Ash alone.

He wanted to be with them. Not because he thought he could do anything that they couldn't, but because Hazel was his friend and she mattered to him, more even than pain. He got as far as clambering out of the car. But the rational part of his brain knew he couldn't move far enough or fast enough to be of any use in the search, and if he came to grief too they'd have three potential casualties to look for. He eased himself back behind the wheel.

He looked at Patience. He took her seatbelt off. 'I guess this is where we find out if you're as smart as you say you are.'

Certainly I am, said Patience.

'I can't do anything to find Hazel, and I couldn't do anything to help her if I did. You can. Even an ordinary dog could. I've seen the *Lassie* films. Go and look for her. Stay with her till help arrives.'

I don't like leaving you here alone.

'I'll be fine,' insisted Ash. 'If Price comes back, I'll lock the doors and blow the horn.' If Price came back alone . . . 'Please, Patience. I need you to do this.'

All right.

He leaned across and opened the passenger door. Even a very smart dog, even a dog that can talk, lacks opposable thumbs.

In a couple of bounds the slim white lurcher had vanished into the undergrowth.

When the last branches parted so that Hazel could see clearly, she slowed to halt, unable to feel the broken ground beneath her feet. Then she sank slowly to her knees and put both fists against her mouth to keep from screaming.

They'd found Saturday. And they'd found him too late.

She thought at first, staring, unable to drag her eyes away or even to blink, that his killer had crucified him. But actually he was tied there, under the waterfall, his arms stretched by ropes to trees either side of the stream, the little cataract crashing down on his head and shoulders. His head was on his chest now, his wet hair in his face, his thin body slumped as far as the ropes would permit. The flash of white she'd seen through the trees was his T-shirt. Whoever had strung him up there had left him nothing that might keep in a little warmth.

Somewhere deep in her brain, where she was not just a friend and compassionate human being but also a police officer, the question was forming: How long had he been dead? How long had he suffered the icy chill of the winter stream beating down on him, exposed, immobile, unable to help himself, before he yielded up his life? Hours, certainly. In Britain, even in winter, healthy young men don't die of exposure in a few minutes. He'd been missing a full day. Had he been here most of that time? Had he been here all night? Had he stayed conscious long enough to feel himself dying by inches? If she'd got here an hour sooner . . . two hours . . .?

A cry wrung itself from her throat, and it didn't even sound human. It sounded like a trapped animal.

Benny Price was on his knees beside her, his arm around her shoulders. 'I'm so sorry . . .'

'Get him down.'

He looked doubtful. 'Should we?'

'Cut him down!' Right now she didn't care that it was a crime scene that needed preserving. All she cared about was that her friend had died cold, miserable and alone; that in all likelihood his last conscious thought had been to wonder where she was and when she would come for him; and she hadn't come. She wasn't leaving him strung up like a beast in an abattoir any longer than she had to. She staggered to her feet. 'If you can't, I will.' She didn't have a knife. But she had fingernails, and a knot that one person can tie can always be picked apart by another.

Price was rooting through the contents of his backpack. 'Wait. I have a knife.' There were other tools in there, too, that chinked and rattled as he searched.

Armed with a sheath-knife, he climbed down into the gulley, crossing the stream sure-footedly using two of the bigger boulders as stepping-stones; from the far bank he reached up and cut the rope securing Saturday's left arm. The boy's whole body sagged towards Hazel's side of the stream. She leaned down, grasped his wrist in both her hands and hauled.

Though he'd grown since she first knew him – a little taller, a little broader – there still wasn't a lot of him. But the water soaking his jeans and T-shirt made him heavier than usual, and the effort required to drag him up the bank was beyond her. She knelt in the mud, oblivious of the cold and the splashing water, tugging fruitlessly and sobbing with grief and frustration.

Benny Price came back across the stream, hooked an arm round Saturday's knee and dragged him up the bank with a grunt. Then he straightened up and, reaching into the nearer tree, cut the rope securing the boy's right wrist.

Hazel eased the body of her friend onto his back. She had nothing to put over him except her own coat. She told herself that would be silly – that it would do him no good now, and she needed it herself. Then she shrugged it off and put it over him anyway. Two sweaters were not enough to keep the winter at bay. Stray droplets from the waterfall burned her skin like ice.

As she leaned over him, Saturday's eyes fell open.

Shock jolted through her. Then she told herself it was just a physiological response to the way they'd been manhandling his body. And *then* she saw intelligence and a flicker of recognition in his gaze, and her jaw dropped.

'Dear God, he's alive!'

Benny Price spun back as though galvanised. 'What?' He peered into the wet face, fish-belly white, and Saturday looked back. He blinked. A tremor ran through him, and Hazel realised he was trying to move, to sit up, but his chilled body wouldn't obey him.

She leaned closer. 'Lie still. Help's on its way.'

Blue lips moved in his white face. A whisper of sound escaped him. Hazel leaned closer, struggling to catch the words.

The words were, 'It was him. He did this.'

THIRTY-TWO

Benny Price was beside himself with rage. Shock too, but mostly rage. 'You're supposed to be dead!'

Hazel just looked at him, stupidly, too confused, too stunned to react.

'I looked it up,' insisted Price. 'On the internet. I looked up how long it would take. There's been plenty of time. He should be dead by now. You' – he glared accusingly at Saturday – 'should be dead.'

All Hazel could think to ask was, 'Why?'

He stared at her as if it was a silly question. 'For you.'

'*What*?!!'

'Miss Best – Hazel – *everything* I've done has been for you. For us. Because some things are too important to let other people stand in the way. People who do have to be . . . moved.'

'Moved? *You tried to kill him*,' cried Hazel. 'For us? There is no Us.'

'Don't say that,' said Benny Price, half a growl, half a whine. 'You saved my life. How does a man begin to repay that? With presents? Well, yes, that was easy enough. Presents little enough to be left on your doorstep, too small to raise eyebrows. I know you have to be careful about accepting gifts. But wine and chocolates were never going to say everything I wanted to say to you. So I left you something better at the shopping centre.'

It took until then for Hazel to fully comprehend what he was saying, and what it meant. He was saying that he'd murdered Trucker Watts. If he'd murdered Trucker, he'd murdered Gillian Mitchell as well. He was her Brother Jam. He was also the stalker, who'd broken into Hazel's house while she was asleep. He'd beaten Ash bloody, and now he'd done his damnedest to kill Saturday.

All of which meant that Benny Price, rambler and ornithologist, maker of rustic furniture and cornerstone of Norbold Council works department, was insane. Actually, clinically, insane.

Even before she met Ash, Hazel had dealt with people who had mental health issues. Every police officer has. At any given time, half the people in police custody ought to be under the care of a psychiatric nurse. Though they could be unpredictable, dangerous to themselves and those around them, she had become modestly adept at keeping them calm until they could be transferred to more suitable forms of care. She knew that, given appropriate treatment and support, many of them would be back in the community, living productive lives, a month later.

Benny Price was something different. She had never met anyone in whom the fires of insanity roared within so carefully defined a hearth. He seemed more than normal, *boringly* normal; but scratch the surface and there was . . . *this* . . . churning volcanically beneath. Somehow, the degree of control he was able to exercise when he had to made his outbursts of violence more, rather than less, frightening.

'You killed Trucker Watts?' whispered Hazel. Only to have him say it: she knew it was the truth.

'After how he treated me on the train? *In front of you?* Of course I did,' he said shortly. 'He had no respect. He didn't deserve to live.'

'And Gillian Mitchell?'

'Yes.' He vented a little sigh. 'I rather regret that, now. She was my sister, you know – the only family I had left. I was fond of her. But she said . . . she said . . .'

'What did she say, Benny?' asked Hazel softly.

'Lies. Terrible, hurtful lies. She said it was all in my head. You and me. She said I had to stop pestering you. She said an attractive young professional woman would have friends of her own and wouldn't be interested in me. She said, if I didn't leave you alone, she'd warn you about me. Tell you what I was like. Tell you not to trust me, that I'd end up hurting you. She said she had all the proof she needed on her computer.'

'The neighbours heard shouting.'

'I lost my temper,' admitted Price. 'So did she. She told me to get out of her house. Like there was something special about it – like I wasn't good enough for Park Crescent! I have a nice house too. You've seen it. She was my sister, but she'd no right to tell me what to do. She'd no right to come between you and me.'

Hazel ignored that. 'So you hit her?'

'She asked me to hang a picture for her. I brought my tools in from the Land Rover. Then we argued, and almost before I knew it, I'd hit her with the hammer.' He reached into the backpack again. 'Not this one. It's a decent enough hammer, but the balance isn't as good as my old one. But it wasn't safe to keep it, not with the police looking for a murder weapon. So I dropped it in the canal and bought this. There was a sale on at the hardware shop.'

There was no response Hazel could usefully make. 'And you attacked my friend Gabriel, and now' – she looked down at Saturday, hovering on the very edge of consciousness – 'this. I don't understand why you'd want to hurt me like this.'

Price's eyes were astonished. 'I don't want to hurt you! I told you – I *love* you. I want what's best for you. These so-called friends, this one and the other one, they're not worthy of you. The other one's an idiot. He talks to his dog. And this one's just street trash. He seems to have come by some money somewhere – stole it, probably – but he's still basically just street trash. I don't like to criticise, Miss Best, but it was poor judgement, letting him move in with you. People will talk.'

'Benny, you tried to *kill* him,' she gasped. 'To avoid *gossip*?'

'You have to have respect,' Price retorted stiffly. 'If you don't have respect, you don't have anything.'

She was desperately aware that time was passing, that Saturday might not have much of it left, that her coat might not be enough to prevent him succumbing to hypothermia, and that if Benny Price decided to use his new hammer to hurry things along she would not be able to stop him. But that was the point. While he was talking, he wasn't hurting anyone. If he wanted to talk, she should encourage him.

But first . . . 'Benny, I need your coat. Take it off.'

He started to. 'You must be cold,' he said solicitously.

Hazel stared at him in disbelief. 'It's not for me!'

Price looked at her as if she'd disappointed him somehow, and shrugged his arms back into the sleeves. 'No.'

'He's going to die.'

'He's *meant* to die.'

'But *why?*'

'I told you. This friendship of yours, it's not healthy. I thought, this way I could get him out of your life and earn your gratitude at the same time.'

'*Gratitude?*' It was a shriek of sheer incredulity.

Price nodded seriously. 'If he went missing, you'd want him found. I could take you to him. Of course I could – I knew where I'd left him. And then, I really wanted you to see this spot. That's why I sent you the photograph. I've always thought it was a bit magical, and I wanted to share it with you.'

'You wanted to show me your special place because you'd killed my friend there?'

Price gave a faintly censorious frown. 'You weren't supposed to know that was me. He was missing and I found him: that was all you needed to know. You'd still have been grateful, even though we found him too late.

'I should probably have left him a bit longer,' he said pensively, as if contemplating a cake that hadn't risen. 'You took me by surprise, stopping me on the road. I wasn't going to call you until later. Then everything would have worked out fine.

'All the same, it should have been long enough,' he added irritably. 'Especially since he spent last night tied to a tree. That one.' He pointed. 'I put him in the waterfall first thing this morning, after I'd read up about hypothermia on the internet.'

Hazel was struggling to stay calm. She knew this man could kill her, was deranged enough to beat her head in with his nice new hammer despite his protestations of affection. Her best chance was to keep him talking until help found them. Ash knew where she was, at least roughly. When she didn't return, he would . . .

Well, he would call DCI Gorman; and Gorman would find out where the area car was, and send it up the Wittering road if it wasn't too busy; and eventually, when she still hadn't reappeared, the crew would make a desultory search for her, at least as far into the wood as they could go without getting their socks wet.

She was so on her own.

She *wasn't* on her own. If she had been, it would have been easy. Basic training had covered situations like that. The first resort, when confronted with a dangerous man, is always to run away and get help; if you can, and if you can do it without dereliction of duty. The second resort is to try talking him down. The third and last is to fight.

Well, she couldn't run. She couldn't carry Saturday, and she couldn't leave him behind because she knew what that would mean. Talking was the next best option. If she could understand something of what had led them here, perhaps she could find a way for them to leave.

'Benny,' she said, as reasonably as she could manage through chattering teeth, 'it isn't too late to get this sorted. I can help – I *will* help – but I need your help first. I need you to lend me your coat. If I can warm him up, there'll be time for us to talk.'

She didn't actually know that. Saturday had gone very quiet again, very still, too cold even to shiver. She couldn't lift him but she pulled him halfway onto her knees, to get him at least partly off the wet ground. It wasn't enough. The icy chill of him was striking through her clothes. She thought he was going to die here in her arms, but she didn't dare ask too much too soon for fear Price would turn on her. One blow mightn't kill her, but if she woke up with a ringing headache she'd find Saturday dead beside her.

Price was looking at the boy. Hazel held her breath. But then he shook his head. 'No.'

'If he dies, there's no going back.'

'There's no going back now.'

Hazel's heart sank. She'd hoped he hadn't realised that. But there was no alternative but to keep trying. 'It's different, don't you see? Trucker Watts threatened you with a knife. And your sister – well, brothers and sisters fight all the time. People will understand that you were upset, and angry, and you struck out without meaning to.

'But if Saturday dies, that's premeditated murder. You *planned* it. You brought him here, you tied him up and you left him here overnight; and then you came back and dragged him into icy water, and left him to die. And even after *that*, you could have helped me save him and wouldn't. No one will understand that, Benny. I don't, and no one else will either.'

'Really?' He leaned forward, peering into her face. 'You still don't understand that I love you? That, beside that, nothing else is important? That, whatever it takes to be with you, I'll do it?'

'You think murdering my friends is going to make me love you back?!!'

Price straightened up with a snort. 'You're just being silly now. Girls are so *silly*. My sister was, Miriam was, and even you are, a bit.'

'Maybe I am,' she said desperately. 'Maybe I am being dense. But I want to understand. Benny, tell me about Miriam. Was she your girlfriend? Your' – she swallowed, got out the lie – 'last girlfriend?'

'She was.' His voice softened for a moment with the memory. 'I thought the world of Miriam. We'd been going out for a couple of months, and then I took her to the joinery shop to show her where I worked.' All the gentleness leached out of his voice and bitterness filled the vacuum. 'The lads there, my so-called friends . . . Dear God, how they laughed! The jokes, the *vulgar* jokes! As if there was something intrinsically absurd about me wanting what other men take for granted. Ho ho, who'd have thought old Benny had it in him? How do you get on with her guide dog, Benny? Never mind, Benny, just our bit of fun. Your lady-friend doesn't mind, do you, dear?

'But she *did* mind. They frightened her. They made her think I was some kind of a freak, and it frightened her. And she left me. She left me.' The heartbreak of it was like a chasm in his voice.

'That was very wrong of them,' said Hazel quietly. She was fighting hard to keep control of herself. She couldn't hope to control the situation if she couldn't control her own emotions. 'You must have been very upset.' Keep him talking, said her inner Sergeant Mole, training supervisor. Make him think you're on his side.

Benny Price barked a mirthless laugh. 'You know what they say: Don't get mad, get even. I burned the place down. They were old men, some of them, they'd never find work again. I thought, Let's see you laugh *that* off!'

It was dignity every time, Hazel realised. It was when he thought people weren't giving him the respect he was entitled to. Then he stopped being polite and helpful and became vengeful instead. The workshop, Trucker, his sister: they'd all threatened his view of himself as someone quietly important. That was what he couldn't tolerate. And Ash, and Saturday? He'd felt slighted because she was fond of them instead of him. And he'd thought that making Saturday disappear, and then finding him for her – too late, but he couldn't be blamed for that, could he? – would make her see him in a more heroic light.

It was madness. Of course it was madness. But she had to work with his madness if she hoped to get her friend out of here alive.

A whisper of sound made her look down. Saturday's blue lips were moving again. She leaned closer.

'You need to go.'

Hazel knew what he was saying. She knew *he* knew what he was saying. She shook her head. 'I won't leave you.'

'It doesn't matter.'

'It matters to me.' She gave it one more try. 'Benny, who knows what the future holds for you and me? I think you're a basically decent man who's not been very well, who maybe needs a bit of help. Somehow we need to get past this, and the other stuff that's been happening, but after that – well, we can talk about it. See where that takes us. Stranger things have happened.'

She was trying not to tell actual lies, not to make promises she had no intention of keeping. She knew that wasn't as important as keeping Benny Price from venting his rage on her and the boy helpless on her knees; but still, she didn't relish trading on Price's regard for her. 'So what do you say? Give me your coat, and help me get him back to the cars, and let's see where things go from there.'

He might have gone for it. There was a moment, and Hazel saw it in his eyes, when he might have been persuaded. But the moment passed. He shook his head. 'I can't. You must see that – I can't. The only way I can be safe is if he stays here, and you come with me.

'Hazel, I can make this right.' He was pleading with her, begging her. There was something almost childlike about it, as if he really believed he could escape the consequences of his actions if he crossed his fingers and wished. 'I can make you forget about him, forget about everything. I can make you so happy. No one will ever love you the way I love you. No one will ever be prepared to do as much for you as I've done – as I will do in the future, I swear to God. All you have to do is come with me. Leave him, and come with me. Please. Oh Hazel, please do what I ask. I promise you'll never regret it.' He stretched out his free hand, the one that wasn't holding the hammer.

What was she going to say then? There's no way you can be safe, you're never going to walk away from this? When you leave here, you're going to Broadmoor? Saying that would leave him with nothing to lose. She might as well beat Saturday's head in herself.

Which left what? She wouldn't run. She might be able to stay ahead of Price – she wasn't sure, but she might – and Saturday might survive the hypothermia long enough for her to bring help. But he wouldn't survive the kind of savage attack that had killed Trucker Watts and Gillian Mitchell. In his current state, he wouldn't survive the kind of beating Ash had taken. She could keep Price talking, but if they talked for too long the result would be the same. And she didn't believe she could defeat a fit, powerful man in a stand-up fight on his own ground.

In the end, all she could do was what she perceived to be her duty, as a police officer and a human being. She would look after Saturday as best she could, and what Benny Price chose to do about that was up to him.

Hazel pulled Saturday's sodden T-shirt off and pressed her own sweater, warm from her body, against him. She rearranged her coat around his thin shoulders. She pulled the polo-neck she'd worn under the warm sweater free of her belt.

Price was watching her every move. He couldn't figure out what she was doing.

She pulled the polo-neck over her head as well. The cold air flayed her cringing skin. With only a momentary hesitation, she unhooked her bra and dropped it on the ground.

Saturday whispered, 'What are you doing?'

'I'm going to warm you up the only way I can,' Hazel said flatly. 'With my own body-heat.' She pulled him higher in her arms and folded him against her, bare flesh to bare flesh, packing her clothes around his back and flanks. It was like hugging a salmon fresh from the fishmonger's slab.

Benny Price was gibbering in mounting fury. 'Him? *Him?* I'm not good enough for you, but you do this for *him*?'

All she could think of to say was, 'I do what I can. And you'll do what you must.'

She sensed rather than saw the movement as the burgeoning rage took him and his arm swung up. She squeezed her eyes tight shut and held Saturday against her, shaking with cold and terror.

Away in the woods across the stream, above the sound of the waterfall, she heard a crack like a branch breaking, and

Benny Price fell back into the leaf-litter. When Hazel finally opened her eyes, he was spread-eagled on the damp ground, the hammer still clasped in one hand, a single bead of blood in the centre of his forehead.

Saturday whispered, 'What happened?'

'Someone shot him.' She wouldn't have believed it if the evidence hadn't been there beside her. Still for long seconds she didn't dare move, in case somehow she'd misread the situation. But then relief began bubbling in her blood like champagne when the cork comes out. Another minute and she would either laugh out loud or start crying.

'Good.'

And it was at that point, when the danger was past and her moment for glory had passed with it, that Patience trotted out of the undergrowth, scimitar tail waving an amiable greeting. Lassie would never have missed her entrance like that.

But the sight of the white lurcher cheered Hazel immensely. If Patience was here, Ash wasn't far away; and though he probably wasn't up to scrambling through this wood right now, she was confident he'd have found other people who were. Including, presumably, the marksman. She called out a shaky greeting. 'Here. We're over here.'

Saturday's breath of a voice asked, 'Do you want your clothes back now?'

Hazel was tempted but shook her head. 'You need them more than I do. I'll risk shocking the search party.' For a moment she eased her bear-hug and reared back far enough to catch his eye. 'And as for you . . .'

The boy didn't know where to look. Hazel thought she detected the faintest of blushes on his cold white cheek. 'What?'

'Think of this as your Christmas present.'

THIRTY-THREE

B y the time he'd spoken to each of them, DCI Gorman had a fair idea what had happened, except for one thing. He didn't know who had shot Benny Price.

Hazel had assumed it was an armed response officer brought in along with the helicopter. Given her track record, most of Meadowvale had assumed it was Hazel.

The mystery was solved – or perhaps it was compounded – when John Carson arrived at Meadowvale Police Station with Leo Harte's solicitor.

'My client is here to furnish you with a full and frank explanation of how he came to shoot someone in that part of the Wittering Woods known as Lubbuck's Gully earlier this morning.'

Dave Gorman was generally rather good at not being surprised; and quite good at not appearing surprised even when he was. But no amount of practice could stop his hedgerow eyebrows from shooting up into his low-slung hairline. 'You mean, he's here to confess to a crime?'

'Well, possibly,' said the solicitor carefully, 'or at least a misdemeanour. If you still deem it in the public interest to prosecute when you've heard all the facts.'

'A misdemeanour . . .?' John Carson putting a bullet through Benny Price's brain might have been the least-worst outcome of the events in the wood that morning, but Gorman's soul baulked at lumping it in with dropping litter.

'When you've heard all the facts.'

Two hours later, DCI Gorman released John Carson on his own recognisance, with the warning that he should hold himself available for further interview and charges might follow. Then he left DS Presley holding the fort in CID and drove up to Highfield Road.

Having used every cushion in Ash's house, Frankie Kelly had then raided the neighbours in order to pad both sofas in the big sitting room. When she showed Gorman in, Ash was nursing his bruises on one, Hazel buried under quilts on the other.

Patience was curled in the chair closest to the roaring fire. Gorman stood over her expectantly.

Yes? Can I help you? she asked politely.

'Just get off and let the man sit down,' said Ash. With every sign of reluctance, the dog did as she was bid.

'You're not going to guess who I've been talking to,' said Gorman.

'Not the hospital?' asked the hump in the quilts that was Hazel, anxiously.

'No,' he said quickly. 'Though I called them before I came out. Saturday's fine. He's asleep, and they'll hold onto him until tomorrow, but they say he's come through it remarkably well. They say . . .' He hesitated, and cleared his throat. 'They say you got to him just in time. And you did exactly the right thing. That you saved his life.'

'Or to put it another way,' she mumbled, 'I nearly got him killed.'

'Oh Hazel,' sighed Gorman, 'don't go off on a guilt trip over this. None of what happened was your fault. Benny Price was a mentally deranged man who got fixated on you only because you were doing your job well. Everything that happened was down to him, not you.' He switched his gaze to the other sofa. 'Tell her, Gabriel.'

'I've *been* telling her,' Ash said patiently, 'since eleven o'clock this morning. It's now' – he glanced at the grandmother clock in the corner – 'a quarter to four. I have every hope that by about eight o'clock this evening she will begin to believe me.'

The mound of quilts grunted. 'Then who have you been talking to?'

'John Carson.'

That brought the top of her head into view, down to the level of her nose. 'Leo Harte's social secretary?'

'The very same. And the man who shot Benny Price.'

Both of them stared at him in a most gratifying way. 'You are *kidding*,' gasped Hazel, with a vulgarity that would have dismayed her mother.

'Leo Harte's *social* secretary?' said Ash, perplexed.

Hazel ventured a bit further out of her warm cave. 'It's his job description. Because *Chief henchman and occasional knee-breaker* doesn't look good in the annual accounts.'

'You know who Harte is?' asked Gorman. Ash nodded. 'Well, Carson's his fixer. And a bloody fine shot with a rifle, it turns out.'

Frankie brought fresh tea. He settled in with a cup – Ash's mother's tea set was nearly as awkward in his big hands as Superintendent Maybourne's – and told the story he'd been told. 'You are not to understand from this that I *believe* what I was told, only that this is Carson's account and I'm pretty sure he's going to stick to it. And I may not be able to break it, even if I try.'

'*If?*' echoed Hazel.

Gorman ignored her. 'Before John Carson worked for Leo Harte he was a soldier, and before he was a soldier he was a bit of a wild lad. Think Trucker Watts but with brains. One of his little earners was poaching – a brace of pheasant here, a roebuck there – not industrial scale, just enough to supply a short-sighted butcher or two. It wasn't even the money so much as the fun of dodging gamekeepers he enjoyed.'

'This must have been years ago,' said Hazel.

'It was. Now, of course, he's a respectable grown-up who does a responsible grown-up job and pays his income tax and votes in council elections and supports worthy charities, and any kind of criminality is far behind him.' Gorman caught her look and interjected defensively, 'I didn't say I believed this crap. I'm telling you what he told me.

'Except,' he resumed, 'every now and then he can't resist the urge to go out into some quiet bit of woodland and knock down a pheasant or two. He doesn't do it often, he doesn't take many, and he sticks to neglected corners of wood where the birds don't really belong to anybody or at least won't be missed. That's what he was doing this morning. Poaching.'

'With a rifle?' said Ash doubtfully.

'That's what I said. He said he'd been a crack shot in the Army, and this was a way of keeping his hand in. Shotguns, apparently, are for cissies. Look,' he said sharply, anticipating

Hazel's interruption, 'I *told* you – this is the statement he gave under caution. I don't believe it either. It's just a low-cost way of explaining what he was doing there.'

'He was there because Leo Harte sent him,' said Hazel.

'Of course he was.'

'Because . . .' Revelation dawned in Hazel's eyes. 'Leo Harte didn't want Benny Price arrested. Benny killed the woman he cared about, and he didn't want justice, he wanted revenge.'

'Exactly. He offered to help you find Gillian Mitchell's killer because he thought you – well, me too but you especially – had a better chance than he had. And he kept watch on you. Where you went, who you spoke to. That maroon hatchback – I bet you kept seeing it around?' She nodded wordlessly. 'That's Carson's. Harte reckoned that if he kept an eye on you, sooner or later you'd lead him to Gillian's killer.'

'At which point he always intended to take over,' guessed Ash.

'Harte had no interest in seeing the man who killed Gillian in court. He wanted him dead. When Carson saw Price pull a hammer out of his backpack, he knew (a) that he had his man, and (b) that he had a scenario he could walk away from. Price had killed before and was about to kill again. Any court in the land would say that what John Carson did then was justifiable homicide.'

'He used me,' said Hazel, anger sparkling with the firelight in her eyes. 'Leo Harte. I thought I was using him, but he was using me.'

'Yes, he was,' agreed Gorman. 'And if he hadn't, you and Saturday would both be dead now.'

'What will you do about Carson?' asked Ash.

But Gorman hadn't decided. 'I could try to get him for poaching. If we can figure out who that scrap of wildwood between the forestry and the farmland belongs to, and if they're prepared to stand up and say that Leo Harte's fixer had no permission to be shooting there. I might get his gun licence revoked. Or I might just send him a cigar.'

After he'd gone, Patience slipped back onto the fireside chair and Hazel emerged from under the quilts and went to raid the kitchen for biscuits. She was no longer chilled, either from exposure or shock, but her body craved something sweet.

Ash said, 'Why don't you stay here tonight? The guest room's made up.'

She was tempted, but only for a moment. 'Tonight I'm going to sleep in my own bed, in the absolute confidence that no one will break in, no one will leave little parcels on my doorstep, and there'll be no stiffened envelopes pushed through my letterbox. A luxury I haven't enjoyed for three weeks.'

'And it was all Benny Price,' mused Ash. 'The man from the council. One of the little people that nobody notices.'

'I feel pretty stupid about that,' Hazel admitted. 'I knew he worked for the council. I saw him standing beside the hole in my road and assumed that was his job. If I'd thought to ask, and been told he was actually the park warden and none of the guys digging the hole knew why he was always hanging round, we'd have got him days ago. We'd never have let Saturday go off with him.'

She was close to tears. She sniffed, and grinned ruefully, and then sobbed.

Ash rose from his sofa like an old arthritic horse, and put one creaky arm about her shoulders. 'It's just reaction,' he reassured her. 'All the time you're dealing with an emergency, your mind prioritises. It filters out the stuff it can do nothing about in order to focus on the things it can. Afterwards, it all comes back and hits you. Have a good cry. You'll feel better for it.'

He was right about that, too. But when she was done, the horror remained. 'We almost lost him, Gabriel. Saturday. We were that close to losing him.'

'Saturday will be all right,' promised Ash. 'He's been through a lot in his time. He's always come out intact, and he will again. He's resilient.'

'You didn't see him,' she mumbled. 'You didn't feel the absolute chill of his skin. I thought he was dead. I thought no one could survive that.'

'But he did,' Ash insisted softly. 'And tomorrow he'll come home, and apart from a disinclination to take country walks or indeed cold showers for a while, he'll be fine.' That made

Hazel laugh, a choking half-ashamed little chuckle that nevertheless brought a smile to Ash's face. 'So will you. It's history now. You did well, and now it's over.'

Except in the back of his mind was the one thing still unresolved. 'Er – what are you going to do about Christmas? Are you going back to Byrfield, to spend it with your father and Pete?'

It was almost as if, with everything that had happened since, she'd forgotten that Pete Byrfield wanted to make an honest countess of her. 'No,' she decided. 'No, I want to spend it here. With you and the boys, and Frankie, and Saturday.' She drew a deep, unsteady breath. 'But then I will have to go back. Pete and I need to talk. Properly. Talk through what we want, figure out what we're going to do.'

'There's no rush,' suggested Ash.

'No. And nothing to be gained by putting it off, either.'

Soon after that she collected her clothes – Frankie had been warming them round the kitchen range, she'd spent the afternoon in Ash's pyjamas with the arms and legs rolled up – and headed home. Saturday's yellow sports car had been left outside her door. There was no sign of the maroon hatchback.

But as she went to open her front door, she caught a movement under the weak street lamp as someone padded across the street. 'Er – miss?'

It was Trucker's sharp-faced little friend, in the same old grey hoodie with the hood up, his gloveless hands shoved deep in the pockets of his threadbare jeans. 'Hello, Neville.'

'It's just,' he began awkwardly, 'there's talk going round. I thought, Get it straight from the horse's mouth. Only people are saying you found who done for Trucker.'

After a moment she nodded. Trucker hadn't had many friends. The Rat was possibly the only one who cared enough about his death to ask the police for information. 'That's right. Do you remember the man Trucker threatened on the train? It was him.'

The Rat's eyes widened. 'That fat little bloke? He got the better of Trucker?'

'He wasn't just a fat little bloke. He was a *strong*, fat little psychopath who used a hammer as an offensive weapon.

There'll be an inquiry to establish the facts, but there won't be a prosecution because he's dead now as well.'

Now the Rat's mouth dropped open as well. 'Did you kill him, miss?'

'No, I didn't,' she said shortly. 'Occasionally, things happen around here that are not my fault. He was going to kill me, except that a man with a gun saw him and stopped him. And that, until the full facts are released, is all I can tell you. I'm sorry you lost your friend, Neville. I hope it's some comfort to know that the man who killed him won't be hurting anyone else.'

The Rat thought about that. Then he nodded, satisfied. But on the point of turning away, he hesitated and looked up at her again. 'Er – miss?'

'Yes, Neville?'

He did the shy smile that had touched her before. The one probably no one had seen since his mother. 'You always call me that. Everybody else just calls me Rat, but you always call me Neville. My mum thought it was a bit classy. A cut above the Waynes and Tyrones and Leroys you mostly get round here.'

Hazel smiled noncommittally.

'Er – miss?'

'*Yes*, Neville?'

'Would you mind not doing?'